The Detective Joanna Best Mysteries
Book 2

The Brothers Crimm

Cenarth Fox

The Detective Joanna Best Mysteries
Book 2
The Brothers Crimm

First published in 2018 by Fox Plays
www.foxplays.com
www.cenfoxbooks.com

ISBN 978 0 949175 19 9

Cover design by Oliviaprodesign

Dictionary of Australian slang/language

Some of the words and expressions found in this novel.

ATO - Australian Tax Office (the IRS)
Billy Hughes - former Australian Prime Minister
bloke - a man
Bluey - nickname of man with red hair
bollocking - a reprimand
boxers - shorts, underpants
cark it - to die
Clayton's - a non-alcoholic drink, the drink you have when you're not having a drink, the leader you have who doesn't want to be leader
codger - man, bloke, fella
Collingwood - popular football team
filth - the police
Glaswegian kiss - head butt to a person's face (Scottish)
Go Blues - good luck to the Carlton football team (the Blues)
jiff - a moment, a short time
jim-jams - pyjamas, pajamas
knackered - tired
lift - an elevator
loo - lavatory, toilet
MCG - Melbourne Cricket Ground (venue for the 1956 Olympics)
Melbourne Cup - a famous horse race (the race that stops a nation)
misper - police talk for a missing person
mobile - mobile phone, cell phone
Nar Nar Goon - small country town
Nobby - nickname of man with surname of Clarke
porkies - short for pork pies i.e. lies
RMIT - a university in Melbourne
rubberneck - person who is a sticky beak often looking at an accident
sheila - a female, often a male's girlfriend (she's me Sheila)
smalls - underwear
socks and jocks - sox and underpants
spray - a vocal attack, a reprimand
Stat Dec - statutory declaration
tyre - tire
Weet-bix - breakfast cereal

For
Eileen Nelson
actress, booklover, friend

1

JOHN FIELDING DIDN'T KNOW IT BUT he was about to be murdered. As an investigative journalist, he upset people and plenty wanted him dead. When it happened, few were surprised.

His current article was about paedophilia in Sydney in the 1980s. The men involved would do anything to keep their secrets hidden. They were powerful, wealthy, and about to be betrayed as Fielding found someone who knew names. Would that someone talk?

En route to the interview, Fielding called at his family home. Only his brother lived there now as their elderly father died last month. John and older brother Martin clashed and Martin hated John. Their old man's will created division with Martin ropeable. He thought about killing his brother. Why not tonight?

It was after 8 pm when John arrived. Martin glared. 'How dare you come here? How dare you.'

'Take it easy,' said the journalist brother.

'Take it easy?' Martin fumed. 'You do nothing for 30 years then waltz in here and take half the old man's estate.'

'I don't want to fight you, Martin.'

'No, just steal what's rightfully mine.'

'We have to honour Dad's wishes.'

'Jeez, for someone who writes about justice, mate, you are the world's biggest hypocrite.'

John offered an envelope. 'This note explains a way forward.'

'Well you know where you can stick that. Now fuck off.'

The angry brother turned into the hallway and grabbed an old ceramic chamber pot their mother inherited from her mother. It was worth a bit and had decorated the hallstand for decades. Martin brandished the ornament.

'Martin, don't be so bloody stupid.'

'Stupid? You've left me without a pot to piss in, so why don't you take this as well? You bastard!'

John started running and fast as the pot flew through the air and shattered on the path. John dived into the street and kept running. Their mother, long dead, did a couple of spins in her grave.

The journalist hoped for better luck with his interview. He was sure the contact could break open his paedophilia story. He parked on a busy road under good lighting, and headed for a block of flats in a side street.

A disinterested architecture student, helping his uncle the builder save money, designed the flats. A "box with windows" was a generous description, and the builder, former *President of Cowboy Builders Inc.*, upheld his work ethic of "cheap 'n quick".

The flat the journo wanted was on the top floor with the stairs open to the world. Fielding reached the landing and walked the length of the concrete walkway. His nerves jiggled. This contact knew explosive secrets about VIPs. The journalist entered a minefield.

Would the contact speak? Would he lie? Was he scared, terrified? Would he go mad, lash out and kill the journalist?

Fielding knocked. The TV was loud. He knocked again. A voice.

'Who is it?'

'My name's John Fielding. I'm a journalist. I want to talk about ...' He dropped his voice, '... about VIPs in Sydney.'

'Wrong flat.'

'Just a few questions.'

'I'm calling the cops.'

'Don't. The cops attract the media. Do you want your face and address on national television?'

The feeble threat worked. Silence. The man inside thought about his past life and its secrets. He softened and whispered. Both men did.

'If I talk, they'll kill me.'

'I'm only interested in them. They'll never know we met.'

'How did you find me?'

'I'm a journalist, it's my job.'

The man in the flat paused. 'Go away.'

'I promise no mention of your name, identity, anything. You'll never be traced. You have my word.'

'Which is worth what?'

Good question. More silence. Fielding was nervous standing in the open. He looked down at the car park, another architectural masterpiece of cracked concrete and faded white lines. He thought he saw a man in the shadows.

Is that a walking stick? God, it's a rifle!

'Please,' almost begged Fielding, 'let me in.'

His skin crawled. It felt like he was back in Syria with rocket-propelled grenades falling from the black sky. He knocked louder on the door. Nothing. He found it hard to breathe.

Then the door opened a little. The tenant stared. Fielding held up his Union card as if it carried some authority.

The man in the flat was Robert Lensbury, a former rent boy who, decades ago, turned pimp, finding young flesh for wealthy middle-aged males. He was more nervous than Fielding.

'Five minutes,' said the journo, 'I promise.'

Lensbury opened the door enabling Fielding to enter. He looked at his cowering interviewee. A wreck of a man, old before his time, Lensbury was on the cheap wine, roll-your-own fags and frozen pizza diet. Use-by date? What's that?

'Who told you about me?'

Fielding shrugged. 'I told you, I never reveal sources.'

'They'll kill me if I talk.'

Fielding thought. *They'll kill you anyway.* He sat. Lensbury twisted his hands. Getting blood from a stone would be easier.

'Look,' said Fielding, 'how about I read out a list of names and you nod if they were part of the ring. Okay?'

Lensbury gave a miniscule nod.

Fielding started to name names. Lensbury got busy nodding. Every name produced a nod. Fielding was worried.

Is he just nodding to get this over with and me out the door?

Fielding threw in a made-up name, nothing to do with his list. Lensbury hesitated then shook his head.

'Thank you,' said Fielding. He paused. This was an ordeal for both men. 'Can we do the same for meeting places?'

'No. No more.' Lensbury took a vow of silence.

Fielding wanted to push on but knew he now had an eyewitness confirm the names he'd been given—a damn good start. He stood.

'Thanks. I really appreciate your help. And I promise your name will never get mentioned, even indirectly.'

'If you mention me, I'll kill you. Before they kill me, I'll kill you.'

Fielding looked at the frightened, miserable man. This was no idle threat. Lensbury had nothing to lose.

'Thanks,' said Fielding, starting to leave.

'I mean it,' snarled Lensbury.

At the door, Fielding looked back at him. Lensbury made a sign drawing a finger, as in a knife, across his throat.

Walking back to his car, the journo heard footsteps. They were good, the person in the shadows. They were there but not there. Fielding's breathing got shorter. His hair turned prickly. He walked faster. The street was quiet and trees blocked the street lighting. He was sure he could hear footsteps and fought against the temptation to look back. He was still a fair way from the busy road and his car.

Suddenly Fielding was whacked and fell. Lying on the path, he expected a knife, not a gun, a knife. No knife. On his skateboard, a teenager had careered out of a driveway, crashed into Fielding, and both were skittled.

'Sorry mate,' said the kid, hopped on his board, and skated away.

Fielding found his satchel and limped to his car. He wanted to get home and write. In his car, he spoke into his phone, recording his thoughts. Then he drove off, looking in his rear view mirror. Nobody.

He found a car spot reasonably close to his home in Princes Hill. He reached his front gate then panicked. His front door was wide open. He raced inside.

'Rebecca,' he cried fearing the worst.

He found her, slumped on the kitchen floor, bruised and bleeding.

'Becky,' he cried, kneeling to help his girlfriend. 'What's happened?'

'He was here. He's only just gone.'

'Cody? Did he do this?'

She nodded. Fielding roared in anger and frustration. 'I'll kill him,' he snapped, trying to make her comfortable.

'Forget him. I've rung the police and the ambulance.'

'No, this has gone too far. This time he has to pay.'

He ran out of the house with Rebecca calling, begging him to stop.

The patrol car received the call. There was a domestic in Garton Street, Princes Hill. The perpetrator had just left the premises. The man has a record of violence. Call for back up if necessary.

Traffic was normal for this time of night in Carlton—heavy. The only quiet time was between 3 and 3.15 am on the third Tuesday of the month in the middle of winter.

The constables hated domestics. They were potentially lethal, and often the victim didn't press charges. Some victims attacked the cops as they tried to arrest the violent offender, usually a male.

You couldn't win.

The patrol car drove along Lygon then into Pigdon and headed for Garton. They put on their flashing lights to get as clear a run as possible. Then, without warning, from the middle of the road, a woman waving her arms raced straight in front of the police van.

The constables swore, and the driver swerved and stopped.

'What the hell?'

Both police undid their seatbelts and got out.

'Help,' blurted the woman. 'He's been attacked.'

The domestic up the road was put on hold as the cops ran with the woman to the wide grassy area. The police pushed through the crowd where a man performed CPR on the victim.

The female constable grabbed her radio and called an ambulance. One appeared en route to the domestic. It was a busy night.

The male constable joined in the life saving routine. The two men worked desperately. It was no use. The man on the grass was dead. The streetlights were strong but beneath the towering palm trees, the male constable shone his torch. The victim had a nasty wound on his head, as if a metal bar had smashed it. His chest had a major bloodstain, and mini rivulets of blood crisscrossed his face.

The constables fought to get the onlookers away and set up an area around the body. The ambos tried resuscitation but failed. The cops interviewed the man who gave first aid. Other witnesses spoke. Nobody saw the attack.

Another police unit arrived. The officers were told about the domestic in the next block so set off. A second ambulance followed the second police car. It was all happening in Princes Hill.

Rebecca, the victim in the domestic, had recovered enough to bathe her wounds. She heard the visitors.

'Police,' they called moving through the still open front door.

'He's gone,' she said.

'Are you okay?' asked one constable.

'I'm fine or will be.'

The ambos entered and treated Rebecca.

The police kept asking questions. 'Who did this?'

'My ex, my mad ex-husband, Dermot Cody.'

'And where is he now?'

'He left, and then my boyfriend came home, and went after him. You'd better catch them because if John finds him, Dermot is dead.'

'And John's your boyfriend?'

'Yes, you've just missed him. Go!'

She fought the ambos, more worried about her boyfriend.

'What does John look like? What was he wearing?'

Rebecca struggled. 'Black. He always wears black. His beard has a shot of grey in it. Hurry, please, if he finds Dermot, he'll kill him.'

The constables went outside and stopped beside their car. One called their colleagues in the next street.

'Jordy, can you describe the victim?'

'Yeah he's about 40, medium build, dressed in black and has a beard. Why?'

'We think we know who he is.'

They went back inside. Rebecca looked at their faces then collapsed.

Detective Senior Constable Joanna Best was asleep on her settee. She'd had a bad night. It started okay with an upmarket TV dinner. Then she watched a football match where her Bombers (Essendon) made her miserable. They lost. To overcome her sadness, Jo attacked some expensive ice cream with an abundance of calories, which would require at least two half-marathons to remove.

She recently joined the Homicide Squad, a job she dearly wanted but after a few weeks got the sack and was back in uniform asking drivers to provide a breath specimen.

In Homicide, she didn't follow orders, did her own thing, and upset victims of crime. It was humiliating, frustrating and bitterly sad.

However, when it transpired that the upset victims of crime were in fact the perpetrators of a double homicide, unmasked by sleuth Jo Best working in her own time, the Homicide boss asked her back—he had to when an Assistant Commissioner praised her to the heavens.

Boy was she thrilled. Her ambition had long been to work in Homicide, and this time she would make her superiors proud. Alas, she didn't know some of her colleagues were already plotting her second and final downfall.

Jo was her own worst enemy. She was clever but prone to follow a hunch. Hunches without evidence can be dangerous. In addition, to make matters far worse, she led a secret life as a criminal. She crossed the thin blue line, and conspired with Michael Chan, a self-employed computer whiz, to steal money from someone's account.

Mind you, this was not your straightforward theft. Jo and Michael stole what had been stolen. They took back what was taken. Long story short, they carried out a sort of Robin Hood routine.

However, Jo and Michael's walk on the wild side was discovered by her fellow cops, and right now, Jo was skating on very thin ice.

Her phone rang. Murder victims are damn inconsiderate. They allow themselves to be bumped off at all times of the day and night.

Jo knew the number. 'Good evening, Sarge.'

'Homicide in Princes Hill, Senior,' said Detective Sergeant Deborah "Billy" Hughes. I'll pick you up in fifteen.'

Right, Sarge,' said Jo already moving to her bedroom.

'And don't keep me waiting,' said the DS before ending the call.

Jo scrambled to dress and fix her hair. Crime scenes were not fashion parades, but she knew male homicide detectives wore a suit, collar and tie so made sure she at least matched the boys.

Waiting in the street, Jo saw the sergeant's car approach and climbed aboard.

'This reminds me of my first day, Sarge, only this time I get to sit in the front.'

'You've been promoted.'

'I was afraid to ask questions on my first murder.'

'Don't be afraid; just keep your nose clean. Do nothing to upset The Pope. Understood?'

'Sarge.'

Jo now knew the head of Homicide was called The Pope. He sacked Jo. She had vivid memories of that event in DI Steele's office—how could she forget? The Pope screamed at her. For him, having to take her back meant eating a massive serve of humble pie. He loathed her, and wanted to sack her, permanently. He'd enjoy that.

The women arrived at the crime scene, which resembled a circus. Uniformed police patrolled the taped off area. Sticky beaks and rubbernecks were everywhere. Forensic officers were doing what they do and Homicide officers, including DI Steele, stood around talking.

'Here's trouble,' said Detective Senior Constable Stephen Payne, as the female detectives approached.

'Sir,' said Hughes to her boss, and Jo mimicked her sergeant.

'Single victim, head wound, plus stab wound, and no witnesses,' explained Steele. 'His phone and wallet are missing but the victim's been identified as a John Fielding, investigative journalist.' He indicated DI Richelieu, the French Aussie with the Parisian accent, and the bluest of eyes. 'DI Richelieu is OIC.' (Officer in Charge)

'Bonsoir Mesdames,' he smiled and Jo was seriously glad to be back in Homicide.

'We have a suspect,' said Steele. 'Dermot Cody, ex-husband of the victim's girlfriend. Cody allegedly assaulted his ex, who lives around the corner. The victim came home, discovered his battered girlfriend, took off to catch her attacker, and got killed for his trouble. Silly man.'

Richelieu continued. 'It is a monumental failure, n'est-ce pas? DS Fleming and DSC Baldwin have gone to collect Monsieur Cody. The victim's girlfriend is close by in the next street. May I ask you ladies to interview her, s'il vous plaît?'

Before Hughes and Best could move, a major event occurred with the arrival of the pathologist, Dr Gabrielle Strange. It was impossible for her to arrive in a quiet or dignified manner. Some in Homicide disliked her but Jo reckoned she was wise, witty and wonderful.

'You do know I've got out of bed for you lot,' she barked.

'Yeah but whose bed?' murmured Payne.

'Bonsoir Docteur Strange,' oozed Richelieu, using his natural charm to welcome the expert. 'This way, s'il vous plaît.'

And so it began, the investigation of the murder of the man in the street. The journalist John Fielding was dead.

Billy and Jo walked from the crime scene around the corner to the house once shared by John Fielding and Rebecca Cody. A soft knocking and the door opened. A female uniformed constable showed the detectives to the lounge-room in which sat two teary women. One was a neighbour and the other, Rebecca Cody, the victim's lover.

Introductions over, the detectives took a statement. Rebecca suffered two nightmares. Her ex assaulted her, and then the man she loved was murdered—not a nice night.

'We're sorry for your loss,' said Billy. 'May we call you Rebecca?'

She nodded. She'd been given a sedative and had run out of tears. 'It was Dermot,' she said wiping her face.

Hughes trod with care. 'Dermot being your ex-husband?' Rebecca nodded. 'And you saw him? I mean you weren't attacked in the dark?'

'The lights were on but I'd know him anywhere.'

'Has he done anything like this before?'

'He's been harassing and threatening me ever since I left him. And I left him because he hit me.'

Hughes paused. 'Did you have an intervention order for him?'

Rebecca moaned. If only. 'John said it would tip him over the edge. Well he was right there.' She broke down again. The neighbour rubbed her arm. 'Have you arrested him?'

'Officers have gone to interview him.'

'Interview him? Surely you'll arrest him?'

'Yes, we will.' Hughes paused. 'Do you think he's capable of murder?'

'I don't think, I know. When he's drinking, he's capable of anything.' More tears.

Hughes tried bridge building. 'I know this is really hard, Rebecca. Just a couple more questions, if you're up to it.' The distraught woman agreed—just. 'Does Mr Fielding have any family?'

'A brother, Martin. Their father died last month. The brothers don't get on. John was afraid of his older brother.'

'Afraid?'

Rebecca was distressed. 'I can't talk about it now.'

'Sure. Can we have the brother's address?'

Rebecca found it and Jo took notes. Hughes led the interview asking the right questions. But Billy, having seen Jo Best in action before, knew her inexperienced colleague was clever, with potential. She looked at Jo.

'Senior Constable?'

Jo appreciated the professionalism, and spoke sympathetically. 'We understand John worked as an investigative journalist.' Rebecca nodded. 'Do you know what he was investigating?'

She shook her head and wiped her eyes. The tissue needed a break. 'He never spoke about his work. He said it was bad luck. And he didn't want me to know anything in case someone forced me to talk.'

'Did he say that?'

Rebecca nodded. 'How bloody ironic he survived the criminals and corrupt officials and politicians and got killed by a jealous madman.'

We don't know that, thought Jo. She looked at Hughes indicating she had no further questions. They were quickly developing a rapport.

Hughes took over. 'We may need to speak to you again, Rebecca. Thanks for being so helpful and the constable will explain the services you can contact. Okay?' Rebecca nodded.

The police officers again offered their condolences and left. They enjoyed working together but had mixed feelings about the murder. Billy thought it straightforward. Jo was not so sure.

2

A WEEK BEFORE JOHN FIELDING DIED, some senior police officers met in a building in the Melbourne CBD (Central Business District). DI Steele from Homicide was there as were officers from the Fraud and Terrorism Squad. An unnamed person sat quietly in the corner. He was an observer from IBAC, the Independent Broad-based Anti-corruption Commission. They investigated corrupt police officers.

DI Handley from the Fraud Squad started proceedings.

'Gentlemen, shall we begin. DS Craven.'

Barry Craven was a solid cop and citizen who nicked fraudsters. He addressed the meeting.

'Last month we arrested David Baggio, aka Ponzi, on charges of deception. He and his mates were selling land in an estate knowing the project would fall over. It did and hundreds lost their savings.'

A picture of Ponzi appeared on a screen. He wasn't smiling.

'Ponzi and his mates made millions. We got him but not his co-conspirators who fled the country. So Ponzi is facing serious jail time. In desperation, he asked to make a deal. We laughed until he knocked us sideways claiming to be working with a corrupt cop.'

DI Steele interrupted. 'If this is a case of police misconduct, then IBAC is clearly involved. But is this a case of a rogue cop, an officer who's committed a crime?'

'I think that's what we're here to discuss,' said DI Handley. Steele backed off. He wanted Jo Best back in Homicide so he, personally, could nail her. 'Sergeant?' Craven continued.

'We asked Ponzi for details. We know he was interviewed as a witness in a homicide. He was not involved in the crime and never charged. End of story. But then he claims that one of the Homicide Squad detectives who interviewed him came to his home.'

'Ponzi's file would have been available during the interview,' added Steele.

'Ponzi claims the officer told him about a secret police set-up involved in locating criminals and stealing the proceeds of their crimes. The officer wanted a criminal who knew about scams to join the team.'

'That's consorting, conspiring and, the misuse of police data,' said Steele.

Craven placed a screed in a plastic envelope on the table.

'Ponzi claimed this document was given to him by the corrupt officer. It details the first scam the group was planning. Forensics found three sets of prints on this screed, but none belonging to the rogue officer.'

Steele was getting impatient. 'So she's smart. We know that.'

We've now identified all three sets of prints. They belong to Ponzi, and to two police officers.'

'What?' Steele was furious. 'Who?'

'Detective Senior Constable Stephen Payne from Homicide …'

'Bullshit,' snapped Steele.

Craven was worried. 'And I'm afraid to say, sir, the third set of prints are yours.'

Steele was speechless, incensed. DI Handley tried to rescue the mission. 'Obviously the officer under investigation took a document handled by colleagues and probably saw this as some sort of a joke.'

'Ha bloody ha,' said Steele. His blood pressure supported his claim. 'Right, can we cut to the chase? We all know the officer. She's part of my squad at Homicide. Her name is Detective Senior Constable Joanna Best and she's a real piece of work.'

'I heard she'd been sacked,' said Handley.

Steele was not keen to discuss Jo's history. 'She was dismissed.'

There was a pause. Craven wouldn't touch this issue. Handley had the rank and did.

'But now she's back in Homicide?'

'She is.'

Handley wanted the facts. 'So she was sacked, and then reinstated. Why?'

Steele snapped. 'She helped solve a double homicide and came back to Homicide. But that was before we knew she's a criminal.'

'And I understand Homicide has a proposal,' said Handley.

Steele did. 'We don't know how big this scam operation is. It could involve many officers all secretly breaking the law. I propose we allow Best to continue in Homicide with a watching brief to catch her in the act. It would involve a joint force from Fraud and Homicide working to trap her and her gang.'

'Her gang?' asked Handley. 'And is Best the boss?'

'Quite possibly which is why we need the joint surveillance.'

Handley wanted more. 'And Ponzi, what happens to him?'

Steele had it all worked out. 'We make him an offer he can't refuse. We hold off on the fraud charges, flag his passport then don't oppose bail on the condition he helps us trap Best. If we get Best via Ponzi, we either waive or reduce his charges.'

Handley was convinced. He looked at the IBAC officer who gave the slightest of nods.

'There's one thing,' said Steele. 'Senior Constable Best is popular with some of her colleagues. If word gets out about her being under surveillance, she may give up her criminal activities. We could miss catching a serious rogue police officer. This operation must be run on a need-to-know basis. I suggest all communication goes through me.'

'Agreed,' replied Handley. 'Sergeant?' Craven agreed.

Steele explained. 'I'll appoint a trusted Homicide Squad officer to liaise with DS Craven.' Craven nodded. The IBAC representative nodded. Handley nodded.

'So,' said Steele, 'let's catch these criminal cops.'

3

DERMOT CODY WAS A TERRIBLE ACTOR. Homicide detectives Justin Fleming and Charlie Baldwin banged on his door about an hour after John Fielding was murdered. The suspect called, complaining in ham acting style.

'What the feck are you doin'?'

'It's the police, Mr Cody. Open the door.'

More grumbling before Cody appeared. The police grabbed him.

'Hey!' yelled the angry Irishman as his over-acting kicked in. 'What are you doin'?'

Fleming made the arrest. 'Dermot Cody, I'm arresting you for assault. You do not have to ...'

'I never assaulted no-one.'

'Anyone,' corrected Baldwin.

'I think your ex-wife would disagree,' replied Fleming.

'She's not my ex, she's still my wife.'

'And battered too,' added Baldwin.

Fleming tried again. 'You don't have to say anything ...'

'Ow, that feckin' hurts, man,' complained Cody resisting arrest and losing. Baldwin made a quick investigation of the messy home including feeling under the blankets in Cody's dump of a bedroom.

Bundled into a police car, Cody was soon in an interview room at Homicide where his pathetic acting saw him plead his innocence.

He tousled his hair. 'I was asleep. You bastards woke me up.'

Lies, as his bed was cold. DS Justin Fleming was old school. He'd just finished a profiling course in the US, but at heart was a Homicide cop, and knew how to cut to the chase. Pretty soon, bad-acting Dermot was prepared to throw up his hands. His anger remained but when he saw the evidence—and this was just from his own phone—of threatening texts, phone calls, and photos, he reluctantly admitted the assault.

'The bitch deserved it,' he growled. 'Now I'm sayin' nothin' more. Charge me, and I'll ask the magistrate for bail.'

'Ah, it's not quite that easy, Dermie, me old mucker,' smiled Fleming. Baldwin didn't smile and most certainly neither did Dermot.

'What?'

'We'd like to have a little chat about another matter.'

The boiling blood returned. Dermot was furious at his ex, livid he'd been caught, and ropeable that he'd almost certainly go inside.

'Something else? No feckin' way, man.'

Fleming stayed calm. 'After you bashed Rebecca, what did you do?'

'Why?'

'Just answer the question.'

'No.'

'What is your relationship with John Fielding?'

'Why?'

'Just answer the question.'

'Feck off.'

'Now Dermot, you're a smart guy,' mocked Fleming. 'Pathetic when it comes to respecting women but I reckon reasonably clever. I'm giving you a chance here to get the police off your back.'

Dermot lost it. 'I've already confessed. I admit it. I bashed me missus. What more do you want?'

'An explanation of your movements after the assault.'

'Oh f'Chrissake, I pissed off. What, you think I hung around for you morons. I only just got home before you pricks started bangin' on me door. Now throw me in a cell and let me get some kip.'

'Not possible, Dermot. We need to talk about murder.'

There was a lull before the storm. Then Dermot lost it.

'Murder! What feckin' murder? When I left, she was cursin' and cryin'. I never killed her.'

'Not her, John Fielding.'

Dermot paused. He was in shock. 'What?'

'He's dead, Dermot, as well you know.'

Dermot paused again. He sensed a fit up, and erupted. The table and chairs got rearranged without any reference to Feng shui. An alarm sounded. Fisticuffs, swearing and fury filled the room.

Additional bodies piled in, the interview ended, and Dermot Cody got a free ride—carried to his overnight accommodation.

Early the next morning, as part of his post-mortem, John Fielding was chilling out on a table awaiting the self-named pathetic pathologist, Dr Gabrielle Strange. At Homicide HQ in the city, detectives gathered in the incident room. Most were sleep deprived. His suaveness the Frenchman, DI Pierre Richelieu, got things moving.

'Merci, ladies and gentlemen, let us begin.' Chatter stopped. 'We 'ave details on the victim.' He looked at Billy. 'Detective Sergeant.'

'The victim is John Fielding, freelance investigative journalist, aged 42. His partner contacted police when she was involved in a domestic with her ex-husband, Dermot Cody. Her current partner is the victim. Fielding came home to find his girlfriend on the floor having been bashed by her ex, and rushed out to catch the attacker. The boyfriend never came home. Heading to the domestic, uniform came across the victim in the street. They identified him thanks to the girlfriend. Fielding's wallet and phone are missing which raises the possibility of robbery.'

'Robbery with a stabbing and head wound for a wallet and phone? Bit extreme.' Charlie Baldwin was not convinced.

DI Richelieu turned to DS Fleming. 'Detective Sergeant?'

'Yes, DSC Baldwin and I went to the home of the alleged assault suspect, a lively leprechaun, Dermot Cody, and arrested him. We interviewed him late last night. In the end he coughed to the assault but furiously denied the murder.'

'And Monsieur Cody is currently enjoying our hospitality, n'est-ce pas?'

'He is nesting par as we speak,' replied Fleming.

The Officer in Charge was a man of meticulous order and precision. 'So, can we back up, s'il vous plaît? We have identified the victim. We have one suspect in custody. We await news from the pathologist and Forensic Services. What else?'

Hughes spoke. 'We need to interview the victim's brother who did not like his brother at all. Bad blood there for sure.'

'Anyone or anything else,' asked Richelieu?

Jo Best had listened to the comments. She remembered her first such Homicide gathering where she spoke up and made a fool of herself, collecting an enemy or two along the way. Nevertheless, she had ideas hopping around inside her head so joined the discussion.

'Do we know what was on his phone and in his wallet?'

Nobody knew and nobody had thought to ask.

'Excellent question, Senior Constable,' said Richelieu with a smile that gave Jo the smallest of thrills.

Jo had the bit between her teeth. 'The motive might have been robbery because of the data in the wallet and on the phone. Maybe Fielding had enemies because of the articles he wrote.'

Steele sat motionless at the back of the room noting the contribution of the young woman he was planning to destroy.

Hughes spoke again. 'His girlfriend said he wrote about corruption in business and politics but never discussed his work.'

A buzz floated around the room.

'OK,' said the OIC, 'allocation of tasks. We need to again interview Mr Fielding's brother, and have another go at Mr Cody. We need reports from Forensics, and the autopsy, and to find Mr Fielding's employer.'

'Employers—he worked as a freelance,' added Hughes.

'Which means what, Sergeant?' asked Richelieu.

'He's self-employed. He writes a piece then sells it to the highest bidder. He probably had several employers.'

'Just Google his byline,' suggested Baldwin.

Jo smiled internally wondering what her grandfather, a former head of the Homicide Squad, would make of "Google his byline".

I'm sure Pop never spoke or ever heard those words.

'Indeed,' added the OIC. 'So our tasks include forensics, the PM and the victim's work 'istory. Interviews include the victim's family, 'is lover again, and the man in the cells, 'er former 'usband.' The way Richelieu said "lover" gave Jo a tingling feeling. The French Aussie continued. 'So unless there is something else, Mesdames et Messieurs, let us away and catch a killer, ...'

The company spoke as one. '... s'il vous plaît.' Some of them, Jo included, added a rich French accent. She loved being back solving murders. But there was a worry.

She didn't want to work with DSC Payne. He hated her and told her so in as many words. She tried to be professional but he was having none of it. Had Jo known that Payne was conspiring with Steele to trap, arrest and ruin her, her loathing for the man might well have exploded. But she couldn't refuse to work with him. A lowly senior constable doesn't get to choose their work colleagues.

Fleming went with Richelieu to catch up on many missing months in Homicide. Billy Hughes took control of her charges. 'Charlie and Jo, see what Dr Strange and Forensics have got.' Jo felt good. 'And find out who the victim worked for? Background and leads, please.'

'Stephen, you're with me.' He was unhappy. How could he keep an eye on the criminal, Best, when not working beside her?

Baldwin and Jo drove to see Gabrielle Strange. Both remembered their last shared car journey. It included a blazing row with Baldwin raging against Jo and sarcastically telling her to get out of his life. There was bad blood between them. The fallout saw Baldwin get an official reprimand from Steele, while Jo got the sack.

Later, when reinstated due to her solving a double homicide, Charlie genuinely congratulated Jo and they were back on good terms. They arrived as Dr Strange was finishing the post mortem.

'Ah,' she exclaimed, looking over the top of her glasses, 'the boys and girls in blue, or is it black these days?'

'Good morning, Doctor,' smiled Baldwin. 'How goes the PM?'

'Better for me than him,' she said indicating the corpse. 'I am yet to complete my opus but am happy to take a stab—pardon the pun dear boy,' she said to the body before addressing the cops, 'that our friend died from a single knife wound which well and truly penetrated his left ventricle. In falling, the victim's head whacked the metal garden seat causing a further serious injury this time to his cranium. Either could have killed him. The killer was right-handed and I would guess of medium height, and reasonable fitness—not a boring old fart like me.'

Jo smiled. Baldwin wasn't sure.

'There are no defensive wounds suggesting our friend was taken by surprise or knew his attacker or attackers.'

'Attackers, plural?' asked Baldwin.

'If he was stabbed *and* pushed, there might have been more than one culprit. Oh, and our journalistic victim had partaken of junk food as his final meal and, amazingly, the turgid repast did not act as a shield against the killer's weapon. I'm told those hamburger buns are rock hard and, as we all know, there's nothing like rock hard buns.'

Jo wanted to laugh. She settled for a smile noted by the pathologist. They had become good friends.

'What about the weapon, Doctor?' asked Baldwin.

'Short 'n sharp,' she replied, indicating the body. Mr Fielding had a zipper from abdomen to Adam's apple. 'Oh, I don't know. Let's say a hunting weapon with a blade about 20 centimetres or 8 inches in old money. And I wager, never to be found.'

'Oh?'

She looked at Baldwin. 'Methinks your killer planned this attack, Detective, and, if so, that knife has vanished. Any arrests?'

'One,' said Jo. The victim's partner was married to an Irishman. She left him for the victim because of hubby's violence.'

'Oh shut the gate,' said Strange. 'An Irish cuckold? Done and dusted, officer.'

Baldwin was confused. Jo was not. Here stood the Madwoman of Chaillot in full flight, Sarcasm-Satire her hyphenated middle name.

'Is that all, Doctor?' Baldwin was keen to escape.

'It is, unless you want to know what he was working on and with whom?'

The detectives froze. Surely, she jests. Surely this was just another of her so-called jokes. They stared in confusion. Strange moved to a table and held up a clear, plastic envelope in which was a tiny book, a diary, which could well have been stolen from the Bronte museum.

'His little black book, I believe,' she smiled. 'Many secrets and clues for detectives in here I wager.'

Jo was stunned. 'But where did you find it?'

'On his person.'

Baldwin didn't believe her. 'No, not true. We searched, *I* searched his clothes thoroughly before I went to arrest Cody.' He moved to collect the package.

'Not his clothes, his body.' Strange held back the package. 'I'd only handle this with gloves, dear boy.' Baldwin produced an evidence bag and the book, itself in a small plastic envelope, was dropped therein.'

'I'm not sure you detectives understand medical terms, but the victim secreted this material up his arse. Well, maybe his bum-crack.'

'Have you looked at it, Doctor?' asked Baldwin.

'His bum-crack? Not the slightest inclination, dear boy.' Jo struggled not to laugh. 'My guess is that if a journalist buries a booklet in his backside, chances are it contains information related to his secretive work. Have a read, my lovelies, but preferably after you've eaten.' She started tidying and called. 'I'll send my report in the fullness of time.' She stopped and thought about her last statement. 'Don't you love that expression? And what's the half-fullness of time?'

Jo nodded towards the exit and Baldwin got the message. Strange winked at Jo who smiled then left to join her colleague as they set off to deliver the mysterious diary to Forensics.

Hughes and Payne arrived at the house of Martin Fielding, older brother of the late John Fielding. Martin was taciturn. Words cost money, folks, and Martin was a miser.

When told his brother was dead, the man didn't react. Nothing. When asked if he had anything to say, he replied, 'Good.'

That got the police interested.

'Would you care to explain, Mr Fielding?' asked Billy.

'I hated him. If you find the killer, let me know. I'll congratulate him. Hell, I'll buy the man a drink. No, I'll shout the entire bar.'

The man who at first appeared mute, now became garrulous, and in doing so, revealed his motive for fratricide.

Hughes took control. 'I need to caution you, Mr Fielding. Your brother was murdered and we are seeking his killer.'

'And you think it was me?'

'Where were you last night between 10 pm and midnight?'

'Here.'

'Can anyone confirm that?'

'No.'

He stared at the detectives, daring them to arrest him. Hughes broke the impasse. 'May we sit down?'

He shrugged and they sat. She went for the jugular.

'Why did you hate your brother?'

'Why?' He added feeling. 'Why?' Payne felt for his firearm. Hughes gave a tiny shake of her head.

'Because he was a selfish bastard. Because he left me to look after our crippled, demented father, spoon-feeding him and wiping the poor old bugger's arse while Mr Almighty Investigative Journalist swanned around righting the wrongs of the world. That's why.'

'I understand your father has recently died, Mr Fielding.'

'And at the funeral, there's my saintly brother glad handing and being comforted by everyone when he barely came to visit or lift a finger to help his dear old dad. I did everything—literally!'

The detectives let the diatribe run.

'And here's the best bit. My dear sweet father only went and left my brother half his estate. Half! I did everything, he did sod all, and the bastard gets half. So when you tell me he's dead and I say "good", I mean GOOD in big fucking capital letters. Now, if that's all, you can get the hell out my house. I can say that because you're in the half I own.'

He stood and stared at the detectives. Hughes stood and returned fire, gentle but with a touch of steel.

'Don't leave town, Mr Fielding. We may need to speak to you again.'

He looked back at Hughes with equal intensity. 'Piss off.'

They did.

Baldwin and Best arrived at Forensic Services with the tiny diary.

'This was found on the murder victim's person,' said Baldwin. 'Apparently he hid same in his rectum.'

'Charming,' said the scientist. 'How come I get all the shit jobs?'

'And after you've finished, we really need to read the contents,' smiled Baldwin.

The scientist smiled back. 'I'll separate the wheat from the crap.'

The detectives returned to their car. Jo worked on her phone. 'I've found Fielding's name on a few articles in *The Age*, *Herald Sun* and *Guardian*. Which do you fancy?'

'Let's go back to HQ. We can walk to *The Age*.'

They did and soon sat in the office of an assistant editor.

'Terrible, terrible news,' he said. 'Everyone knew John, and his work was highly regarded.'

'Why did he work as a freelancer?' asked Jo.

'Some journos like the risk, reckon it makes you work harder and chase bigger stories knowing you've got no salary to fall back on.'

'Do you know what he was working on when he died,' asked Baldwin.

The editor shook his head. 'No idea. John never discussed his work until he was ready to publish. But one thing I can tell you, it would have been big. He had no fear. He'd tackle corporations, politicians, institutions, the lot. And if ever a journo was likely to be killed for what he wrote, John Fielding was it.'

Having learnt everything and nothing, the detectives walked back to Homicide. At the entrance, Jo stopped.

'Fancy a drive to Princes Hill?'

'No.' He paused. 'Why?'

'Have a look at the murder scene. We can be there in ten minutes.'

'I've warned you about hunches. Remember your last disaster?'

'And look how that turned out.'

'Yes, all right, mea culpa.'

'We're not talking to anyone, just looking at the scene of crime. Daylight, better viewing, who knows, we might find something.'

'Forensics spent hours on it.'

'Come on, nice drive in the country, it'll do you good.'

Jo's comedy swung the deal. The murder was in the adjoining suburb, nowhere near the country.

They parked by the murder scene and wandered around the bench. Hard to believe a few hours ago a man was stabbed to death on this very spot.

'Right, Sherlock,' said Baldwin, 'what are we looking for?'

'We'll know when we find it,' she said as they both looked in vain.

After a few minutes, Baldwin gave up. 'Come on, this is useless.'

Jo walked along the grass median strip, calling as she went. 'This was the way he came.'

'Jo,' he called. She ignored him and, frustrated, he followed.

'He turned here.' She pointed. 'There's his house.'

She moved towards it. Baldwin worried. On a recent case, he followed her to an address also in Carlton, and got a bollocking from The Pope. Jo was sacked. Never again.

'Jo.' His voice now contained anger.

She reached the house once shared by John and Rebecca. Jo looked around. Baldwin was about to take her arm and lead her away when the front door opened and two young people came out. They looked like uni students. The boy helped the girl who was crying. The couple stopped because Jo stared at them, almost blocking their way.

'Hello,' she said, showing her ID. Baldwin felt sick. 'We're police officers investigating the death of Mr John Fielding.'

The female cried even more. The male comforted her. He explained.

'We knew John pretty well. He was helping us with our uni course.'

Jo turned on the charm with Baldwin searching for his rosary beads. The four of them walked around the corner, sat in the police car and the students told their tale.

John Fielding was a part-time lecturer in Media Studies at RMIT University, and both Tommy and Hannah were students in his journalism class. More than that, he was their mentor.

'He was a terrific lecturer and a great guy,' said Tommy.

Jo probed. 'Did you know what he was writing about?'

The students looked at one another. Tommy answered. 'No.'

'Not even a hint?'

Heads shook. Lips were sealed.

Baldwin let Jo ask the questions and breathed an enormous sigh of relief when the two 20 year-olds finally went on their way.

'Please,' he begged, 'no more fishing trips.'

'And here I was about to offer you smoked salmon sandwiches.'

He blew a long breath and eventually laughed.

4

JO HAD AN IMPORTANT DATE. Nothing romantic; this was strictly business. The young man, Michael Chan, recently saved her bacon, well, Jo's mother's bacon—her life savings. Shirley Best, mother of Detective Senior Constable Joanna Best, was a lonely divorcee, who went from being scammed and broke to being well off and elated. Michael, with help from Jo, rescued Shirley's savings. They broke the law as Michael hacked the scammer's bank account.

Now reciprocity was a major part of Jo's DNA. She was determined to return the favour, and after work arrived at Michael's Northcote abode, his converted warehouse.

He knew she was coming thanks to his electronic wizardry and spy apparatus. He opened the door and produced his mini smile.

'Greetings Detective, it's nice to see you again.'

Her smile was bigger. 'And the same to you, good sir.' They were now solid friends with trust a given. They pulled off the amazing heist of a criminal's ill-gotten gains. He stole it from Jo's mother and they stole it back—with interest.

Their success brought enormous joy and their adventure still produced sweet memories, but a new task beckoned. Michael's father too had been scammed, not in the same way but still defrauded. The computer whiz and the homicide cop faced a new challenge—how to steal back a second pile of stolen money.

'How's your mother?' he asked.

'She's a new woman, Michael. Thanks to you, her health is bursting with goodness.'

Just talking about her mother made Jo smile, and Michael lapped up the good vibes. The fact that the fraudster was behind bars was the icing on the cake.

'But enough about my family, let's fix the finances of your Dad.'

'I like your enthusiasm.'

'If we can save my mother, we can save your father. So please, tell me his tale.'

They settled. 'My father's been in business forever. Today he owns a number of furniture and homeware stores. He imports furniture from Asia, even Europe, and is very successful. He made sure his children went to the best schools. My sister's a radiologist.'

'I didn't know that,' said Jo.

'About a year ago, Dad was approached by some Chinese Australian businessmen, who offered him a business venture. They were investing in a booming manufacturing company in China where dividends were expected to be solid. My father looked into all the details and made a modest investment of $20,000. Over the next few months, the overseas business continued to grow and my father received some generous dividends.'

'Sounds like our friend Ponzi was involved.'

'They were the Chinese version of Ponzi. Long story short, my father was offered a part-ownership of the Chinese company. The sweetener being he would get a generous discount on any of the goods made by this new and growing business.'

'I think I know what happened. He made a large investment and the Chinese company collapsed.'

'There never was a company. The video, pictures, profit and loss statements, everything my father saw was of another company and the dividends he received were paid from his initial investment.'

'Hello Ponzi.'

'Hello Ponzi indeed.'

'Did he try and retrieve his money?'

'Yes and no. He discovered the men he dealt with were stooges acting for two brothers, gangsters who extort members of the Chinese community. He contacted them and suddenly his business was raided by the Drug Squad.'

'Ouch.'

'Nothing found of course but it was a warning. The brothers called on my father at night and told him straight. Say anything and we'll make your life a misery.'

'Did he go to the police?'

'No. Of course he was intimidated but he was also ashamed. He saw the loss as being his fault—caveat emptor.'

Jo shook her head. 'So tell me about the criminals.'

'Their names are Ernie and Joe Sim. They extort fellow Australian Chinese and get away with it. They're clever and evil and anyone who doesn't pay protection gets hurt. They rule by terror.'

'Michael, we have to go to the police.'

'I have, I've gone to you.'

'No, seriously. This is a major crime. You need the heavy hitters.'

He didn't like her suggestion. 'You need to understand. My father is like your mother. He's ashamed of his stupidity, and does not want his misfortune broadcast to the world.'

Jo fell silent. She was in a bind. She promised to help Michael but now reckoned Michael's problem should be a police matter. When they first met they made a deal. He would help her mother then Jo would help Michael's father. Jo Best was never going to welsh on that deal.

'Okay, well not only do I want to see your father's money returned, I want to see the brothers Sim behind bars.'

'Their nickname is the brothers Crimm. They're criminals who get away with murder.'

'Can I ask why your father told you about his loss?'

'He didn't, well not at first. I could see he was troubled, and I kept asking. He brushed it off saying business was bad but I knew he was hiding something.'

'Been there, done that,' said Jo.

'One night he broke down and cried which was really scary as my father is such a proud man.'

'Been there, done that,' repeated Jo.

'He made me promise I would never tell a living soul about his loss. And yes, I know what you're going to say.'

They spoke together. 'Been there, done that.'

She chanted as in a kids' game. 'What's the plan, Mister Chan?'

He frowned. 'I'm not sure.'

'What about some more of your magical hacking?'

'The problem is we know who scammed my father and these people are not Sunday school teachers. Yes, I've thought about the police but they may not retrieve my father's money, and my father would die if the matter became public. Any court case would take months.'

'Tell me about the brothers.'

'They're thugs who'll maim even kill you and your family in a heartbeat. With Cornelius Kruger, we had one vicious criminal. Here we're up against two.'

Jo exhaled a long breath. This was tough. Surely it was time to call in the Fraud and Extortion Squad.

'I don't like this, Michael. Are you sure we can't make it official?'

'I promised my father I would say and do nothing.'

'Well you've already broken that promise.'

'Ha ha. Look, how about I try something and if it doesn't work, we call the cops.'

She looked at him. He was in torment. '*We* try something, Michael. I'm in this too, remember?' He nodded. She spoke softly. 'Can I ask the amount?'

'A lot—more than your mother's.' Jo sucked in air, not knowing what to say. 'I've got a possible plan,' he said.

Now she felt excited—scared but excited. 'I'm listening.'

'We set up a scam on behalf of the government.'

Jo was stunned. 'We what?'

'A scam like the one they used for my Dad, would never work. They'd see through it immediately. But if the Australian Government set up a tender scheme, that would not look like a scam. Done the right way, it could look like a serious proposition. I reckon the brothers Crimm might go for it.'

'I'm impressed—again. Tell me about it.'

'We set up an official looking Australian Government web site. It's on the Dark Web and password protected.'

'You've lost me already but please, keep going.'

'We leak details to the Sims who are hooked and check out the site. It looks impressive. The deal on offer is seriously good, and to deter time wasters, would-be bidders have to pay a holding deposit. If a bid is unsuccessful, there's no problem getting your money back because you're dealing with the Federal Government.'

'And?'

'And that's it. These criminals will want to win the tender so they pay the deposit. We send the funds offshore and shuffle it around making tracing it nigh on impossible. Then the funds appear in my father's bank account and I tell him the good news. He must never say or do anything; just keep quiet and take the money—his money.'

'Will he keep quiet?'

Michael shrugged. 'He'll be curious, and worried I've put myself in danger.'

'Which you have, but will he be grateful?'

'Of course—but he won't be able to love me any more than he does already.'

Jo stopped. She saw yet another side to this young man.

'And will the crims come looking?'

'Will they ever? But again, everything disappears. No web site, no emails, no trace of their money.'

'*Your* money.'

'They'll have no one to complain to which will make them even more determined to find who scammed them.' He puffed his cheeks. 'Let's just hope they never do.'

'Will they?'

'Cornelius Kruger did.'

Jo grimaced. Scary memories surfaced of what that man did to them and Jo's mother. They stared at one another.

'So what do you think?' he asked.

'Where does Ponzi fit into this?'

'He doesn't. I don't like him. I reckon he's dangerous.'

'Michael, we don't have to like him. I think he's a creep but he knows how to scam and perhaps we need a thief to catch a thief. His advice could get us over the line.' Michael wasn't convinced. 'Why don't we keep him in reserve, just in case?'

'Maybe, we'll see.'

They both wondered if Ponzi was a good fit for this, their latest enterprise.

5

IN THE INCIDENT ROOM, BILLY HUGHES and DI Richelieu stood with their backs to the notice board. Every Homicide Squad member was present. The photo of John Fielding, the murdered journalist, was front and centre. The discussion began. Whodunit?

Hughes reported on the grieving girlfriend. Fleming reported on her ex, Dermot Cody, his hatred of the victim, and his violence and threats during the interview. Payne reported on the victim's brother and his passionate loathing of his dead sibling. Baldwin reported on Strange's early PM comments, the victim's freelance writing gigs, and the hidden diary. Many leads, much information but no arrests.

Work piled up. Forensics and the PM report needed chasing. Another interview with Dermot Cody was required. Martin Fielding, the victim's brother, needed a background check, and the miniature diary was, so far, the only physical evidence.

Jo loved her working life. That scam business with Michael Chan was hairy but being back in Homicide got her heart pumping. It went faster when she was paired with the French speaking DI, he with the mouthwatering blue eyes, and the dress sense of a fashion designer.

They drove to Forensics. Jo studied her boss en route.

How old is he? That greying at the temples is exquisitely sexy.

'So Mademoiselle Best,' he oozed, 'do you like life back in 'omicide?' He barely sounded the letter H in *Homicide*.

'I do, thank you, sir. I'm hoping to stay a little longer this time.'

He smiled and that in itself was an experience worth savouring.

They called on Dr Strange who reacted in a way, which matched her name. She stood taller, smiled wider, and spoke sweeter. Jo was puzzled.

Surely, she's not fallen for the Gallic charmer.

The post-mortem report was complete and a typed copy handed to the Detective Inspector. The pathologist explained some points. As he perused the document, the two women looked at one another. Jo suddenly saw a different side to her friendly pathologist.

My God, she does fancy him and she thinks I'm competition.

'Merci beaucoup, Docteur,' smiled Richelieu. 'Au revoir.' He smiled also at Jo. 'Mademoiselle,' he said then turned and left.

Strange grabbed Jo's arm and whispered. 'I saw him first, you little minx.' Jo was shocked then twigged. Gabrielle winked and they suppressed their laughter. Richelieu looked back.

'Mademoiselle?'

Jo took off after her boss, turned back, and blew the doctor a kiss.

The officers went to Forensics and collected the tiny diary found on or apparently *in* the victim's body. The only prints on the diary were Fielding's. In the car, Jo read the PM report.

'Anything catch your eye, Senior Constable?'

'Not really, sir. I think the main interest will be found in the diary.'

'Then good luck.'

'Sir?'

'It is your task to examine the diary, Detective. I expect a full report on my desk before the end of the day.'

'What am I looking for, sir?'

'Names, dates, places, anything and everything. If there's an entry which says, "The name of my murderer is Monsieur So-and-So", then make sure you note such a find, s'il vous plaît.'

He grinned and Jo unconsciously fluttered her eyelids.

My God, I can't help myself. Steady girl. He's old enough to be your ... lover!

She sat at her desk and studied Fielding's diary. It was strange. There were numbers on certain dates but little else. Some of the numbers were underlined and some had one or two dots after them. Why? What did the numbers mean? Was this a well-known cipher? Did Fielding have his own secret code? Bloody hell.

I'm guessing here—not even that.

After half an hour, she knocked on DI Richelieu's door.

'Entrer,' he called.

Jo opened the door and stopped. Her favourite Frenchman was in conversation with another DI, her bête noire, the boss of Homicide.

'Oh, sorry, sir, I'll come back.'

'No, no, no, Detective.' He beckoned. Do come in, s'il vous plaît.'

She did and nodded to the Pope. 'Sir.'

'Problem, Detective?' asked Richelieu.

'It's the victim's diary, sir. It's written in some form of code.'

'Surely not a problem for an intelligent officer, Mademoiselle?'

'I'm afraid it is, sir.' She hated admitting defeat but had a plan. 'I have a friend who is brilliant with codes. I could show it to him if you agree.'

DI Steele joined the conversation.

'Who is this friend?'

'His name's Michael Chan, sir.'

'How do you know him?'

Jo hesitated. 'Ah, a colleague in Fraud introduced us, sir.'

'Why?'

'Why, sir?'

Steele persisted. 'Yes, why would a Fraud Squad officer recommend a computer expert?'

Jo tried to control her panic. She started to feel funny, no, more like sick. She knew Michael was never big on publicity, and here she was announcing his name to senior police officers, and almost talking about his and Jo's secret life as criminals.

What am I saying?

'I needed some help with a technical issue, sir.'

'And did he help?'

'He did, sir.'

'An excellent suggestion, Senior Constable,' smiled Richelieu. 'Let me know 'ow your code-cracking goes. Au revoir.'

Jo got the message. 'Sir.' She nodded to the Pope and left.

Phew.

Arriving in Northcote, she found wunderkind Michael busy on his latest scam—*their* latest scam.

'Good morning,' he said wondering why she had turned up.

She held up the diary. 'Michael, this is business, police business.'

She explained the diary and her confusion. He opened it then stopped. 'Please, help yourself to coffee.'

'Thanks. Oh, hello Alan.' Leg rubbing was in from Alan the cat.

Michael called. 'His favourite topics are Philosophy and Fly-fishing. He knows a bit about Eastern Religions, and a hell of a lot about salmon fishing on the Tay—fish, you see.'

Michael returned to the diary and, in the kitchen, Jo chatted with the feline.

A coffee and feline chat later, Jo approached her partner in crime. When Michael Chan was quiet, you knew something was brewing. She hesitated to interrupt. He looked at her and smiled.

She dared to ask. 'Any luck?'

'Henry Huckster.'

Jo looked blank. 'Who is?'

'Who was a poor man's Edward de Bono. Most of Henry's ideas were whacky but he claimed he invented a kids' cipher.'

Jo had no idea what Michael was talking about. 'A kids' cipher?'

'Yes, it's pretty simple. This first series of numbers reads Robert Lensbury 8/17 Denton. Then here it's Charles Brittain 2/66 Beaching.' He looked at her. 'The numbers are listed on different days. Mean anything?'

She was still in shock. 'Is there anything you can't do?'

Thanks to Michael, Jo got a break. But she needed help.

He explained. 'Henry's full name was Henry Reginald Ralph Huckster. His parents conveniently named him using 26 letters so each letter in his name is a number with H for Henry being A and *r* in Huckster being Z. There are repeated letters and he used tiny dots for the second *h* and so on. For numbers he used real numbers and underlined them, so using Henry Huckster's cipher you get these names and what I'd say are part addresses. Because each name appears on a particular date, you could assume the diary owner had business with that person on that day. The suburbs aren't listed but perhaps he already knew them. If he had the street and house number, that's a fair assumption.' He looked at her. 'Do you know this … Robert Lensbury?' She shook her head. 'Or Charles Brittain?'

'Never heard of them.'

'Well the owner of the diary did or planned to. According to this little black book, he was due to meet Mr Lensbury last Tuesday.'

Last Tuesday meant something to Jo. John Fielding was murdered.

'I can give you the names, addresses and dates if you like.'

'I like,' was all Jo said still recovering from Michael's expertise.

He wrote the details on a piece of paper. 'Just remember Henry's full name.'

'Henry Reginald Ralph ... Huckster,' she said.

'That's him. It's childlike simplicity and a cinch to decipher. I don't think the owner of the diary ever worked for the CIA. Have you read *The Adventure of the Dancing Men*.' More head shaking from Jo. 'Sherlock Holmes.'

'My Pop read me those stories when I was a kid. I should call you Sherlock.'

'He solved a cipher in *The Adventure of the Dancing Men*.'

'Okay, that's my next book to read.'

'All your diarist has recorded are names and addresses sans suburb or town, and placed this info in dates. I hope that helps.'

'I'm sure it does, Michael. Thank you yet again.'

Michael produced his potted grin and handed her the diary.

'So what's this all about? Or aren't I allowed to know?'

Jo explained how the diary was found on the body of a murdered man, and she was trying to figure out what the entries meant.'

'Well I'd bet they're meetings.'

'So would I.'

'Now as you're here, how about a sneak peek at the latest scam?'

'You've done it already?'

Jo was stunned. Michael opened a web page, which looked like an official part of the Australian Government's Department of Foreign Affairs and Trade (DFAT) web site. The logo, the font, the photos, the text—everything looked to be a dead ringer for the real thing. It wasn't. It was a hoax. The whole darn shooting match was the work of one, Michael Chan.

'I don't know what to say,' she said.

'You like?'

'You've topped your own super-high standard, Michael.'

'It needs some fine tuning, and I'm not sure of the wording of the final pitch.'

'Should we run it by Ponzi?'

Michael expelled air. He didn't like Ponzi. 'I'm still not sure about him. He's the weak link. If he gets arrested and rolls over, we're sunk.'

'Well how about we tell him nothing about the scam, just show him the text on plain paper, and get his feedback?'

Michael took a very long breath. 'I'll think about it.'

Jo sat in her car and studied the diary wondering why an experienced journalist would use a child's code.

She had names, part addresses and dates. Charles Brittain in 2/66 Beaching was listed for next week. But last Tuesday, the day Fielding was murdered, he had a meeting with a Robert Lensbury who lived at 8/17 Denton Street or Road or whatever. Lensbury was a definite lead.

Should I ring Billy and report this discovery?

Jo used her phone to look for Denton. There was a Denton Street close to Princes Hill. She tingled some more. On her way back to Homicide, she could check out that address.

She called Homicide and spoke to Charlie Baldwin. She told him her friend had cracked the code, and she'd be in as soon as possible. She didn't tell Baldwin she was about to investigate someone named in Fielding's diary. Will she never learn?

Jo found the block of non-descript flats and climbed the stairs Fielding climbed the night he was murdered. She knocked on Flat 8. Silence.

Not at home, at work.

She was about to turn away when the door opened a smidgeon.

'Oh hi,' said Jo. 'Robert Lensbury?'

'Are you the police?'

'Yes I am.' She showed her ID.

Why would he ask that? Is he expecting me?

He opened the door. 'You've gotta help me.' Jo entered. He closed the door. 'They're gunna kill me. I need protection. I need it now.'

'Okay, take it easy,' said Jo. 'What's the problem?'

'Why are you asking? I've already told you.'

'Not me personally, sir. So who's going to kill you?'

'I told the police when I rang.'

'Yes but you didn't tell me.'

Jo was telling white lies. She was going it alone, the very thing that got her into trouble and sacked not long ago. She couldn't help herself and kept playing the game.

'I told that reporter guy all the names.'

'What reporter guy?'

'Fielding, John Fielding.' Jo's pulse leapt out of the blocks. 'He said he wouldn't use my name but I think he has. I know he has.'

'How do you know that, Mr Lensbury?'

'Are you a cop? You're a woman.'

'Very observant, sir and yes, I am a cop. I showed you my ID. So what were these names you told him?'

'He asked about the VIP paedophile ring in Sydney. He read out some names and I nodded if I knew a name.'

'Which paedophile ring are we talking about?'

'I knew them all. Every name I knew—except one.'

'Mr Lensbury, where were you, on Tuesday night between 10 pm and midnight.'

He stopped and stared at her. 'Why do you want to know?'

'Just answer the question, please.'

'He's dead isn't he?'

'Who?'

'That reporter, Fielding. They killed him after he left here.'

'Who are they?'

He panicked. 'They'll kill me next. They're powerful and ruthless. They told me. Talk to the police or the press, to anyone, and you're dead.'

'I think you should come with me,' said Jo not knowing whether to arrest or rescue the distressed man.

He pulled back. 'Are you mad?' His voice oozed fear. 'If they see me with a cop, I'm dead.'

'You said you wanted protection.'

'I do.'

'Well I'm a detective, in plainclothes.'

'They can tell. They'll have your picture. They'll know.'

'Right, I'll go first, and wait by my car. I'm right outside.'

'No way.'

'Mr Lensbury, we can't protect you if you stay here.' He thought about that. His eyes screamed for help. Jo gave him her card. 'Take this. Come into town and ask for me at the front desk. You'll be safe.'

He took the card, sniffed and blinked—a lot.

'Okay.' He got the shakes.

'Are you sure you won't come with me now?'

'No.' He could not have been more definite.

'Then I'll wait for you in town. How will you travel?'

'Carefully.'

Jo opened the door, looked at the terrified Lensbury, then left. As she walked back to her car, she had a sinking feeling in her stomach.

Have I stuffed up again?

She reached her car when a police van pulled into the street. She held up a hand and showed her ID.

'Have you come for the guy in Flat 8?' They had. 'He's scared. He needs protection. I think he's in real danger. He's a witness, and possibly a suspect in a homicide. Can you take him into town?'

The two uniformed constables headed into the carpark of the flats. Jo got into her car when her phone rang. It was her father. She was about to switch to voicemail then decided to answer it. He normally rang at night.

'Hi Dad. How are you?' She was polite but businesslike. She expected him to invite her for a meal with his second family, his trophy wife and their two young kids. Jo had a half brother and sister young enough to be her own kids. Her father's response wasn't quite what she expected. His voice sounded weird, scary. Gone was the pushy, enthusiastic, real estate agent she knew. Her father sounded desperate.

'Jo, please, you've gotta help me.'

'Dad, what's happened?'

'I've been arrested.'

6

JO PARKED IN HARP ROAD, KEW near the large and modern police station. She fronted Reception.

'Can I help you, madam?' asked the constable.

'Yes, hi.' She showed her ID. 'I'm Detective Senior Constable Jo Best from Homicide but I'm here ...

'For your father,' said the constable. 'He said you were coming.'

'Right. Can I see him?'

'Sure, come through.'

Jo entered the heart of the station and stopped outside an interview room. The constable indicated the door.

'I'll tell Senior Sergeant Greeves you're here.' He disappeared.

Jo wasn't sure what to do. She knocked softly and opened the door. Her father jumped to his feet and gave his daughter a strong hug.

'Jo, thank God you're here. It's a bloody nightmare.'

'Okay, Dad, take it easy.' He couldn't. 'Sit.' He even found that difficult. She sat. 'What's happened?'

'I've been arrested.'

'I gathered that but why?'

'Natalie threw me out.'

'What? Why?'

'She believed the woman who said I assaulted her.'

Jo was genuinely shocked. 'What woman?'

'It's not true, not even remotely true.'

'Dad, slow down. Who said you assaulted her? And why?'

'I don't know. That's what's killing me. Jo, if this goes to court, I'm finished. I'll never work in real estate again. Who'll buy a house from a pervert?'

'Dad, try and calm down. What have the police done?'

'They arrested me at a home we're selling—thank God I wasn't at work—brought me here, interviewed me, then charged me with assault.'

'What about Natalie?'

'I've rung her and she said she doesn't want me back in the house if the police charge is true. She doesn't want the kids near a criminal. Oh God, my own kids. And the whole thing is a lie, a total fucking … sorry, lie. I never assaulted anyone.'

Malcolm's head slumped. He silently cried. Jo saw a shattered man.

'Are they keeping you in tonight?'

He despaired, his voice a wail. 'I don't know.'

'I'll talk to them.' She stood. He grabbed her arm.

'I've got nowhere to stay. My brother hates me. Caitlyn reckons I spoil her kids. Can I stay with you? Please Jo?'

She was stumped. 'Let me talk to the arresting officer.'

'Okay, thanks. But please, Jo, I've done nothing wrong and I've got no-one except you.'

She grimaced and forced a weak smile. She spoke to Senior Sergeant Greeves who agreed to release her father into his daughter's care. Malcolm was devastated. Shock, shame and fear smothered his body. He stood in front of the officer who warned about the conditions of his release. 'Don't miss your court appearance, Mr Best,' said the senior sergeant. Jo stood close to her father trying to give support and, at the same time, struggling to believe they were in this situation. She'd been in many cop shops but this was a first.

They finally left and Malcolm walked as if tipsy.

Is my father drunk? He doesn't smell of grog.

'Where's your car?'

He wasn't sure. 'Ah, back at the house in Deepdene.'

'We'll get it later. Get in.'

They drove back to Jo's flat in Clifton Hill. Her father had his phone, wallet, keys and the clothes he stood up in. Great.

Jo felt pressure. She abandoned a distressed witness, possibly a murderer. Her latest spot of criminal activity with a new scam was about to kick off. And now her father, it was her mother last month, was in a frightening situation with his marriage, career and health under serious threat.

'Listen, Dad, you can stay here till we get this sorted.'

'Thanks, Jo. I really appreciate it.'

'I'll go to your place and get some things.'

'You're a star. And please, tell Natalie it's not true—none of it.'

'Sure. I'll need your house keys.'

'You won't, she'll be there. And don't be surprised if your sister is too. They're as thick as thieves.'

'That'll be interesting. Just stay here, don't go outside or answer the door. I'll be back in an hour.'

'Love you, Jo,' he said as she left.

'See you soon.'

Steele and Payne were in the Pope's office. The topic of discussion was one Jo Best.

'She's disappeared, boss. She interviewed a witness without authority, left uniform to bring him in, and now she's gone AWOL. A week in and she's shot herself in the foot.'

'Get a grip, Payne.'

He looked confused only because he was. 'Boss?'

'First we're not sure she's done anything wrong—stupid maybe, but not necessarily wrong. And second, if I sack her, we miss the chance to catch her breaking the law. The aim, in case you've forgotten, is to catch her in the middle of her fraudulent racket, and have her not only sacked but charged and put inside.'

Payne twigged. 'Sure, boss, sorry.'

'A mate at Kew rang to say she called in to rescue her father who was arrested for assault. If that's serious it might excuse her stupidity and keep her here in Homicide.'

Payne got excited. 'Crime runs in her family.'

Steele looked at the grinning constable and wondered why he was working with an idiot while conniving to remove a brilliant detective.

Jo pulled up outside her stepmother's Canterbury home. It was a grade above classy, and worth a squillion dollars with hot and cold running gardeners. Jo and Natalie were not close. Having a stepmother about the same age provided a challenge to both women and particularly Jo. Not to Jo's sister Caitlyn, but that's another story.

The doorbell had its own set of stereo speakers. Natalie opened the door and couldn't decide between a smile and a scowl so settled for a smowl.

'Hi,' said Jo. 'I've come to collect some things for my Dad.'

'Oh,' replied Natalie. 'Come in.'

Jo followed Natalie into the kitchen. There, enjoying a skinny latte, sat Jo's big sister, who wasn't big, Caitlyn.

'Hi,' said big sis.

'Hi,' said little sis.

'Coffee?' asked the stepmother.

'No thanks, I can't stay.'

Then followed one of those pauses where everyone thought of something to say but no one did. The elephant in the room swapped chairs.

'Well,' said Natalie, 'I'll show you where to go. Do you need a bag?'

'No, I'm fine.' She would later regret that decision.

Natalie headed upstairs and Jo followed. The sisters didn't even exchange a glance.

At the door to the master bedroom, Natalie indicated. 'I'll leave you to it. I'm sure I can trust the police.'

That last comment got filed under *Unnecessary* or *I wish I hadn't said that*.

'Thanks,' said Jo and got to work.

This was a first for Jo and, frankly, weird. Collecting smalls for your father was not an everyday occurrence for many daughters, Jo included. She chose toiletries, shirts, shoes, socks and jocks.

Is that enough? What about jim-jams?

With hands full, she went downstairs and called. 'I'm off, ladies.'

Natalie hurried out and opened the front door. Caitlyn followed.

'Thanks,' said Jo and left. Her sister chased after her.

'Jo, wait.'

They stopped in the garden and looked at one another. 'I don't know what's going on,' said big sister.

Jo paused. 'Join the club.'

'It's really unfortunate.'

'Look, Dad called me and asked for help.' She indicated the clothes. 'That's what I'm doing.'

'Great. And thanks for not wearing your uniform.'

'Sorry?'

'Thanks for not rocking up looking like a cop.'

'I am wearing my uniform.'

Caitlyn looked puzzled. 'What?'

'I'm a detective in the Homicide Squad.'

Caitlyn reacted. 'Oh, since when?'

Jo realised the connection between some members of the Best family was not so much broken as non-existent.

'A while.' She headed to her car. 'I'll see ya.'

Jo was about to drive home but took a detour to see her mother. Shirley opened the door with a smile to power a generator.

'Jo, my favourite, favourite daughter.' Mother's hug matched her smile and vocabulary.

'I was in the area,' fibbed Jo. 'How are you, Mum?'

She was fine, obviously, and gushing. Having enjoyed a recent financial windfall, Malcom X's ex had moved to the land of Bliss.

'I've got some news, my darling. I'm going on a cruise.'

'Wow,' said Jo in a meek voice. She nearly said, "No problem with the expense, hey Mum?"

'And I'm not paying a cent.' That rocked the detective, while the next sentence poleaxed her. 'I've met someone.'

Okay, I'm guessing you mean a romantic type meeting.

'Really?' Jo thought that sounded surprised so added, 'I'm really happy for you, Mum.'

Then Jo had a terrible thought. *My mother's got money, and a new fraudster has moved in for the kill.*

'And I know what you're thinking,' said Shirley. 'I've met another fraudster who only wants my money.'

'Well, I couldn't bear to see you hurt again, Mum.'

Shirley smiled. She was like a teen describing her new boyfriend.

'I met him at the U3A, his name's Antony, he comes from Italy, he's 71, and as rich as Croesus.' Shirley saved the best till last. 'Jo, I've found a sugar daddy.'

There's not a lot you can say when your mother babbles like so.

'Well, good for you, Mum. When's the trip?'

Shirley was on a high. 'But wait, there's more. My daughter's a cop, and her father's a crim.'

Shirley grinned. She took pleasure in her last statement. Jo didn't react and that surprised Shirley.

'You're not shocked?'

'I know about Dad. I helped get him released, and I don't share your glee at his suffering.'

Right, that pricked Shirley's balloon. It went phut in a nanosecond. She lost the attitude.

'Yes, I'm sorry. Of course, you know. Did your sister tell you?'

'Mum, Dad told me. I just said I helped get him released.'

'Oh.' The visit ended. Shirley offered coffee. Jo had to go. She didn't say to deliver her father's smalls. Shirley knew she blew it with Jo.

The detective arrived at her flat in Clifton Hill carrying her father's goodies. At her front door, her phone rang. It was Baldwin.

'Charlie, I can't talk right now, family emergency.'

'Sorry but I thought you should know the Pope's on the warpath.'

'What else is new? I'll be there as soon as I can.'

She ended the call and struggled with the flat door. Rather than put everything on the ground then find her key, she knocked and called.

'Dad, it's me. Can you open the door?'

Nothing.

'Please.'

Still nothing.

Muttering, she dumped the goodies, found her key, and opened the door. Picking up the items, she entered her flat.

'Dad, it's me. Can you give me a hand?'

Nothing.

It didn't take long to check the flat. Malcolm X had gone.

MICHAEL STUDIED HIS FAKE WEB SITE. He was picky but even he reckoned it looked okay. His scam was simple. A government department wanted to appoint an Australian company as a trade ambassador. The Department of Foreign Affairs and Trade invited expressions of interest. Certain criteria applied, and applicants must:

* Speak fluent Putonghua (standard Chinese).
* Have an established business reputation in Australia.
* Have solid business connections in China.
* Lodge a substantial holding deposit.

Any business deals struck between Sino-Australian companies would earn the trade ambassador, a percentage of the deal.

Say that again.

The proposal screamed out for applicants. It was a license to print money. The Federal Government wanted to employ someone to help Australians do business in the world's biggest (or second biggest) economy. China was huge. How good is this job? It's money for jam.

Michael kept thinking the scam was too obvious. No sensible crook would fall for it. But then he remembered he once managed to hook a scammer in Cornelius Kruger, and relieve him of a small fortune in what they called the Code of Monte Christo. Could this scam work too?

The text on the fake web site looked okay but Michael was no copywriter. This was where David Baggio, alias Ponzi, alias criminal and now police informant, came in.

Michael and Jo didn't know Ponzi had been arrested on fraud charges and, to save his skin, had agreed to spy on Jo Best and report any news about her scams to the police. Michael and Jo had no idea the third member of their team was a rat.

Ernie Sim was Australian by birth and Chinese by ancestry. He and his less intelligent brother Joe, known as Dim Sim, were both what some call an ABC, an Australian Born Chinese. They liked to think of themselves as white-collar crims, although thuggery and violence were their calling cards. Ernie and Joe had stitched up Michael's father, David Chan, who was too proud to fight back, and afraid of the terror the brothers would bring down upon his business and family if David complained.

The Sim brothers made an excellent living from crime. Extortion via protection was their main line of business. 'You pay us for insurance and we'll not set fire to your business.'

They managed to avoid arrest because they were careful, and because of the fear they spread amongst their victims, David Chan being a perfect example.

However, David's son wanted to fight the Sim brothers. He fancied a game of *David and Goliath*. Michael was determined to retrieve his father's money. Michael's scam for Jo's mother worked. Could he do it again? And, if so, would the criminals react with violence? Michael sent a text to his favourite Homicide detective.

Monte Christo tonight.

Right now, Jo was not in the mood for meetings of any kind. Her father, with whom she didn't enjoy the closest of relations, had been arrested for assault, thrown out of home, begged for help from his younger daughter, and now had done a runner. To where? And why?

She laughed inside. Parents take responsibility for their kids. Of late, she was taking responsibility for her parents. She rang her father. Voicemail. She left a message.

'Dad, I've left some of your things at my place. Call me.'

She went to work. Things weren't happening with the investigation of the murder of John Fielding. Leads weren't so much thin on the ground as non-existent.

'Everything okay,' asked Baldwin?

'Fine, bit of a worry with my Dad but I think it's sorted.'

'You think?'

'He's fine. Did a guy called Robert Lensbury get brought in?'

'He's being interviewed by Billy and the Cardinal as we speak.'

Jo had forgotten that DI Richelieu was known as the Cardinal. She slumped at her desk. Life was not going swimmingly, and had the potential to get far worse.

'How did you find Lensbury?'

'Through Fielding's diary.' Baldwin looked at her. His look told Jo she'd goofed again. Her learning curve was about to get steeper. 'What have I done this time?'

'Sorry to be picky but taking the evidence out of the station ...'

Jo hit back. 'Charlie, I had permission. Richelieu in the presence of Steele gave me specific authority to show the diary to my friend who's an expert with codes.'

Baldwin waited. He wanted Jo to lose her anger and frustration.

'Known and understood,' he said, 'but going off on a personal errand while hanging onto the evidence is not wise. If something had happened to that diary, you would have been in really deep shit.'

Jo twigged. She kept the knowledge she got from Michael to herself for hours. That knowledge might have provided a lead to the killer. She was still sitting on it. *Damn.*

She tossed the diary onto Baldwin's desk. Neither said a word. He studied the tiny book and tried to repair the damage.

'And you've cracked the code. Well done.'

His compliment was too little too late. But he was right. She'd mucked up again. She ignored advice and orders, and found another way to do the wrong thing. And to rub salt into her wound, Payne entered accompanied by his smirk.

'Ah, Detective Best, welcome back. All well at home, I trust?'

Jo spied a therapy ball on Baldwin's desk and moved to grab it and hurl it full pelt at Payne. As she grasped the ball, Billy Hughes entered.

Everyone stared at Jo. She had the smoking gun in her hand. She grimaced, squeezed the ball and placed it back on Baldwin's desk.

Hughes broke the silence. 'Senior, well done with Lensbury. You found a valuable witness or perhaps our murderer. He's one screwed up individual but well done you.'

'Thanks Sarge.' Jo lost some of her fury and frustration.

'What's happened with your family matter? All okay?'

Does the entire squad know about my private life?

'Getting there,' said Jo.

'Good. Now I'm buggered.' She spoke louder. 'Who's for a drink?'

Such words have become universal in police stations. "Who's for a drink" is only bettered by "I'm buying". The room cleared faster than any fire drill, except for Jo who returned to her desk.

Baldwin called. 'Come on, Jo. It's my shout.'

'Thanks Charlie but I've got a naughty parent to find.'

He understood and left. Jo tried her father again. It went to Voicemail. She looked again at Michael's message. She liked their code —*Monte Christo*—and Michael never requested a meeting unless something important was in the air.

Two hours earlier, Malcolm Best sat in his daughter's flat and couldn't believe his predicament. Arrested for anything was likely to end his real estate career. Arrested for assaulting a lone female during a house tour was, in career terms, akin to murder. The fact that it was a fit-up meant nothing. There's no smoke without fire and Malcolm X got burnt. He'd been cooked, well done, and on both sides.

He replayed the incident in his mind. He could see everything in living HD colour. The woman was attractive and polite.

'I'm sorry,' she said, 'but my husband's been delayed. Can I still see the property?'

'Of course,' replied the estate agent. 'Come on in.'

Malcolm's memory got busy. A man had booked the viewing and asked specifically for Malcolm claiming he showed the couple a house in Deepdene a year or more ago. Malcolm understood. *I've been set up.*

The inspection was normal. At the downstairs cloakroom, Malcolm opened the door then stood back. The woman entered and touched the handrail and door handle. *Is she superstitious?*

Malcolm turned to head towards the kitchen when the woman suddenly took off screaming, unbuttoning her blouse as she ran. Malcolm froze. She ran through the house, out the front door and down the drive. A neighbour saw her and called.

'Are you all right?'

Highly agitated, the woman ran straight to the neighbour.

'Call the police, I've just been assaulted.'

The neighbour, a retired gent busy in his garden, was in shock. The woman looked back at the house she'd run from and saw a confused Malcolm heading towards her. She pointed.

'There he is. Help me, please!'

The gardener escorted her indoors where she rang the police.

Malcolm stopped at the driveway of the house and called.

'Hello? Is everything all right?'

The neighbour was adamant. 'Keep away. She's calling the police.'

'The police? Why? What for?'

'Just keep away,' replied the neighbour who closed the door.

A stunned and confused Malcom went back to the house for sale, rang his office and reported the incident, checked the doors and windows were locked and opened the front door. There to greet him were two uniformed police officers. His nightmare began.

Now, waiting in his daughter's flat, Malcolm pondered.

I've met that woman before. But where?

He remembered. He met her at a staff barbecue, when she was a brunette sans specs. Now she was a blonde with glasses. And when they met, she was the girlfriend of an agent Malcolm had the unpleasant task of firing.

I've been stitched up.

He took a cab to his car outside the house in Deepdene then drove to the house in Burwood where his former work colleague lived. The man liked a drink, and Malcolm had sometimes driven the sacked agent home. Malcolm parked and walked down the drive. The house was quiet. He rang the doorbell. No response.

Hanging around felt strange so he went for a walk. At the end of the street, he crossed to the other side and started walking back. Then he saw a car arriving at the former agent's house. Malcolm rang Jo as he started to run.

'Hi, Dad, where are you?'

He spoke between puffs. 'I've worked it out. I've been framed. I can see them now. Can I make a citizen's arrest?'

Jo struggled. 'Don't do that. Dad. *Dad!* Where are you?'

Malcolm kept running. 'They're right in front of me. I'll call you when I've arrested them.'

'Dad! Stop! Don't do that!'

The phone went dead. Beryl from Reception entered with a message for Billy Hughes.

'Problems?' asked Beryl.

'If it's not one, it's the other.' Jo didn't making sense.

'Sorry, love, you've lost me.'

'Parents, Beryl, don't have them.'

Jo rang her father. Voicemail. She left a brief message. 'Dad. Ring me now.'

He couldn't. He was busy preparing for middle-aged male fisticuffs.

Malcolm reached the top of the driveway, puffing and determined. Out from the vehicle stepped the agent he once sacked plus his partner, the woman who accused him of assault. She looked different; no wig, no glasses.

'Hey!' shouted the emboldened Mal.

The couple looked back and saw an angry Malcolm trespassing on their property. He headed their way.

'Get off my property,' yelled the driver.

'Call the cops,' yelled the woman.

'Call them,' yelled Malcolm, 'and let's find your wig and glasses.'

Malcolm got closer. Thoughts of his younger daughter screaming at him flashed through his mind. He should have stopped but couldn't, well, wouldn't.

The former agent wasn't having the prick who fired him barging down his driveway. The two men moved closer. Blood was boiling. The sacked agent could never allow his testosterone to be bested by any challenger, and certainly not in front of his woman.

'Get him, Gordy,' she snarled as the men raised their fists.

Jo stood at Michael's front door thinking. *Twice in the one day.*

He appeared and spoke. 'Twice in the one day, Detective.'

Great minds, she thought.

They sat in front of their latest scam. 'I'm almost finished,' he said. 'But reluctantly I reckon we need Ponzi's help. The text's the killer. I'm no copywriter and that's the key. The site may look terrific and convincing, but the wrong words could help the scammers smell a rat. I like your suggestion. We show Ponzi just the plain text. We tell him nothing about the scam. He simply comments on the pitch.'

'Fine,' said Jo. 'Do you want me to contact him?'

Michael put his hands on his face. 'Any method is dangerous. If you meet face to face and are seen, we're in trouble. If you phone or email, you'll leave some sort of footprint.'

'I used a computer in a public library once.'

'I can re-route stuff. We'll try that. Just sound him out. Maybe he won't be interested.'

'If there's money involved, he'll be interested.'

Michael, as Jo, sent an exploratory email to their "partner" who responded almost immediately.

'He's interested,' said Michael showing Jo the reply from Ponzi.

'Okay, let's send him the text and ask him what he thinks.'

They did and after a few minutes, Ponzi replied.

I can improve your pitch if I know some details about the project.

Michael was unhappy. 'This is not good. He doesn't need to know anything about the scam.'

'But how can he get the pitch right?'

'He's up to something. He's lying or playing games. The more we tell him, the greater the risk we'll fail.'

Jo was not so suspicious. 'Maybe he's just angling for more money.'

Neither spoke. This was a crucial moment. Sloppy or ineffective text could kill the project. Too much detail to Ponzi could kill the players.

Michael had an idea. 'How about we invent a scam which has nothing to do with our current one, but uses the same text?'

Jo was cautious. 'Okay but what's our imaginary scam?'

Michael pondered. Jo could detect but not imagine. He grimaced.

'How about we're scamming a real estate mogul who has siphoned off funds from his clients?'

Jo threw back her head and laughed. Michael caught her joy. He tapped out a new email. Jo read it and kept laughing.

Hi Ponzi

We are dealing with a major real estate player who has helped himself to funds belonging to his clients. How can we change our pitch to obtain his interest?

The pitch followed. They sent it. Ponzi replied. Dead straight. No irony in sight.

'He's played it straight,' said Michael. 'And he's improved our text. Thanks, Ponzi, you're a star.'

What they didn't know was that Ponzi was currently on the phone.

'Fraud, DS Craven speaking.'

'G'day, it's David Baggio here.'

'Ponzi, hello,' replied the detective waving to a colleague wanting her to listen to the conversation. 'What's happening?'

'That cop and her mates are running another scam.'

There was a pause. Craven wanted more. 'And?'

'It's happening soon.'

'That's all good, my friend but we need details. Who are they scamming, when and how?'

'It's real estate.'

Craven stifled a laugh. 'Real estate?'

'Yeah, they're after some guy who embezzled funds from his clients.'

Craven suddenly changed tack. 'Ponzi, is this a windup?'

'What? No.'

'Are they trying to scam you?'

The criminal exploded. Craven's ear copped a dial tone. He phoned Steele. The game was afoot.

<h1 style="text-align:center">8</h1>

SOME MURDERS ARE SOLVED IN FIVE MINUTES, some take an age, and some are never solved. The murder of journalist John Fielding proved tricky. There were three known suspects—Martin Fielding, Robert Lensbury and Dermot Cody with Dermot the short-priced favourite. But damning evidence didn't exist. Motive and opportunity, yes, but with no DNA, witnesses, weapons or confessions, no charge had been laid—yet.

Homicide detectives reviewed the situation. Richelieu invited Hughes to report on her interview with Robert Lensbury. She pointed to his photo on the board.

'We located this guy through Fielding's diary. It's in some kind of code which was deciphered by Senior Constable Best.' Jo felt good. Payne didn't.

'Fielding interviewed Lensbury just before the journo was murdered. Fielding was writing about an alleged VIP paedophile ring operating years ago in Sydney with Lensbury supposedly some sort of go-between.'

'He was a pimp for paedos,' said Payne.

'But is this Lensbury for real?' asked Fleming. 'If he's telling the truth, why haven't we investigated him before? We keep hearing from people who claim politicians and captains of industry were paedophiles decades ago but are these claims true? I mean, is Lensbury a fantasist?'

Hughes replied. 'Lensbury's being interviewed by Serious Crime re his paedophile claims. We need to know if he killed Fielding. Lensbury told us Fielding put him in danger, and admitted he threatened Fielding.'

'So 'e certainly 'ad motive,' added Richelieu.

'But why would he say that if he did kill him?' asked Baldwin.

'Double bluff,' said Fleming.

'He asked for protection so he'll be in a safe house,' replied Hughes.

'OK, next, s'il vous plaît,' said Richelieu. 'What do we know about the brother, Martin Fielding?'

Payne was assigned this task. 'He's one angry man. He hated his brother because of their father's will. Martin reckoned he should have received more than his brother. He told DS Hughes and me he wanted to thank whoever killed his brother and he has no alibi for the night of the murder. Could he have done it? Yes. Did he do it? Not sure. Did he have a motive? Too bloody right.'

The meeting drifted. Richelieu brought it into line. DS Fleming, our Irish friend, s'il vous plaît .'

Dermot's photo glared out from the noticeboard. 'Cody was interviewed soon after the murder.'

'How soon?' This came from Steele.

'An hour and a half. When we got to his place, he said he'd been in bed for hours but it was cold. He'd just got home having belted his ex, Fielding's lover. Dermot is not like the other two suspects. We can place him at the murder scene when it happened. He confessed to bashing his ex but furiously denied murder.' Fleming shrugged. 'Again, no evidence for the homicide.'

The mood in the room was flat. Many believed if you couldn't crack a case within 48 hours, you were in for the long haul.

Richelieu looked around. 'Mesdames et Messieurs, do we 'ave anything to add?'

Jo had plenty on her mind and reckoned the search was too narrow. 'Are we stuck on only these three suspects?'

'No, indeed,' replied Richelieu. 'And you, Senior Constable, as a reward for deciphering the code of the victim's diary, will produce a list of every name therein.' Others jeered. 'Together with background notes on each person, s'il vous plaît.'

Richelieu smiled and Jo inclined her head.

'Oui Monsieur.' Secretly, she was delighted.

The others looked at Jo. Was she ambitious, showing off or possibly smart? Or all three? Billy Hughes had a strong opinion.

More discussion followed before the meeting broke up. Jo returned to her desk and started diary reading. Unable to do anything for her father who could be anywhere and in even more trouble, she opened the Fielding diary and made a list.

Thanks to Michael Chan, she knew the names of individuals and their street name and number. She could make an educated guess as to the suburb. She knew Robert Lensbury and his address but who were the others and why were they in Fielding's diary?

She used Google Maps. The street name Beaching produced the suburb of Port Melbourne. Nice houses. But so what? Then she tried a White Pages search of the person's name and their address.

Bingo. For Charles Brittain of 2/66 Beaching Parade, Port Melbourne, up came a landline phone number. She rang it.

'Charles Brittain,' said the male voice.

'This is Detective Senior Constable Joanna Best from Victoria Police.' Jo had learnt to pause after such an introduction. Silence ran down the line. 'Are you there, Mr Brittain?'

'Yes.' He suffered an attitude change.

'I'm conducting a murder enquiry. Can you tell me why your name and address are listed in the diary of a man called John Fielding?'

'I've no idea what you're talking about.'

'Have you been interviewed by a journalist called John Fielding?'

'I've never heard of him.'

'Do you know anyone who's been contacted by Mr Fielding?'

'No. Look, I don't know who you are. What's your name?'

'Best, sir, Detective Senior Constable, Homicide Squad.'

'Well assuming you are the police, I've answered your questions, I've never heard of John Fielding and I'll thank you to leave me alone.'

The called ended promptly and with feeling.

Baldwin looked up. 'Any joy?'

'No, but interesting.' Jo worked through the diary. There were five names in total. One was deceased, another in care suffering dementia, and the third left the country months ago with whereabouts unknown. Hardly promising. The other names were Lensbury and Brittain.

She searched for Lensbury. Nothing. She searched looking for news items on paedophile cases back in Sydney in the 1980s. That produced results. Several stories appeared with names but none rang a bell. Then she saw a photo. It was grainy and its reproduction hardly HD (High Definition), yet the face looked familiar.

Using a magnifying glass, she poured over the snap. It nagged her. It was a teenager, someone she thought she knew. But the name didn't fit—Rupert Lenton. Hang on. It couldn't be. It could be. It was. Rupert Lenton looked like a very young Robert Lensbury.

Goosebumps played Chasey under her shirt. She searched for Rupert Lenton. Hooley Dooley. Up in Sin City many moons ago, young Rupert was in trouble with the Vice Squad. Lots of charges, lots of not guilty pleas, lots of sentences. And then the thunderbolt.

Nearly 20 years ago, Rupert was found guilty of manslaughter over the brutal death of a man said to be a police informer. Oh my.

Jo made copies of documents, checked her notes then went looking for DS Hughes.

Don't grandstand. Work through the chain of command. Involve Billy Hughes. She's backed me. Start with her.

Hughes was super impressed but didn't show it. Inside she glowed with pride. Her initial opinion of Jo Best being an outstanding detective was gaining credibility by the case.

'Excellent work, Jo. Not sure how we missed this. Puts Mr Lensbury in a whole new light. Let's tell the Cardinal.'

He listened and praised. 'Brilliant work, Mesdames, magnifique.'

'It's Senior Constable Best's work, sir. I had nothing to do with it.'

'And modest to boot,' he said smiling at Jo. 'Leave this with me. I will consult with Major Crime. Methinks, Mr Lensbury, aka Lenton, 'as some explaining to do, n'cest par. Adieu and merci.'

The women departed and wandered along the corridor.

'You know you're making life extremely hard for DI Steele.' Jo looked blank. 'You know he wants you out, and this kind of result makes you invaluable to Homicide.'

Jo was about to express her gratitude when her phone rang. She looked at the caller.

'I have to take this, Sarge.'

'Sure,' said Hughes and returned to her office.

'Dad,' whispered Jo in a panic. 'Where the hell are you?'

'Malcolm spoke in a strange way. 'St Vincent's Casualty.'

'Oh God. Are you okay? No, don't answer that. Stay there. Dad?'

'Yes?'

'Stay there.'

Long story short, Malcolm X had become a detective like his younger daughter. Through swollen lips he told his tale of the sacked real estate agent and the vengeful girlfriend, his accuser.

'I went to their place, and when they came home, I walked down the drive to confront them.'

'You idiot,' said Jo, and meant it.

'I did what you said and tried to make a citizen's arrest.'

Jo growled. 'Dad, I said exactly the opposite.'

Malcolm X moved and groaned. 'The woman invented a charge of assault so I tried to arrest both of them hence this.' He indicated his face with the scars of battle. 'I got lucky. A neighbour called the cops. They called an ambulance and here I am.'

'And arrested, again.'

'Ah, afraid so. But now I can fight them in court. I know it was a false complaint. It was a revenge attack because I sacked the woman's boyfriend.'

'Where are you staying tonight?'

'I think they're keeping me in overnight.'

'No they're not.'

A voice spoke from outside the dividing curtain. It was pulled back and Natalie, wife number 2 appeared. She walked around the bed to avoid Jo, moved close to her bewildered husband and gently kissed his swollen head.

'I'm sorry, darling. I called your office and they said you reported the incident. You're coming home. I never doubted you for a minute.'

Bullshit.

Malcolm X shed a tear. Just the one as he had a masculine image to maintain, and a black eye to flaunt.

Jo squeezed her father's hand.

'I'll be off, Dad. Look after yourself.' She smiled—well, sort of—at her stepmother and left.

At her car, she received a text message from Mr Chan.

Monte Christo.

9

WHAT'S THE WORST NEWS YOU CAN HEAR? You've been robbed? Your house has burned down? Your partner's run off with your best friend? You've lost the first-prize winning ticket in the lottery? Your nearest and dearest has died? These are all heartbreaking in their own way. But so too is this.

Your child is missing.

That news, surely, must be rated as terrifying and devastating.

The Saturday after John Fielding was murdered, Donna White suffered a fright. She chatted with another mother of a young child in the playground at Citizen's Park in Richmond. Donna's 4-year-old daughter Candice, known as Candy, was having a grand old time on the climbing apparatus and slide. This was a regular gig for Donna and her girl. Usually Candy's father, Gavin was there unless a game of Australian Rules Football drew him away. He was with his family today only on the nearby oval with a mate watching some kids playing football—that's AFL, the local Australian game.

Donna and her new friend, Kate, chatted about life with a toddler, and Donna regularly looked across at the playground to see if Candy was okay. She was having a ball running or climbing, and laughing with friends new and old. Donna went on chatting.

Time went by and she took another look—no daughter. Donna stood.

'What's up?' asked Kate.

'I can't see my daughter.'

Kate stood. 'What's she wearing?'

Donna moved from the picnic tables to the playground covered in pine bark. It's softer than asphalt and fun to pick up and throw.

Donna moved around looking. She called. 'Candy?'

Children kept playing, squealing and having fun. Donna called louder. Parents stopped and stared. Donna's voice revealed her emotions. Fear crept into the playground. Parents grabbed their kids.

Donna panicked. She screamed. 'I can't find my child. Where's my child. Somebody's taken my child!'

No acting required here. This was real. A man and a woman approached the distraught mother.

'What does she look like?' asked the man.

'What is she wearing?' asked the woman.

Donna slurred her words. She kept turning, looking, praying, hoping and becoming more distressed with every passing second.

Kate asked a sensible question. 'Could she be with anyone else from your family?'

Donna felt enormous relief. 'Yes, my husband. He's on the oval.'

'What's his name?' asked the man next to her.

'Gavin, Gavin White.'

The man took off. He jumped the fence and ran towards the adults watching the kids. He called.

'Gavin White!' People turned. The running man called louder.

Gavin heard his name and panicked. This had to be bad news. He ran towards the messenger.

'I'm Gavin White. What's happened?'

'Have you got your little girl with you?'

Gavin's heart copped an arrow. 'No,' he gasped. 'Why?'

'Your wife can't find her.'

Gavin ran. His wife looked at the oval and saw her husband racing towards the playground. Her heart froze. She moaned in agony.

Soon every adult was looking for a little girl with blonde curly hair, a large straw hat, white leggings and a red jacket. Candy was the word on everyone's lips.

The man who ran onto the oval spoke to Donna and Gavin.

'The cop shop is just up the road. I can tell them if you like.'

Donna convulsed and Gavin held his wife while nodding. 'Please. And thanks.'

The police were soon informed.

Donna needed help. She was due to collapse. Any parent in this situation can't stop thinking certain thoughts.

My child's been taken by a monster. My child is being tortured. She wants her parents. Is she safe? Is she dead? Where is she?

The mental agony of Candy's parents was difficult to describe.

Two constables arrived and spoke to Gavin as Donna was a mess. The constables radioed their station, 100 yards away. This appeared to be a genuine missing child. The event was logged as a Misper, a Missing Person, to wit, a child. This looked like abduction.

Donna's grief was multiplied by the fact that she was caring for her little girl at the time. Candy disappeared on her mother's watch. Had Donna been keeping an eye on her daughter, right now she'd be safe.

But how could this happen in broad daylight in a busy playground? Did Candy wander off and was now in someone's garden? Was she taken by chance? Was this planned? No one knew and no one knew where the little girl was at this very moment. Candy disappeared.

Not long after she vanished, and with no sign of Candy, DI Ronald Graham, soon to retire, was appointed to lead the investigation. A family liaison officer was sent to the little girl's Abbotsford home to help the parents at this horrendous time.

The police knew that the longer the child was missing, the more likely the victim would either not be found or be found dead. Of course they would never say that to the family or anyone not working on the case. Pressure began to build.

It was inevitable the media would get involved. This was lead story material. In this situation, the fourth estate can do a power of good. People see a photo of the missing child, what she was last wearing, and keep an eye out for the precious youngster.

The midday news bulletins reported the case. The TV news carried a picture story of little Candy. By the time the afternoon and evening news came along, the parents appeared in a press conference with the police, pleading for help. Tears and wringing hands added pathos to the nightmare. Parents with young kids felt a flash of terror. Without thinking, they looked to confirm the safety of their child or children.

More police action began with a team of detectives drawn into the case. The usual lines of enquiry began. Who were the known sex offenders in the area? Are there paedophiles operating under the radar? What is the family's background? Is the marriage sound? Who else lives in the house? What do family, friends and neighbours know? Have there been any suspicious people or vehicles in the area?

Anyone with a direct link to the missing child was to be interviewed, and asked to verify their movements in the last 24 hours.

Volunteers and Emergency Services people began a detailed search of the entire park and surrounding streets. Forensic officers examined the playground. The search became a major operation.

The public was asked to help. Do you know anything about this missing girl? Can you help? Did you see a person, a vehicle, anything you think might help? The key phrase became "no matter how small".

Social media came alive once the TV appeal screened. People were distressed and disturbed. Those distressed issued thoughts of hope, and best wishes. Those disturbed gave their opinion—uninvited. They knew what had happened. They knew why. Or so they thought.

The father did it. Did you look at his eyes? The mother was putting on an act. I bet it's someone in the family. It always is.

Who are these people some call trolls? One definition of a troll is a strange dwarf-like creature living in a dark cave; scary folk.

A modern-day troll is a housewife, a pervert, or church-going, law-abiding citizen, seated in a dark room with a laptop, spewing vile lies.

What drives an Internet troll to do what they do? What drives them to post comments about the guilt of a parent or anyone for that matter? Why accuse someone of evil, a person you have never met, without a shred of evidence? Are trolls human? Were they once online teenage bullies who've grown down and found another platform?

And why are they anonymous? Surely if people had no access to social media unless they had to identify themselves, that would make the world a better place. Trolls are brave because they are anonymous. Shine a light on trolls and watch them scuttle deeper into the darkness.

48 hours can be a lifetime in the search for a missing child. There were no sightings, several false reports and many dead-end leads. Interviews and searches produced nothing.

The sky turned black. The temperature dropped. The police despaired, and it was impossible to describe the condition of the parents.

10

CHARLES BRITTAIN RANG HIS YOUNGER BROTHER. Paul had wealth, power and influence. Charles had a dog.

'Charles, what can I do for you?'

'Can you talk?'

'About what?'

'A police officer asking me if I knew anything about the murder of a journalist called John Fielding.'

Paul took a deep breath. His older, quieter, poorer brother was a real pain. Over the years, Paul pulled strings to save his brother's skin, not because Paul loved Charles but because if Charles got into strife, and it became public knowledge, Paul would suffer. The saying, "There's no such thing as bad publicity" was definitely not true when it came to developer Paul Brittain.

You've seen those media reports with a certain headline. The *brother* of footballer so and so or the *mother* of TV star X is arrested. The media take an interest because the person in trouble is related to a public figure. The public figure has nothing to do with the issue and if the arrested person had no famous relative, the story would be unreported or appear on page 29.

So in this case, a possible media story would be, "Charles Brittain, brother of developer Paul Brittain, was last night arrested blah, blah, blah." Paul loathed bad publicity. As a developer and friend of politicians, Paul needed a squeaky-clean image. He could not afford any scandal.

'What did you say?' asked Paul.

'Nothing. I told her I didn't know the man.'

'Her?'

'What?'

'You said I told *her.*'

'Yes, the cop was a woman. They do have them you know.'

'What's her name and rank?'

'Ah Best, I think. Yes, Detective Senior Constable from Homicide.'

Paul made a note.

'Was that the guy stabbed the other night?'

Charles knew it was but spoke softly. 'Probably.'

'Well if you don't know the dead journo, why did she ring you, how did she get your name, and what was he investigating?'

'I don't know.'

That sounded like a lie only because it was. There was a pause. Both men knew what the dead journalist was investigating, and why his death had the cops calling Charles.

'I'm sick of your bloody lies, Charles. We know why he was killed.'

'How many more times?' groaned Charles. 'I was living in Sydney but had nothing to do with their sordid little hobby.'

'Oh it's a hobby now?'

'I'm sick to death of this guilt by association.'

Neither spoke. Both were upset but for different reasons.

Paul relented. 'Let's hope the murder kills the story. Keep your head down and say nothing.'

Charles breathed a sigh of relief. 'Okay. Thanks.'

'Who killed him?'

'Who?'

Paul spoke slowly. 'Yes, who killed the journalist?'

Charles hesitated then spoke in a whisper. 'I thought you did.'

Click.

If Paul was angry before, now he was furious. He summoned his associate—great word that—associate. It has 47 meanings.

Danny Fortune played many roles. He was Paul Brittain's right-hand man, bodyguard, driver, his Mr Fix-it, and his associate. Fortune was the gatekeeper on steroids. Nobody got to Paul Brittain unless through Danny Fortune, and very few made it.

Danny knew more secrets than an elderly priest, and if the associate ever rolled over, Paul was cactus. Danny arrived.

'What's up, boss?'

'My brother's had a call from a Homicide cop, a woman, Detective Senior Constable Best. Check her out.'

'Can do.'

'And find out who murdered a journalist called John Fielding.'

'That it?' Brittain nodded and Danny left.

He didn't waste words, our Danny. And he was good. He'd have the answers in a day, if not sooner. He was wasted working for a CEO who cloaked his criminality in respectability. If Danny became a cop, the crime cleanup rate would triple overnight.

Paul's phone rang. He knew the caller. Redmond Latimer was a high-ranking Victorian state politician with a burning desire to reach the top. Redmond fancied himself as Premier material and having the backing of a big-end-of-town developer was vital.

'Redmond, how goes it?'

'Mate. Are we still on for tonight?'

'Of course.'

'Good. There's something I need to run by you.'

'It'll cost you.'

Both men laughed.

'See you tonight,' said Redmond and ended the call.

11

WHAT A DAY! Jo buzzed as she drove to Northcote. She broke a new lead in the current murder investigation. Her father became a detective, got assaulted then arrested. Her houseguest left, thank God, and her partner in crime sent her his famous code.

Michael was edgy. 'I think it's time,' he said leading Jo to his space-age control centre.

'You're the boss, Michael. If you say we launch, we launch.'

They looked at the landing page of the fake web site.

'I've added Ponzi's revised text. He knows his marketing stuff.'

Neither spoke. They knew this was risky, even dangerous. They knew the names of the criminals they were targeting, the brothers Sim. These men were local with greed their inspiration, and fury their calling card. Cross them at your peril.

For Michael and Jo, it was more than retrieving the stolen cash; it was staying alive. The sting in the tail was that winning could mean losing. Forget about being sprung by the cops. If Jo and Michael succeed, they could die.

The geek and the cop looked at one another. Into the valley of death they rode as Michael tapped a key, and the Dark Web now housed a web site supposedly owned and operated by the Federal Government of Australia. That in itself was a serious crime. Obtaining money by deception was a do-not-pass-go but a go-straight-to-jail card.

And to prevent the web site being seen by the world, Michael needed to bury it deep, and advise only the Sim brothers of its existence. The brothers wouldn't know that. They would think the world and its mother were all over the site and lining up tenders. So the Dark Web it was.

Ernie was the brains in the Sim family, brother Joe the brawn. Mind you both were handy with the violence, and the fear they generated made their victims keep schtum.

Michael Chan needed to figure out a way of telling the Sim brothers about the fake web site without telling the world. Michael hit on the idea of a mistaken email. His father had told Michael about the brothers Crimm including a phone number. From that, Michael had discovered Ernie's email address—one of them.

Michael would deliberately send an email to the Sim brothers making it look like it was for someone else. Simple mistake. The email was to a prominent Chinese Australian businessman talking about the new Department of Trade web site. The advice in the email was to check it out and not to talk about it. The body of the email mentioned the recipient's name, Ernie Lim, hopefully fooling Ernie Sim into thinking the wrong email address had been used.

Oh dear, simple typing mistake; it's Ernie Sim, not Ernie Lim.

Would it work?

It did as Ernie was intrigued. He smiled when he saw the single keystroke error the sender made.

Ernie's smile got bigger as he read the email. When he clicked on the link to Michael's web site, adrenaline flooded his body.

'Joe, get in here,' he called to his brother. Joe arrived.

'What?'

'Look at this.'

Joe was not the smoothest chopstick on the banquet table, and needed an explanation.

When Ernie finished the lecture, Joe was as keen as his sibling. 'And we get a cut of every deal Aussie companies land in China?'

'That's what it says. And it's backed by the government? No, it *is* the government.'

Joe gesticulated. 'Well what are we waiting for?'

'Easy,' said Ernie. 'There's a contact number here for all enquiries. Maybe there's a way to reduce the odds.'

He rang the number, and put the call on speaker. A recorded message kicked in.

"You have reached the office of Dee-Fat, China Australia trade department. All our officers are busy at the moment but if you leave ..."

The recording stopped and a "real" person spoke.

'Hello, you've reached DFAT, Mitchell Collins speaking.'

'Oh, good morning, Mitchell,' said Ernie. 'Or is it afternoon?'

'Will you hold the line please, sir.'

Ernie put his hand over the phone. 'They're busy.'

Joe whispered. 'What's Dee-Fat?'

'Department of Foreign Affairs and Trade.'

The official rejoined the call. 'Hello, are you there?'

'I'm here.' Ernie smiled. He was well and truly there.

'How can I help you, sir?'

I'm enquiring about the tender for the China Australia Trade Commissioner.'

'How did you hear about that?' The voice was sharp, almost angry. 'That's supposed to be confidential.'

Ernie was thrown. 'It's online. I'm looking at it now.

Ernie heard the DFAT official call to a colleague. 'That damn fool hasn't taken down the site. Get him in here, now.' The official's voice turned soft and friendly. 'I'm sorry about that, sir. There's been a communication breakdown. The site should have been taken down.'

Ernie's initial excitement turned sour. 'You mean the tender's closed?'

'Well technically not until the site comes down but that will be as soon as my colleague arrives here in my office.'

Again Ernie could hear the official yelling off-mic. 'Get that lazy bastard in here now!'

'Hello?' Ernie sounded desperate. 'Hello, are you there?'

'I'm terribly sorry, sir, and for any inconvenience. Is there something else I can help you with?'

'Yes. I mean I want to place an expression of interest in the tender process for the China Australia trade position.'

'I'm afraid the site's about to close, sir.'

'Wait, wait! Please!'

'I assume you've read the criteria for submission, sir?'

'Yes, everything,' almost shouted Ernie. Joe nibbled his nails.

'You'll understand, sir, because this is such a huge undertaking, we can't afford to waste time with small operators.'

'That's me, I mean *not* me. Our business is one of the biggest in Australia. We're Chinese Australians. We deal with Chinese companies all the time.'

'Well, all I can say, sir, is that the site will be down in about an hour. If you wish to submit an expression of interest, then good luck.'

'Thank you. Thank you very much.'

'I'll let you get on with your submission.'

'Thank you,' said Ernie for the umpteenth time. He hung up and started preparing his application. At the sub-branch of DFAT, in a warehouse in Northcote, the official "Mitchell Collins" collapsed on the floor. Michael Chan shook like a leaf in a gathering storm. And if only Michael knew, a real storm was gathering.

Robert Lensbury scowled. His pleas for protection looked like happening then hit a wall. Serious Crime had a chat to him about his VIP paedophile ring allegations but Robert proved slippery.

Serious Crime grew impatient. They wanted specific details. He offered few. It was obvious Lensbury was looking for a way out.

'I'm saying nothing without a guarantee of protection.'

'And all in good time, Mr Lensbury.'

He stalled. The cops were frustrated, and when a call came from Homicide, they were happy to send him back.

'Where am I going?'

'Just go with these officers, Mr Lensbury.'

He kicked off. 'Where are you taking me?'

They were bigger than him and Robert had no choice. He moved departments.

He sat and fumed in a Homicide interview room back where he started. Two detectives entered—The Cardinal and Billy Hughes and Senior Constable Jo Best watched through a window.

'What's going on? I told you people all I know. If you don't protect me, the people who killed that journalist will kill me.'

'Take it easy, Robert,' said Billy Hughes. She paused. 'Or should I say Rupert?' Silence roared into the room. 'You *are* Rupert Lenton?'

He tried for the brave face and failed. He tried for the bluff and denial posture and failed.

Hughes attacked. 'You've not been honest with us, Rupert.'

'Big deal, I've changed me name.'

'But not your spots.' He had no idea what Billy meant. 'You're a nasty piece of work, Mr Lenton. You've played this victim card when all along you know how to look after yourself. You killed a man.'

'It was fucking self-defence,' bawled the now worried suspect.

'You told my colleague, Detective Best, you were too scared to go outside for fear of being killed.'

'I was. I am. Those paedophiles will kill to protect their reputations. Look what they did to that journalist.'

'*They* did or *you* did?'

Hughes left the question hanging. Rupert shook his head. 'Ah no. No way. No, no, no—you ain't pinning that on me.'

'Come on, Rupert; let's go over your statement. Fielding came to your flat and got you talking. You said you were reluctant to do so.'

'I was.'

'Yet you gave him the names of the VIPs in the ring.'

'I was trying to get rid of him.'

'You thought if Fielding published his story, you'd be exposed.'

'He swore he'd keep my name out of it.'

'But you didn't believe or trust him. You had to stop that story.'

Jo watched, fascinated. Billy Hughes had a plan and stuck to it. She went on the attack with facts and an almost soft manner. She pulled on a velvet glove to cover her iron fist. There was no shouting, table thumping or finger pointing. She just nagged away, building pressure.

Remember this technique, Jo. One day you may be DS Hughes.

'So Fielding gets you to name names.'

'I never told him no names.'

'You said you nodded when he named someone who was in the VIP paedophile ring.'

Rupert was weakening. The facts built pressure. 'I told you, I wanted him gone. I nodded to get rid of him.'

'Oh so now you lied.'

Lenton struggled. 'I can't remember.'

'Your flat is not far from Fielding's house. You followed him.'

'No!'

'You followed him to his home and you hung around.'

'I was nowhere near his place.'

'So you know where he lives?'

Lenton panicked. 'No. I never met him before.'

'And you couldn't believe your luck when suddenly he came out, looking for someone. He was distracted, looking for the bloke who just bashed his girlfriend. He came running towards you. The man you have to kill.'

'I never killed him.'

'What, not in self-defence, like that time in Sydney?'

Lenton was close to confessing or breaking down or reaching across the table and scratching the face of the woman who hammered him with difficult questions and claims. Billy kept attacking.

'Here was the man who could ruin your life, and send the VIP paedophiles straight to your door.'

Lenton screamed. 'I wasn't there.'

'It's dark. He runs up to you and gets a surprise. You're not the wife beater. You're the witness he's just interviewed. Fielding goes from angry to calm then curious. Has the witness followed me to tell me more facts? Fielding relaxes. It's perfect. You're not a threat. You've just helped him write his story. He likes you. He tells you who he's looking for. He looks around, not looking at you. It's too easy.' Hughes paused and plunged in her verbal knife. 'You stabbed him and ran.'

Rupert sprang to his feet and the Homicide cops reacted. He pointed at Hughes.

'You can't fit me up. I know names and I'm going to talk to Serious Crime, not you.'

Everyone stood and stared. It was a showdown without guns—much more of a whimper than a bang. It was over.

Jo liked the Billy Hughes interview technique. But there was no confession, no smoking gun, or, in this case, no bloodstained knife. It was great theatre but no Tony nomination.

Rupert suffered a mix of rage and fear as officers took him to a cell, and, back in the incident room, the squad reviewed the situation.

Steele wanted the case solved. 'Well? Do we charge him?'

'Close, sir, but not close enough,' said Hughes.

'He's admitted Fielding was in his flat shortly before the murder.'

'And 'e may 'ave slipped up,' said Richelieu. 'Lenton admitted 'e knew where Fielding lived.'

'So he followed the victim or went to his home,' said Steele.

The Pope looked at his detectives. They couldn't join the dots. Frustration festered. It was not enough to charge him.

'Right,' said Hughes, 'we need another search of his flat and of the route he would have taken to the murder scene.' She looked and sounded more like the OIC than did the Cardinal.

Steele grew impatient. 'Well if we can't charge him, we'll have to release him.'

Richelieu objected. 'Not if 'e's in danger, sir. 'is concerns about being killed for revealing secrets are all on record.'

'Serious Crime say he won't talk. They think he's a fantasist who wants money or fame or God knows what.'

'I think 'e's an at-risk prisoner, sir,' argued Richelieu.

The two DIs went head to head with Steele on the attack.

'He's got a choice, Monsieur Inspector. He confesses to murder or co-operates with Major Crime. If he won't do either, he walks.'

Hughes was unhappy. 'But we hold him for now, sir, surely?'

'Yes, for now. Search the crime scene again, CCTV for his route to it, and his flat. Interview him again. If you get nothing, and Major Crime don't want him, set the gentleman free.'

Steele walked out leaving the Squad in two, even three minds.

12

MONTE CHRISTO TRIUMPHS. Jo stared at her phone. She got the same three-word text from Michael a few weeks ago when he handled her mother's stolen life savings. Surely not the same thing again? Surely not now, not already?

She followed procedure. Phone or email contacts only in a dire emergency. Michael never defined *dire*. She drove to Northcote. Not easy during peak hour. He opened his door with his face a blank expression. Neither moved. Finally she spoke.

'Is it true?'

He nodded, stepped back and she entered his warehouse. The last time they shared this news, they hugged, laughed, cried and celebrated like Melbourne Cup winners. This time there was no celebration.

They sat in front of a monitor and Michael put up a screenshot of his father's bank account. Only an hour ago, less, his account received a major injection of funds. David Chan's money was returned with interest, thanks to a generous donation from the brothers Sim.

Jo was stunned. 'I'm not in the least surprised you've done what you've done. I would have been shocked if it hadn't worked. But so soon. It's like you spoke to them on the phone and told them to hand over the cash.'

Michael paused. He was still recovering from that phone call. 'I did.'

Wow, talk about a showstopper. That statement demanded an explanation. Jo couldn't speak. When she did, her mind ran ahead of her words.

'Sorry? You spoke to the criminals? A live conversation?' Michael nodded. Jo gasped. 'Give me strength.'

'I only spoke to one brother but I could hear the other one in the background.'

'Michael, I don't want an explanation. I'm afraid to ask. It's gobsmackingly unbelievable.' She paused. 'But I'll die of curiosity if you don't tell me. Please, what happened?'

He explained his DFAT chat with Ernie Sim leaving Jo shaking her head. A few deep breaths helped her think like a normal person again.

'Have you told your father?'

'Of course. He would have seen the transaction and rung the bank thinking someone had made a mistake.'

'What did he say?'

Michael thought about his reply. 'Very little.'

'Very little? You've recovered his fortune and he said very little?'

'If you met my father, you would understand.'

'He sounds like a remarkable man. Describe him—please.'

Michael thought about his answer. 'He's hard-working, honest, loyal, loving and caring.'

She looked at him. 'You're talking about yourself, Michael Chan.'

That floored him but his mind was elsewhere. He wondered if right now the brothers Sim had discovered the scam.

They hadn't. They put in their tender submission, deposited the Government-guaranteed, fully refundable deposit and left it at that. The thought of them being ripped off didn't exist. First, because the Sims took, they never gave, and when the Australian Commonwealth Government is running the show, it's impossible to lose. You might not win the tender process but your money is as safe as houses.

Not quite.

So while Michael and Jo endured stress and lived in fear, the brothers Sim got on with life.

They gathered names of Australian companies they could encourage to trade in China. They assumed they'd win the tender and, if they didn't, they'd contact the winner and make them an offer they couldn't refuse. For the Sims it was all systems go.

That night they dined well. Celebrate lads because tomorrow you kick start your new squillion dollar enterprise.

Next morning, Ernie fired up his laptop and clicked on the URL he used yesterday for the DFAT site. He double clicked. It wouldn't open.

'Bugger,' he said clicking again. Still no joy. He snapped at his brother, still breakfasting.

'Have you been using my laptop?'

'Me?'

'I told you not to touch it.'

'I didn't.' Joe wandered over. 'What's wrong?'

'The link's not working.'

Joe knew nothing about computers but was curious. 'Did we get the tender?'

Ernie kept tapping as he replied, getting louder as he spoke. 'That I can't say because the fucking link is broken.' He lost it.

'Call 'em,' suggested Joe, for once the calm one.

Ernie gave up and agreed. He typed DFAT into a search engine and up came the government web site. He relaxed. It looked just like the site he worked on yesterday. Everything was cool.

He scrolled up and down the Home Page. He opened drop down menus. Where is that page from yesterday? Everything wasn't cool. His anger level got going again. Suddenly he slapped the desk.

'Of course, they've taken it down. They said they would just before we applied.'

'Why don't you ring that guy you spoke to yesterday?

Ernie resumed fuming. 'Because I don't know his name or number.'

Joe grew impatient. 'Just call the main number and ask for the guy you spoke to.'

Ernie's impatience matched that of his brother. 'I just told you. I don't remember his name.'

'You called him Mitchell.'

Ernie got excited—a little. 'I did. Mitchell what?'

'I dunno. Johnson?'

'That sounds right,' said Ernie who found the DFAT switchboard number and dialed.

A woman answered. 'Department of Foreign Affairs and Trade.'

'Hi,' said Ernie. 'I'd like to speak with Mitchell Johnson.'

'One moment, please.'

Ernie put his hand over the phone. 'You sure it was Johnson?'

Joe shrugged. 'Just ask for Mitchell in the China job.'

'What was it called?'

More shrugging from Dim Sim. 'China Australia Trade something.'

Ernie held up his hand as the switchboard operator returned.

'I'm sorry, sir. I can't seem to find Mr Johnson. Do you know which department he works in?'

'Yeah, it was the China Australia Trade department.'

'Just a moment, sir. I'll put you through to our China department.'

Ernie got some middle-of-the-road-nothingness think music.

'What's happening,' asked Joe.

'I'm waiting.' He snapped at his brother. 'Can't you see I'm waiting. Am I talking to somebody? No. So that means I'm fucking waiting.'

Joe worried. If big brother lost it, that meant big trouble.

The meaningless music changed and became more meaningless, if that were possible. Ernie's breathing changed formation. 'Come on, come on,' he snarled at the phone. Then, a response, and it wasn't a woman. Ernie's blood pressure fell markedly.

'China department, Matthew Dingxiang speaking.'

'Oh hello,' said a mightily relieved Ernie. 'Look I wanna talk to somebody about the tender process Dee-Fat is running.'

'What tender process is that, sir?'

'It was to find a company which could bring together Australian and Chinese companies to set up trade agreements with each other.'

Joe looked on with interest. He wanted to know if they won.

Mr Dingxiang had no idea what Ernie was on about but feared there was a programme within DFAT with which he was not familiar.

'Can you hold the line a moment, sir. I need to check with my supervisor about this tender process. Please hold.'

Ernie's blood pressure did a U-turn not helped by another verse and chorus of aural anesthesia.

'What's happening,' asked Joe?

'Nothing—typical public servants, our taxes at work. They couldn't organise a piss up in a brewery.'

'What happens if we don't win? Do we still go after the company that does and get 'em to sell it to us?'

'Dunno. I'm getting seriously pissed off with this. I reckon we grab our deposit, and tell 'em to fuck off.' Ernie held up a hand to Joe as the man from DFAT returned.

'Sorry for the delay, sir. I've asked my supervisor about this tender process. Can you give me some more details please?'

Ernie groaned. 'Look, we went online to your Dee-Fat site and checked out the page with the China Australia tender thing.'

'On the Dee-Fat site?'

Ernie's patience was so thin it had its own diet. 'Yeeees, on your site. And then we phoned you, not you, Mitchell Johnson, and he told us the tender was closing soon. So we put in an expression of interest and today I notice the web page has been taken down. So I'm ringing to see if we were awarded the tender. Is that clear enough for you?'

'Very clear, sir, thank you. May I ask your name, sir?'

'It's Ernie Sim.'

'Could you spell that please.'

The boiler, aka Ernie Sim, was hissing steam with an explosion about to happen.

'E r n ...'

'I meant your surname, sir.'

'Sim. S i m.'

'Thank you, Mr Sim.'

Ernie got curious and almost nasty. 'And what's your name?'

'Matthew Dingxiang. Would you like me to spell that for you, sir?'

Now the red rag was being waved in front of the bull.

'Look Mr ....

'Dingxiang,' said the helpful public servant.

'All I want to know is who was awarded the tender, and if my company didn't, I will want a bloody good explanation as to why.'

'Well the problem we have, Mr Sim, is that we can't trace the particular tender you are talking about.'

More steam from the boiler. 'You can't trace it? It was a whole fucking web page with the Dee-Fat logo splattered all over it. Are you blind as well as stupid?'

Joe chewed his nails. He didn't like his brother going crazy. When this sort of thing happened, bad things happened. Ernie going nuts spelt trouble.

'Personal abuse won't help, sir.'

'Okay, okay, I'm sorry. Look, can you please find Mitchell Johnson and let me talk to him?'

'Well that's another problem, Mr Sim. We've searched our records and there is not nor ever has been a Mitchell Johnson working for the Department of Foreign Affairs and Trade.'

'But I spoke to him.'

'The only Mitchell Johnson I know, Mr Sim, is a cricketer although he may have retired by now.' Ernie seethed in silence. 'Are you a cricket fan, Mr Sim?'

Ernie and cricket were not well acquainted. But as the boiler's nuts and bolts started to loosen, Ernie made one final plea.

'Look, Mr Dingbat, ...'

'Dingxiang, it's Dingxiang.'

'Well Mr Dingxiang, my company has paid a lot of money to be considered for this tender, and I would now request, no, I demand that Dee-Fat return our deposit and today would be just fine. Do you understand?'

'I do, sir, but I think you need to prepare for some bad news.'

Mr Dingxiang knew the news would hurt. He was like a nurse about to stick a needle in a patient's arm. "This might sting a little". But in this case the sting would not be little. He tried to break it gently.

'You may have been the victim of a scam, Mr Sim.'

'What?' Ernie went pale and Joe mimicked him.

'I'm sorry to tell you there's a possibility you and your company may be the victim of a hoax.'

The boiler's nuts fought like buggery to stay in place. Ernie's blood pressure was so high it needed oxygen.

Joe looked at his brother. Never had so much sweat been secreted by so many glands from so few crims. Joe's fingernails became collateral damage.

Now, to Ernie, the word *hoax* had teeth. It bit hard. Had the DFAT officer confessed to sleeping with the mother of the Sim brothers, and given a graphic description of her skills in various sexual positions, Ernie would have not been more enraged than he was by the word *hoax*.

Right now, apoplexy was slipping into its costume preparing for a grand entrance. Heavy breathing sounds scurried along the line.

Mr Dingxiang continued. 'Are you there, Mr Sim?' Nothing. Ernie's brain couldn't get its act together. *Hoax* and *victim* were words of a foreign tongue. Ernie needed a translator.

'Mr Sim, the only advice I can give is that you contact the police and report a fraud.' Still nothing from Ernie, and Joe looked like he was holding back a very large stool.

The word *fraud* was introduced, and together with *hoax*, created a thought Ernie was unable to handle. He hadn't cried since he was a child and had forgotten how.

The reality of the situation tippy-toed into his brain. It did so being terrified of Ernie's skull. Health and safety had condemned Ernie's brain as a place not fit for thoughts of any description.

Slowly, the gangster put down the phone. Michael Chan had pulled down Ernie's pants, so Joe dropped his in sympathy. He needed to anyway.

The boys had been scammed. Had they ever? Whoever pulled off the scam on the Sim brothers had better take cover. The chase began.

13

RUPERT LENTON WANTED OUT. He was genuinely scared and called the cops for protection. But when the police discovered his real identity and criminal record, he refused to talk. If he spoke to Serious Crime about his so-called involvement in VIP paedophile activities decades ago, he might get charged, and he certainly knew the men he fingered would finger him; with bullets or blades or both. If he went to jail, the inmates would bash him. Help.

He knew Homicide were gunning for him for the murder of journo John Fielding. To them, Rupert chose the *No comment* route.

DI Steele addressed his detectives. 'Right, we've searched the route from his flat to the murder scene, his flat, and the murder scene, again, and found nothing. Right?' Murmurs of assent from the squad. 'And no DNA at all? Nothing?'

Baldwin had been to visit the technical officers. 'Forensics found the victim's DNA all over the crime scene, and some of it could be from Fielding's brother. But there was nothing from Lenton. Obviously, there was a lot of DNA from the park bench but nothing from anyone known or the suspects. Not having the murder weapon is the problem.'

'This is going nowhere fast,' sneered Steele. 'We've got a savage murder in the street, people everywhere, and not a single witness.'

'It was dark, sir,' added Hughes. 'No-one reported a scream or cry for help. Fielding's been stabbed, possibly by someone he knew, he's fallen, hit his head and died. He wasn't discovered for a minute or more, and by then the killer's long gone. People crowding in to help the victim, trampled the crime scene. People only start looking for the killer after they've checked on the victim. By then, he's disappeared.'

'Or she,' said Baldwin.

'It's gotta be close to the perfect murder,' said Hughes.

As OIC, Richelieu felt under pressure. 'I fear we 'ave to release Monsieur Lenton.' Groans from disgruntled detectives. 'Then we go back over interviews and witness statements looking for anything which points to a new suspect, or we find a weakness in the statements of any of the three we already suspect. I am awarding a Moët Impérial Magnum to anyone who uncovers the clue to crack this case, and if she is a woman, then flowers and chocolates will naturally follow. Au travail, Mesdames et Messieurs.'

This caused a stir. Males grumbled and some females, especially Joanna Best, enjoyed a momentary feeling of pleasure. Champagne and flowers from Detective Suave sounded okay.

The case remained unsolved.

Danny Fortune, the gatekeeper cum minder, sat down to chat with his boss, Paul Brittain. Danny's contacts had been busy.

'The cop is a young woman, new to Homicide. She got the chop then solved a double homicide when back on the beat.'

'Smart girl.'

'Her grandfather was once the head of Homicide.'

'Who?'

'Robbo Robertson.'

'Squeaky clean,' remembered Brittain. 'And the journo murder?'

'Not sure. Word is it's a crim from Sydney, Robert Lensbury.'

'Who is?'

'Who was Rupert Lenton, a minor crim in Sydney in the 80s. He's got a history with VIP paedo rings, and the murdered journo was chasing him for names.'

'Did he get them?'

'Again, not sure. The journo's phone and wallet were nicked so whoever killed him would probably have that info.'

Paul Brittain pushed his hands through his hair.

Fortune guessed. 'Is it Charles?'

Brittain sighed. 'Who else? I sometimes wish the prick would die.'

'So?' Danny only needed the word from his boss.

Brittain looked at his fixer. 'No, no, not family. But check out this Rupert Lenton. I need to know what names he gave the journo, and who killed him. See if there's any mention of Charles.'

Fortune stood. 'Can do, boss.' He headed off to work.

Jo was super keen to do things the right way by first running them past her immediate boss. She went to DS Hughes.

'I've had a thought about Fielding's part time job.'

'Which was?'

'Charlie and I met two students coming out of Fielding's house. He taught part-time at RMIT and those students were in his class.'

'And?'

'I thought I'd have a word with their lecturers.'

'Agreed. Take Payne.' Jo froze. Hughes looked up. 'Problem?'

'Oh come on, Sarge. He hates me. How can I be effective with a colleague who belittles me and rejoices when I stuff up?'

Hughes removed her glasses. 'How long are you planning on being in this job, Senior Constable?' Jo dropped her head. She knew the answer. 'You need to work with your colleagues, and follow orders. Shit happens, madam. Deal with it.' Hughes grimaced and finger waved. 'Bye-bye.'

Jo went back to the office and stood beside Payne's desk.

'Hello, here's trouble,' he smirked.

'DS Hughes has asked me to interview staff at RMIT where Fielding gave the odd lecture.'

Payne minced his words. 'Oooo, how odd is odd?'

'She said you're to come with me.'

He grabbed his jacket. 'Well, call me Mr Lucky.' Jo thought he was being sarcastic. He indicated the door. 'Right, Senior Constable, lead on, Macduff.'

Jo knew Payne should have said *Lay on, Macduff.* She also knew Payne was DI Steele's bagman but didn't know he was spying on her.

In the car, Jo asked if she could lead. Gone was Payne's cruel and sarcastic manner. He readily agreed although couldn't resist one dig. 'Of course, the double homicide sleuth gets the nod.'

They entered the Media Studies Department at RMIT University and met the senior lecturer in Journalism, Hesketh Spade. They explained the reason for their visit and entered his office.

'I'm still in shock. It was terrible to hear of my dear friend. Please, officers, take a seat.'

Jo copied the interview technique used by DS Hughes.

'We're asking people who knew Mr Fielding if there's anything they can tell us about him or his work which might help us find his killer.'

Hesketh must have had hessian undergarments as he scratched a lot. 'Well his journalism work was pretty much a private affair, I guess because by talking about his investigative stories he might give someone else the idea, who would then beat him to the punch.'

'People steal stories?' asked Jo.

'People steal anything; surely you know that Detective?'

'Did he confide in you about any problems he may have had?'

'He did actually. There was a family dispute with his late father's estate, and John's brother was pretty upset about the terms of the will.'

'Can I run a couple of names by you, Mr Spade, and ...'

'Hesketh, please, everyone calls me Hesketh. Named after Hesketh Pearson the actor and writer, and I'm sure you young officers wouldn't know him from Adam.'

Jo shook her head. Payne hadn't heard of anyone.

'Do you know these names, Hesketh? Robert Lensbury?'

'No.'

'Rupert Lenton.'

'No.'

'Desmond Cody.' He shook his head. 'Martin Fielding.'

'Ah John has a brother, Martin.' He looked sad. 'Sorry. I wish I could be of more help.'

'Perhaps you can. Was Mr Fielding close to any of his students?' She knew he was but waited to see if the witness could help.

'He was. He got on well with all his students but two in particular; Tommy Glenister—I suppose it's really Thomas—and Hannah Vine. I think they're close friends, what today we call an item.'

Jo made notes. 'And what made them close to Mr Fielding?'

For a moment Hesketh thought the police were poking into privacy matters suggesting something improper. Then he recovered.

'Well if you're readers, you'll know what I mean.' Payne's reading days were yet to begin. 'They were his Baker Street Irregulars.'

Hesketh was right. Neither officer understood. He chided them.

'I can't believe the police have never heard of Sherlock Holmes.'

Oh Sherlock, why, even Payne had heard of him, and Jo now knew what Hesketh meant.

'Do you mean they ran errands for Mr Fielding?'

The look on Hesketh's face was worth bottling. Someone under 40 knew something about classic crime fiction. To be fair, Jo got it from her grandfather when Pop read her the Conan Doyle tales. Payne was adrift in the Ignorance Ocean.

'Well done, officer,' beamed Hesketh.

Jo continued probing. 'How do you know this, Hesketh?'

'John told me. He gave them safe tasks to find background information. He said they were brilliant students who would make outstanding investigative journalists. And that's the real tragedy here. We haven't just lost a good man and a fine journalist, we've lost a brilliant teacher and mentor. Those two students will be devastated.'

Jo already knew that. But she also knew those same two students told her and Baldwin they knew nothing about John Fielding's work. Interesting, because Hesketh claimed the exact opposite; he said Tommy and Hannah were gophers for the dead journo. Someone was telling porkies.

The police, well Jo, chatted some more then thanked Hesketh and left. Back in the car, Payne was in good form.

'Well, what a complete waste of time that was.'

Jo gave him some rope. 'You reckon?'

'I mean his name's Hesketh. We could arrest him for that alone.'

'You don't think the Baker Street Irregulars might be a lead?'

'Nah.' Payne looked at his colleague. His ignorance flourished. All he wanted was a sign, some evidence she was planning or working on a scam. Alas Payne, like the Sim brothers, was not yet in the loop.

14

DANNY FORTUNE KNEW A NASTY BLOKE. Gary Black hurt people for a living. Threats and violence were second nature to him. His conscience had been disconnected, which suited Fortune who hired Gazza whenever something nasty needed doing for his boss, Paul Brittain. Black got good money to get his hands dirty.

If Danny and Gary ever met Ernie and Joe Sim, perhaps they could have done business together. They could barter brutality.

Danny Fortune knew what was needed. Paul Brittain wanted to protect his brother Charles from scandal simply to save Paul's reputation. Bugger Charles. Paul had major business interests and was a close mate of the top politician, Redmond Latimer. Neither could afford any scandal.

Paul needed Rupert Lenton investigated and, if necessary, tortured to discover what he told the murdered journo, John Fielding. Gary Black was a pro. He left no trace and got results. Look out Lenton.

Danny gave Black the address. The standover merchant took his dog for a walk past Lenton's block of flats. Black needed to get inside, "chat" to the occupier, and search the joint for anything useful. He went home planning to return after dark.

He did sans pooch. He stood in the shadows and got lucky. A bloke came out of Flat 8 carrying a bag of garbage. He walked to the bins in the art nouveau cement brick holding bay—another architectural gem.

Lenton dumped his rubbish, stopped to light a fag, and felt something hard press against his spine.

'Move and you die.' Lenton didn't resist. It would mean death. He guessed the VIP paedophiles had sent their hitman. Black growled. 'Walk slowly back to your shithole. Any tricks and you die.'

The way Lenton's life was going lately, dying appealed. But his survival instinct kicked in, and the men made it inside the flat. Black shoved Lenton onto the sofa and waved his knife.

'I've not said a word, nothing,' spat Rupert.

'Tell me the names you gave the journalist.'

'I've not said a word to the cops. They let me go.'

'F'get the filth. What'd you tell the fucking journalist?'

Lenton spoke slowly. 'I … never … said … a … word.'

'Smart answer. How about this? The journo told you names of old paedo mates, which you confirmed. Correct?' Lenton stalled. Black turned up the evil. 'Listen scumbag, I need the names you gave the journo and what you did with his phone and wallet.' He paused, sheathed the knife and produced a gun. 'Tell me or you die here, now.'

Black produced a silencer, attached it to his gun and pointed the weapon at Lenton's groin. He whined and soiled himself. He feared pain. He feared death. He feared that whatever he said or did would not change the result. He was convinced he was about to die—slowly.

Black made Lenton sit in a chair, tied his hands behind his back then ransacked the flat. Black found nothing linked to Fielding; no notes, phone, wallet, nothing. Black confronted Lenton again.

'Tell me the names you gave to the journo. Tell me or you'll bleed to death on the floor in this shithole.' Black suddenly screamed. 'Tell me!'

'If I don't tell you, you'll kill me.'

'Bingo.'

'If I do tell you, you'll kill me.'

Black raised his gun. 'Your choice, arsehole.'

Lenton wanted to live. He tried to remember. He started saying the names Fielding spoke. Lenton's list included Charles Brittain.

'Who?' snapped Black.

'Brittain,' croaked Lenton, 'Charles Brittain.'

Black let him keep listing names then stuffed the gun in his belt and moved to his pathetic prisoner.

'God, you stink,' said Black who wanted to vomit as he started to put a gag around Lenton's mouth. The victim suddenly had hope. His hands were not well tied. Mistake? Lenton fiddled. Then with hands free, he grabbed Black's gun and leapt back pointing the weapon.

'Now let's see who stinks,' spat Lenton. 'You people make me sick.'

Black corrected him. 'You people make me *stink*.' Black was not alarmed or afraid. He knew something Lenton didn't know.

'Yes, I told that journalist the names and if he published them then I'd be dead. But somebody got to him before he could publish and I'm still alive but not you, you bastard.'

He pointed the gun at Black. The seconds before death ticked louder. Lenton had been looking over his shoulder most of his life. This last week brought everything to a head. The press, police and now paedoes or their pals all gave him grief. But he survived and beat them.

Black took a quick step towards Lenton. Rupert squeezed the trigger. Click. Nothing. Another squeeze. Click again. Same result.

He looked at Black in despair. The end was quick. The grinning assassin moved forward and stabbed Lenton. A gurgle, a stifled scream, and Rupert Lenton died a miserable and lonely death.

Paul Brittain made his money from high-rise cheap tower blocks gaining government approval thanks to party political donations. With many overseas students wanting cheap accommodation close to Melbourne universities, demand for Brittain's boxes was never-ending.

But the biggest risk to his business was scandal. His older brother Charles was a deadest liability. He once mixed with wealthy toffs who fancied under-age sex. That was decades ago and while only the odd rumour remained, the threat of exposure seemed minor. But once John Fielding got involved with Rupert Lenton, and Fielding was murdered, the sordid past burst into life. Charles got a mention.

So Paul had his mate Danny investigate, and he in turn asked hitman Gary Black to sort the problem. He did and reported back to Danny. Soon after, Paul and Danny had a meet. It was actually a meeting but modern texting demands change to our battered language.

'It's good and bad news,' said Danny. We know the crim from Sydney told the dead journo about Charlie.'

'Shit,' snapped Paul.

'We couldn't find no notes or phone from the journo, but like the journo, the crim won't be saying anything ever again.'

Brittain sniffed. 'Thanks.'

'The story's dead and buried, like the journo and his source. Just make sure your brother keeps his trap shut.'

Brittain nodded. 'Beer?'

Lenton's body remained undiscovered for days. Complaints brought police to the flat. What a job. Uniform broke in and blocked their noses. Who'd wanna be a cop? Still, someone's gotta do it.

Homicide got the call. Body in flat. Bad news. It was one of their suspects in the murder of journalist John Fielding. Robert Lensbury aka Rupert Lenton was dead, stabbed and lying in his filth.

Forensics people wore masks anyway but in this case they were needed. The stench leapt out and grabbed you by the throat.

Soon there were several people in or outside Rupert Lenton's shithole. Scenes of Crime officers were wrapping up their business. Homicide detectives were outside on the landing ready to enter, and inside, Dr Gabrielle Strange, the pathetic pathologist, was her usual chirpy self.

'My God, I need danger money. Anyone got a peg I can borrow?'

Richelieu called. 'Can you see if there is any connection between this man and the murdered journalist, Doctor, s'il vous plaît?'

'Yes,' she called in reply. 'There's a very strong connection.'

'Which is?'

'They're both dead.'

Hughes didn't like it. 'If Lenton killed Fielding, we may never prove it. If he didn't, we're looking for a killer who murdered twice.'

'Or for two killers,' added Richelieu. Jo arrived. She was the only cop who'd been in this flat. 'I gather you are not surprised this man 'as been murdered, Senior Constable?'

'No sir. He was scared of the powerful people he once worked for.'

'If 'e named names to Monsieur Fielding, these powerful men 'ave spoken. Kill the journalist and kill 'is source.'

Jo had a hunch. 'There might be an alternative, sir,' she said. 'I've interviewed two uni students who worked for John Fielding. They were in his class at RMIT.'

'And?' asked Richelieu.

'They respected Fielding, almost hero-worshipped him. If he told them that Lenton threatened him, and if they believed Lenton murdered their mentor, they may have killed Lenton out of revenge.'

The detectives thought about Jo's theory.

'That's a long bow,' said Billy. 'Good idea but no evidence.'

Richelieu was more encouraging. 'It's worth exploring. I think you should do a background check on the students, Senior Constable. No stone unturned as they say, s'il vous plaît.'

'Sir,' replied Jo and saw Hughes raise her eyebrows.

What does that mean? Does she think I'm wasting my time?

Jo was about to leave when Gabby Strange came out looking like the sister of the abominable snowman. Richelieu and Hughes entered the flat. Strange saw Jo.

'Well, well, if it isn't the deranged detective. How are you, Missy?'

'Fine, thank you, Doctor. Can I give you a lift?' she asked softly.

The detective had heard a tale about the pathologist, the drink drive laws, and a licence suspension. Jo kept the tale under her hat.

'Too kind,' smiled Strange.

Jo handed her car key to the doctor. 'That's me, double-parked in the carpark. I'll be down in a jiff.' Jo joined the detectives but was soon glad to escape the stench and drive the pathologist home. In Dr Strange's comfy cottage, they continued discussing the case.

'Some of the aromas I've enjoyed in this job never leave you,' the medico said stripping off her jacket and throwing it into the laundry. She called from the back room. 'I once dealt with a corpse which gave off indescribable aromas, and dry cleaning proved useless. But I got rid of that smell.'

'How?' called Jo.

'I burnt my clothes. This might be another bonfire job.'

She came into the kitchen and gasped. The detective stood there grinning and holding a bunch of gorgeous red roses.

'Happy birthday, Doctor,' said Jo handing over the blooms.

Gabrielle was close to tears, too close.

'Thank you,' she whispered, quite emotional. She placed the blooms on her kitchen table and embraced the young woman. It was a long embrace.

'How did you know?'

'I'm a detective.'

The pathetic pathologist had a unique laugh. They chatted then chatted some more. Jo had come to regard Gabrielle as a friend in the former meaning of the word. They were not Facebook friends. This was a relationship where each could be open and honest and know their comments would never be repeated, and where what they said was relevant. For some time now, Jo had been worried about her own criminal behaviour. Her latest scam with the brothers Sim only ramped up the stress. She wanted to talk to someone she could trust.

'I have a secret, Doctor.'

'Oh goody,' replied Gabrielle with one eyebrow higher than the other. 'I love gossip. Lots of sex I hope.' She dropped the joking face.

Jo let rip. She explained her mother's tale of woe, how Shirley was defrauded out of her life savings, and how Jo and an unnamed computer genius pulled off a stunning scam to retrieve the dough.

'I love it,' exclaimed Gabrielle. 'What a brilliant job, and I adore happy endings.' She went all quiet. 'Haven't had too many m'self but we won't go there.'

Jo paused. Gabby's face announced sadness. Jo continued.

'Yes but if the facts get out, I'll not only lose my job, I'll go to jail.'

Gabrielle scoffed. 'Bullshit. No jury would ever convict a daughter helping her mother who'd been cheated.' Jo grimaced. She wasn't so sure. Gabby took control. 'Just forget it. Put it behind you. It's something you did in the past, years ago.'

'It happened last month.'

'So what? It's gone and you're back on the straight and narrow.' Jo grimaced again. Gabrielle saw her expression. 'Oh dear, you've sinned again.'

Jo nodded. 'I had to, it was part of the deal.' She explained the situation with Michael's father.

'Jesus Joyce,' groaned Gabrielle. 'If the men you've scammed are vicious bastards, they'll come looking for their money.'

'It's not their money and it never was.'

'Tell that to the Marines. Listen, Missy, you could be in trouble here. That fake web site is trouble for impersonating a government department, and really big trouble from an angry criminal or three.' Jo looked at her and felt bad. Gabrielle spoke the truth. 'You need to solve these two murders, me darling, the journalist with the diary up his jacksie, and that wretch tonight. You need all the brownie points you can get. But more importantly, you need to stay alive.'

15

DISAPPOINTMENT REIGNED AT HOMICIDE. No-one had been charged with the murder of John Fielding. Frustration. Now one of the murder suspects had himself been murdered. Was this payback? If the interviewee killed the interviewer, how could they prove it? Was it worth proving the murder victim was a killer? If so, he'd already got justice. More frustration. Jo went to see Billy.

'I've been thinking, Sarge.'

'Don't.'

'In Fielding's diary there was one live lead, a Charles Brittain.'

'You rang him.'

'I did and he became short and angry.'

'A lot of people are like that when the cops knock on their door.'

'But that's just it, I didn't. I rang him. How about we knock on his door and see his reaction? He'll probably deny knowing the journalist but the question remains, why is his name in the diary?'

Hughes pondered the suggestion. 'My mistake,' she said grabbing her jacket and bag. 'That should have happened. Come on.'

They arrived at the fashionable Port Melbourne townhouse. A dog started yapping. Footsteps and then the door opened, a little. Both women held up their ID. The dog couldn't read so continued yapping. Billy explained the situation to Charles. He was going to seed. Once he was a comb-over chap, who would never shave his nut. Now he was Mr Straggly, and not happy.

'I've told you. I've never met or even heard of that murdered man.'

'Which murdered man would that be, Mr Brittain?' asked Billy.

That threw him. He thought they were talking about the journalist. They were but now had another name to run by him. He was about to tell them to get lost when the upstairs neighbour arrived back from her walk. She too had a dog and it joined the yapping conversation. To settle the barking beasts, and avoid the embarrassment of having two official looking people on his door step, Mr Brittain scooped up his hound and invited, well, ushered the police inside.

They sat in his sitting-room with mine host seething. Fido settled.

Charles glared at them. 'Can we make this as short as possible?'

'Certainly. We have a confession to make, Mr Brittain,' said Hughes, playing the ignorant police officer. 'We have a murdered journalist's diary in which your name and address appears, and in code. Why it's there at all and why in code we have no idea. We would love to eliminate you from our enquiry, Mr Brittain. Can you please assist?'

Jo was impressed. Hughes nailed yet befriended him.

'I can't help you. The name means nothing to me and why Mr Fielding had my details, again, I have no idea.'

'What about the name Robert Lensbury?' Charles shook his head. He genuinely didn't know the name. 'Or Rupert Lenton?'

Charles hesitated, not for long, but enough to let in a chink of light. He knew that name, oh boy, did he ever?

'No, never heard of him.'

'Mr Lenton was murdered.'

Charles put on his blank face. 'Well I'm afraid you're wasting your time. I can't help you with any of those names, and certainly I can't help with any murder investigation.'

'I wasn't thinking you killed them, sir.'

He felt better and prepared to stand. 'Well thank goodness for that.'

The women didn't budge. He had no choice but to remain seated.

'Before he was murdered, Mr Lenton told us he gave the murdered journalist some information. We're interested in that information.'

Brittain took the "total ignorance" position. Hughes changed tack.

'Have you ever lived in Sydney, Mr Brittain?'

He didn't like where this was going. Lying seemed a poor option. He tried a different response.

'Should I have my solicitor present?'

'That's up to you, sir. We could conduct this interview at police headquarters with your solicitor present. Would you prefer to do that?'

Jo admired Billy's maneuvering. Whatever Brittain chose, he was still in for a grilling. He stalled.

'Can I let you know later?'
'Let us know what, sir?'
'If I want my solicitor.'
'You can let us know now, sir.'
'Now?'
'We can drive you to the police station and have your solicitor meet you there. Or we can drive you and not involve your solicitor. It's your choice entirely, Mr Brittain.'

Jo loved this technique. Whatever you choose, you lose. Charles was losing and it showed. He tried one final throw of the dice. 'Can we finish this interview here, now, without my solicitor?'

'We can indeed,' said Hughes, who then turned the screws. 'But I should make it clear, sir, this is a double homicide investigation, and I stress the importance of you giving full and accurate answers.'

Charles wanted to scream at the police about him not being a liar but something held him back. Hughes allowed him to catch his breath. He could never catch his blood pressure; it was out of sight.

'Now, sir, about your living in Sydney?'
'I was never involved.'
The detectives were surprised.
'I'm sorry?' said Hughes.
'I know what Rupert Lenton did in Sydney back in the 80s. I knew some of the men he knew. But I had nothing, I repeat, nothing to do with their sordid lifestyles—nothing.'

Hughes was genuinely grateful for this admission. She was doubly grateful to Senior Constable Best who pushed to interview this man in person. His evidence may prove useless. But now they had someone who knew Rupert Lenton. Jo wondered where Billy would lead next.

'Thank you, Mr Brittain. Can you think of anyone who might wish to silence, to murder John Fielding or Rupert Lenton?'

He paused. 'How many would you like?'
Now things got really interesting.
'We would appreciate your frankness, sir.'
'But I won't give you any names. I wasn't in the VIP ring, I am not nor ever was a paedophile, and even if I knew who did what, to tell you would be signing my own death warrant.'

The chat stopped. Hughes was unsure how to proceed. She looked at Jo who took the hint.

'Do you still see your friends from Sydney, Mr Brittain?'

This frightened him—another examiner and a direct question. He wished his solicitor were present, or his powerful brother, or both.

He stood, and this time had no intention of sitting.

'I've said all I'm going to say. Either arrest me or leave.'

He stared at them. Hughes made a decision and stood.

'Thank you, Mr Brittain. We may need to speak with you again. We'll see ourselves out.'

That was easy as the door was a few paces away and in full view. The women departed and sat in their car.

'Interesting,' said Hughes. 'Your thoughts?'

'I think he still sees his mates from Sydney.'

Hughes was curious. 'Psychic are we?'

'And the hallway photos were interesting.' Hughes missed them. She remembered how Jo cracked the double homicide in Elsternwick having seen a photo of the housekeeper in an unrelated house.

'Well spotted,' said Hughes.

'The deputy leader of the State Opposition was there too.'

Hughes looked at Jo. 'Where did you learn your detection skills? Don't tell me, your grandfather was once the boss at Homicide.'

Jo grinned but not for long. Neither knew where this investigation was going.

They drove back to HQ. 'Can you drop me at the RMIT Uni, Sarge?'

'Don't tell me you're doing post-grad study?'

'I'd like to get details of those two students Charlie Baldwin and I interviewed outside Fielding's house.'

'Oh yes. Why?'

'They said they knew nothing about Fielding's cases, but the senior lecturer at RMIT told us they were the gophers for the journo.'

'Students lying? Whatever next?'

'If they were working for Fielding and knew Lenton was a key source for the VIP story, they may be involved in Lenton's death.'

'So the students killed Lenton? Jo, these hunches are getting weird.'

'They clearly admired Fielding. We saw their reaction to his death. If they thought Lenton killed their hero, there's your motive—revenge.'

'I'm going to start calling you Cider.'

Jo didn't understand. 'Sarge?'

'Long Bow,' she said.

'I think that's Strongbow, Sarge.'

'Whatever.'

Jo kept thinking aloud. 'Or, if they went to see Lenton to get the VIP names because Fielding's killer stole them, Lenton may have fought them and been killed in the fight.'

'Students as murderers—whatever happened to guitars and dope?'

Hughes pulled over near RMIT Uni.

'Listen to me, Missy. Names and addresses only and for God's sake do not conduct any formal interviews, make an arrest or do anything which will upset the Pope. Understood?'

Jo laughed as she got out of the car. '*An* arrest? Sarge, you know I only make multiple arrests.'

'I mean it,' called Hughes as Jo closed the door.

Charles Brittain was on the phone as soon as the female detectives left.

'What now?' asked brother Paul.

'I'm fine, thank you, Paul.'

'I'm busy.'

'I've just had two Homicide squad detectives in my townhouse asking all sorts of questions. I thought you said you would handle this.'

Big brother lost the attitude. 'What did you say?'

'Oh what do you think? Nothing, of course.'

'The matter's been sorted.'

'So why were the cops on my doorstep?'

'Because they're fucking hopeless. Now take your dog for a walk and stop bothering me.'

'Don't underestimate them, Paul. They're smart.'

'Who are they?'

'A DS Hughes and the other was the woman who rang me.'

'Senior Constable Joanna Best.'

'That's her. She's the still waters run deep type.'

'For the last time, leave it with me.'

Charles was disconnected.

'Hello Hesketh. Remember me?' Jo smiled and the lecturer pointed, politely mind, and took a stab.

'Homicide detective, Senior Constable ... Best.'

They shook hands and exchanged grins.

'I'm impressed, and please call me Jo. Look, I won't keep you. I'd like a quick word with the students, Tommy and Hannah, we met at John Fielding's house. They might help us find the breakthrough we so desperately need.'

'Of course.'

'If I leave my card, will you ask them to contact me?'

'I can do better than that. They're here now and their lecture finishes in about ten minutes. You can have a chat when they're free.'

'That's brilliant' said Jo hearing the words of DS Hughes. "For God's sake do not conduct any formal interviews, make an arrest or do anything which will upset the Pope".

'Come and have a coffee while you're waiting.'

They sat in Hesketh's office and Jo let him ramble. Fielding's death obviously hit him hard. The journo was certainly well-liked and highly-respected. Was he a saint? Was he killed because of the VIP story? Or was it simply a lover's tiff involving Dermot Cody and his ex?

She kept thinking about the students, and particularly Hannah. She remembered Hannah crying outside Fielding's house. Was John Fielding more than a mentor? Some female students are attracted to older male academics. Some male lechers fancy a nubile student.

Hesketh interrupted her thoughts. 'The lecture's about to end. Come and I'll show you the way.'

They waited in the corridor. When the students filed out, Hesketh waved to Tommy and Hannah. They remembered Jo and the trio went back inside the lecture room to chat. Jo thanked Hesketh who left.

'I'm sorry to trouble you guys but I wanted to go over a few things.'

'Sure,' said Tommy without confidence. Hannah looked worried.

'I remember you told me that Mr Fielding never shared his stories with you, about the things he was writing.'

'That's right,' said Tommy.

'But someone told me you did research for him. Is that true?'

Big silence from the students before Tommy tried to cover.

'It was nothing.'

'What was nothing?' Jo remembered the technique Billy Hughes used. Keep it polite but firm, and try to paint them into a corner.

'We only did checking of facts, that's all.'

'What sort of facts?'

Tommy didn't want to be in this interview. 'Just facts.'

'Can you give me an example?'

Tommy seemed to be thinking. 'I can't remember.'

Jo looked at Hannah. 'What can you remember, Hannah?'

'Nothing.'

Jo tried a different tack. 'I'm not sure if you know this but the man who spoke to Mr Fielding, the man who helped John write his latest story, has been murdered.'

The students exchanged glances. Their worries multiplied.

'Did you know him?'

The students spoke as one. 'No.'

'I mean did you know the man had been murdered?'

Again the duo spoke in unison. 'No.'

'Did you know the man, Robert Lensbury?'

Oh no, a trick question. When did you stop beating your wife?

Tommy took a deep breath. He wanted out. 'Only by name.'

Jo kept nagging but always with the same voice—a level pitch, and the same volume.

'What did Mr Fielding tell you about Robert Lensbury?'

That was worse than a trick question. That was a give-the-man-enough-rope type of question.

'Not much,' mumbled Tommy.

Jo sensed a breakthrough and went for the kill.

'The police are currently investigating two homicides which may be linked. This is serious. Anyone hindering police can be arrested and charged.' She paused looking from one to the other. They were not returning the eye contact. 'So I'll ask you again.'

Then, from nowhere, came a thunderbolt.

Hannah blurted. 'Shouldn't you have warned us we are being treated as suspects?'

The fact that Hannah spoke at all was surprising. The fact that she challenged Jo on a relevant point of law added to the impact. And for Jo, this caused her to worry. *Have I stuffed up again?*

Now the panic was on the other side. Tommy gained strength from his girlfriend's attack. Jo was on the back foot and struggled to regain control. She fought back.

'Tommy Glenister and Hannah Vine, I'm cautioning you that this interview is being notated and you are advised you do not have to say anything. Do you understand?' They slipped back into misery. It was as if they had something to hide. Jo went even harder. 'So what did you know about the story John Fielding was writing when he was killed?'

'Very little,' said Tommy. Hannah shook her head.

'What did you know about Robert Lensbury?'

More hesitation from Tommy. 'He was the man who knew about the VIP paedophile rings in Sydney in the 1980s.'

'Do you think he killed John Fielding?'

Jo knew that question would never be allowed in a court. She left it hanging. Neither student spoke.

'Where were both of you on the night John Fielding was murdered?'

The hesitation and nervousness continued with Tommy and Hannah refusing to speak. Then Tommy became stronger.

'Why are you asking this? We've done nothing.'

'You lied to the police.' Hannah started to cry and Tommy put his arm around her. 'You told us you knew nothing about John Fielding's writing projects when in fact you were his support team.'

'So what?' snapped Tommy. 'That doesn't prove we killed Lenton.'

Jo pounced. 'Lenton? Who's Lenton?' Tommy was flummoxed. Jo went harder. 'You said you knew Robert Lensbury. Who's Lenton?'

Tommy started to panic. 'You're confusing me.'

'Who told you Robert Lensbury was Rupert Lenton?'

'I can't remember.'

'Was it John Fielding?'

Hannah joined in. 'Stop saying his name. He was the kindest man and he helped us. He helped us with our studies and with our personal lives and now he's dead so stop saying his name.'

She cried even more and Tommy kept comforting her.

'I'll ask you again, where were both of you around 10 pm on the night Mr Fielding, your lecturer, was murdered?'

Hannah looked at Tommy and shook her head. He looked at Jo.

'We don't have to answer your questions.' He stood and helped Hannah to stand. 'Leave us alone. Why don't you catch whoever killed John? Why don't you do your job?'

Jo made an instant decision. 'Tommy Glenister and Hannah Vine, I'm arresting you on suspicion of the murder of Robert Lensbury.'

No,' shouted Hannah.

'You can't do that,' snapped Tommy.

Jo produced her cuffs and reached for Hannah's arm. She pulled back. 'I warn you, Hannah, I warn both of you, resisting arrest is a serious offence.'

Jo paused. The students looked at one another. Jo did what she thought was the right thing. She cuffed the couple together. Her mind again heard DS Hughes. 'Do not make an arrest.'

Sorry Sarge, too late now.

'We'll walk out to the street and hail a cab. We'll all sit in the back. If you want to put a jacket or jumper over the cuffs, that's fine.'

Hannah removed her scarf and placed it over the cuffs. Jo looked at them. She couldn't tell if they were miserable or furious or scared.

They walked out of the lecture theatre and along the corridor. They were almost home free when Hesketh came out of his office.

'Everything okay?' he called.

'Everything's fine,' replied Jo. 'Thanks for your help.'

Hannah looked back at Hesketh then lifted her scarf revealing the handcuffs. The lecturer's face was a picture. Fortunately, at that exact moment, the wind did not change direction.

16

STEELE AND PAYNE WENT TO THE FRAUD SQUAD. They gathered in an office with DS Craven, the man running Ponzi in the project to trap Joanna Best, the cop running scams.

'Your Senior Constable is back in business,' said Craven.

Steele was all ears. 'I'm not surprised. Doing what?'

'She's running a scam defrauding some real estate mogul who has siphoned off funds from his clients. Coming from Ponzi, I think that's what you might call ironic.'

Steele didn't smile. Years ago he had an operation to remove whatever remained of his sense of humour and irony.

'Stuff ironic, I want her nailed. No officer in my squad breaks the law and gets away with it. So, what evidence have you got?'

'Ponzi was contacted by Best asking for advice on the wording of her latest scam. Ponzi delivered. He's keeping all her correspondence.'

'No phone calls?'

'Not as yet.'

'Do we have a tap on her phone?'

Craven hesitated. 'Hmmm, might be tricky in light of cases she's working on.'

'She's working on breaking the law.'

Craven wavered. 'I'll run it past DI Handley, and get back to you.'

Steele wanted results and the sooner the better. 'What have you discovered about other officers working with her?'

'Nothing.'

'Nothing?'

'Ponzi says she's the only person who makes contact.'

'But didn't he say she originally talked about a group of police working these scams?'

'Possibly.'

Steele seethed. 'Possibly? Look she can't be doing this alone. We need to find her partners. Can we get Ponzi to have a meet with her?'

'Too risky,' replied Craven.

'For Ponzi? Who gives a shit about him?'

'For the operation. She's obviously smart. She gave Ponzi a screed with your prints on it, and cracked that double homicide.'

Steele was sick of hearing about her triumph. 'We know she's smart but she's also a crim. Victoria Police has a serving officer who is not just breaking the law, she's making megabucks. Can you imagine the media frenzy if this got out? We'll be toast. We need to trap her.'

Steele's anger and frustration made the others uncomfortable.

Craven tried to pacify the Homicide boss. 'At least we know she's currently active. We've given Ponzi pointers on how he might draw her out but so far, all we've got are broad details.'

Steele was unhappy. Payne tried to cheer up his boss.

'What about that code guy, boss?'

Craven sparked up. 'Code guy? What code guy?'

Steele shot daggers at Payne. He wanted to keep this info as a bargaining chip.

'Best had trouble with a murder victim's diary. It contained details we couldn't understand. She took the diary to a computer bloke who cracked the cipher.'

'And?' Craven wanted more.

'That's all.'

'What's his name? Maybe he's part of the scams.'

Steele was annoyed. He knew Michael Chan was known to Craven's colleague in Fraud. Steele liked to keep information to himself.

'DI Richelieu is the OIC.'

'Well can you get him to ask Best for the guy's name?'

'I can but he'll want to know why and that could spread the news that Best is under surveillance.'

'You can't trust your DI?'

Steele started to lose it. 'It's not a matter of trust, it's a matter of not letting Best have any chance of discovering we're on to her.'

The meeting fell silent.

Payne tried again. 'Would it help if I went to see Ponzi and gave him a bit of encouragement?' Payne meant to intimidate Ponzi.

'No,' said Craven in a firm and decisive way.

'Hang on,' said Steele. 'That might work.' Craven had no idea what *that* meant. Steele explained. 'Why don't we throw the cat among the pigeons? Let's send Ponzi to Homicide to ask for Best. She comes to Reception where everything is public. When he leaves, we tail him to see if she meets him away from the station. Ponzi wears a wire.'

'Could work,' said Craven.

'That's brilliant,' smirked Payne.

And so the sting was nutted out with Ponzi the leading actor. Was he any good? And would Detective Senior Constable Best fall for it?

Jo entered Reception at Homicide with a couple of uni students. They seemed to be holding hands in the conventional way but also happened to be wearing handcuffs.

'Two arrests, Sergeant,' said Jo indicating her party.

'From what I've heard, Senior Constable, everything has to be done in multiple numbers with you.' He grinned. 'What's the charge?'

'Suspicion of murder,' she said without any emotion.

The exhausted students approached the counter. Jo removed the handcuffs. They were booked in and placed in separate cells.

Jo went upstairs to Homicide.

'Where have you been?' asked Baldwin. 'Billy's looking for you.'

'I've just made two arrests for the murder of Rupert Lenton.'

Wow. Talk about a bombshell. People stopped work as Hughes came into the room. She looked at an almost smiling Jo Best. The smile disappeared in a nanosecond.

'Senior Constable, what did I specifically say not to do?'

'Sarge, I had to.'

'No interviews and no arrests. So you conduct an interview and make arrests. Why didn't you tell me you wanted to be sacked—again?'

By now spectator numbers had grown. Police officers were rubber necking a traffic accident. Here was a fight and everyone loves a good scrap, and between a couple of sheilas. Will there be hair pulling?

Jo tried to explain. 'Sarge, please, I had no choice.'

'What part of "no interviews" do you not understand?'

'They were there, Sarge. The lecturer took me to meet them.'

'What part of "no arrests" is incomprehensible?'

'I caught them lying to police. What was I supposed to do? Let them go? They have no alibi for the night of Lenton's murder. They knew what he did with the VIP sex ring. They worked for Fielding, were huge fans of the journo, and hated Lenton. They reckoned he killed Fielding. I had to arrest them.'

Hughes snarled at the gawping officers. 'Get back to work, all of you.' They did. 'But you, madam, you're with me.'

Hughes stormed out and Jo followed. She didn't storm. They entered an interview room and Hughes closed the door.

'Shut up and listen. Even if you are completely correct, have done everything by the book, and these two are found guilty of murdering Lenton, have you not got the message? Steele wants you out. You give him the slightest opportunity, and you're gone and this time, never to return. Do you understand?'

It took Jo a while to answer. She thought she had, as the Americans say, done good. Instead she copped a spray—a biggie. It seemed not only unfair but wrong.

Don't they want to solve homicides?

Jo nodded. 'Sarge.'

Hughes took over and conducted the formal interviews with the students, one at a time. Billy allowed Jo to sit in. They started with Hannah. Hughes didn't waste time on niceties.

'When you first met Senior Constable Best did you tell her you didn't work for John Fielding?'

Hannah nodded.

'For the tape, please.'

'Yes.'

'Was that true?'

'No.'

The questioning continued. Hannah got deeper into trouble. She was returned to her cell, crying, and Hughes interviewed Tommy. His mother had money and a solicitor sat beside the young student.

The questions continued only this time the interviewee declined to answer. His solicitor was adamant. 'Let them prove their case,' he had said to Tommy and the young man did just that.

No progress meant Tommy returned to his cell. Hughes and Jo discussed their next move.

'There's nothing there, Jo. The best we can prove is lying. You've got to learn. Get hard evidence. Build a case. *Then* arrest and charge. All you've done is waste police time and, if they *are* guilty, you've given them plenty of warning. Surprise is a great weapon but you've thrown that away.'

Jo hit rock bottom. She was right but she was wrong. Her catalogue of mistakes grew by the case. But she refused to quit.

'Sarge, can I check with Forensics to see if either left any DNA?'

'After you've released them, and apologised, yes. You need to learn the difference between being determined and being dumb.

Jo knew Billy was right and cringed when next she spoke. 'And you'd better get ready to cop the boss's wrath.'

Jo looked at Hughes. 'Is it that bad?'

'You might get away with it, but if one of the students puts in a complaint, Steele will go ballistic.'

Baldwin knocked and entered. 'The Pope is acting really strange.'

Billy spoke for Jo. 'Meaning?'

'He's almost calm.'

'He knows Jo made the arrests?'

'He does and that's why it's strange. Good luck.' Baldwin left.

'Something going on,' said Hughes. 'Why hasn't Steele lost it?'

Then they heard a PA announcement. "Would Detective Senior Constable Best report to Reception."

'I spoke too soon,' said Billy.

Jo felt sick. Here was her second and final sacking and this time it would be a public affair.

'Good luck,' said Billy and sent Jo on her way.

She headed to Reception. Being sacked once was awful. Twice would be shattering. How could she face her beloved grandfather? How could she face her colleagues in uniform? She entered Reception and froze. Smiling at her was the well-known criminal, David Baggio, aka Ponzi.

17

HENRY DUNN WAS A SUBURBAN SOLICITOR, soon to retire and glad to do so. Wills and conveyancing dominated Henry's practice, which he inherited from his old man, also Henry. Life was winding down for Henry Jnr in many ways. His son, Ralph not Henry, was a documentary filmmaker with no interest in the law. On the quiet, Henry's modest law practice was up for sale—resale value, not a lot.

It was a normal morning meaning business was slow. Henry's right-hand woman, Jean, had collected the mail, made the tea, and telephoned her daughter who was due to give birth any day now. For Jean, this would be grandchild number 6—gender unknown.

Into this peaceful, ordinary, slow-paced world burst a lunatic armed with what looked like a homemade bomb strapped to his waist. He brandished a knife and bloody big and sharp it was too.

'Key,' screamed the madman. 'Give me the key.'

Jean didn't have time to scream. 'It's in the door,' she squeaked.

The crazed interloper locked the front door, pocketed the key then indicated the woman should move through the only other door. 'Get in there,' he ordered. 'Move!' he hissed and Jean hurried.

Henry heard the commotion and was on his way to investigate when Jean burst in without warning. That in itself was a serious incident—she always knocked—but when the deranged bloke with her entered waving a knife, wearing a bomb, and making threats, well, Henry's day became remarkable.

'How do we lock this door,' demanded the intruder, now that all three were in Henry's office?

Henry thought he knew him. 'Mr Fielding?'

Martin's fury ramped up. 'Where's the key?'

'It's in your pocket.' said Jean. 'It's the same key for the front door.'

Martin Fielding, older brother of the late journalist, John Fielding, produced the key and locked the inner office door.

'Right, both of you, sit,' he commanded.

Henry and Jean exchanged glances then sat.

'What can we do for you, Mr Fielding?' asked Henry, treating the intrusion as if it were a normal lawyer client consultation.

'I want the truth,' growled Martin, 'and I ain't leaving till I get it. If you lie to me, I'll detonate this bomb. I don't care about dying, and if you wanna join me, do something stupid.' He threatened. 'I'm serious.'

'We can see that,' said Henry who, given the circumstances, was remarkably calm.

'I want the truth,' shouted Martin. His pent up frustration and anger poured out.

'What truth would that be, Mr Fielding?'

'My father's will—was it ever changed? Tell me.'

'Well if you let me get the file, I can tell you.'

Henry stood. Martin waved the knife. Henry moved to the files. Suddenly the phone started ringing.

'Leave it,' ordered Martin.

'We should answer it, Mr Fielding,' said the solicitor.

'No.'

Jean butted in. 'If we don't answer it, people may come to the door wanting to know why.'

Martin thought about that. 'Okay, but say nothing about me.'

Henry nodded to Jean who picked up the phone. 'Hello, Henry Dunn, solicitor, Jean speaking.' She listened. 'Mr Dunn is unavailable at the moment. Can I get him to call you back?' She listened. 'Certainly, Mr Hand, I'll get him to return your call. Goodbye.' To her boss, she said, 'Trevor Hand.' Henry nodded.

Martin's anger was dripping on the floor. 'Tell me. Did my father change his will in the last two years?'

Henry examined the file. 'He added a codicil last year.'

'What does that mean?'

'Your father wanted to be sure there would be no argument over his estate. The codicil made clear that the house would be sold if you and your brother couldn't agree on living together.'

'Living together? We hate each other. Why would we live together?'

'I have no idea, Mr Fielding.'

'What happens now my brother's dead?'

'Yes, I was very sorry to hear that,' said Henry, trying to calm Martin and defuse the situation.

'What happens now he's dead?' shouted Martin.

'Well if a beneficiary dies then their share is divided amongst the living beneficiaries.'

'So I get everything?'

'Yes, that is what should happen.'

'Should happen? Why should?'

'Well I believe your brother was murdered and ...'

'He was.'

'I mean if he was murdered by a beneficiary, ...'

Jean gasped and Martin turned red.

'You mean if I killed him, I'll get nothing?'

'That is my understanding, Mr Fielding.'

Jean could not believe her boss would raise that point. But then he was scrupulously honest and had been asked a specific question.

'So you believe the cops? You reckon I did a Cain and killed my so-called able brother?'

'I don't reckon anything, Mr Fielding.' He paused. 'But did you?'

Martin ignored the question, and paced about checking the bomb. Jean and Henry exchanged glances. He stopped and pointed at Henry.

'If the police can't prove I killed that hypocritical bastard, then I get the lot. Right?'

Henry looked at the distraught man and nodded. The phone began ringing again. Jean picked it up without asking.

'Hello, Henry Dunn solicitor.' She paused, listening to the caller, then looked at Martin and handed him the phone. 'It's for you.'

Martin recoiled. 'Me?'

'It's the police.'

Martin's face looked more dangerous than the bomb. 'You bastards. You told them.'

Henry remained calm. 'Perhaps the police know you're here, Mr Fielding, because people saw you in the street wearing that ... that device.' Martin looked at that device. 'The police want to speak to you.'

Standoff time began. Jean held the phone, the police held their breath, and Martin held his nerve. Finally, he took the phone.

'Hello?'

The police officer, trained in dealing with hostage situations, ran through the standard spiel. Martin was having none of it.

'Listen, mate, I want a guarantee you won't shoot.' The voice started speaking. 'And I want a guarantee you won't frame me for the murder of that toe rag, my brother.' More sensible words from the negotiator. They didn't work. 'You're not listening. I've been cheated out of my inheritance, and now the police are framing me for my brother's murder meaning I lose twice.' He shouted into the phone. 'It's my house and my money—all of it—so unless I get a written guarantee I won't be charged, I ain't shifting, and if you try and storm the place, the bomb goes off and the people, all the people in here get killed. I've got nothing to lose but they probably want to stay alive. There are five of them.' He lied and the two others looked at him. They wanted to live. Martin snapped at the officer. 'They want to live. Okay?'

The police negotiator gave another answer. Martin didn't buy it.

'Last time, mate, either I get that guarantee in writing in the next 30 minutes or the six people in here get to play pass the shrapnel. Do it!'

He slammed down the phone and Henry and Jean drifted closer to being seriously scared. Jean wanted to see her new grandchild. Henry wanted to see his retirement. Martin was a loose cannon—literally.

He looked at his hostages. 'And now we wait.'

Jo was stunned. She thought she was about to be sacked but when she arrived in Reception, there stood her former, and in some ways current partner in crime, Ponzi. Jo hid her surprise. People watched.

'Hello Senior Constable,' smiled the fraudster offering his hand. He used a trowel to apply his faux bonhomie.

Jo played it cool choosing to pretend not to know him. 'Sir?'

'Remember me, David Baggio. You interviewed me over that stabbing in Frankston—Ola Hatton and her brother.'

Jo continued to pretend her Ponzi relationship was not as he tried to portray. 'Of course. What can I do for you, Mr Baggio?'

'You told me if I ever remembered anything more to do with the case, I should come and tell you.'

Now Ponzi was good. The words he spoke and the way he spoke all looked and sounded legit. They were legit. Anyone listening would have given this routine the big tick for being normal.

Jo was thinking on her feet.

What the hell does he want? How should I handle this?

Ponzi was running the show. 'Can I make a statement? I've got some evidence you might find interesting.'

Jo smelt a rat. She reckoned this was baloney but she had little choice. People were looking, listening. If she told Ponzi to get lost, there could be problems. If she took him deeper into the station, she'd be playing with fire. She chose.

'Come this way, Mr …'

'Baggio,' said Ponzi impressed with her acting.

They entered an interview room and Jo closed the door. Something pinged in her brain about dropping the fourth wall.

In live theatre, (or in a film) when an actor directly addresses the audience as him or herself, it is said they have stepped through the fourth wall. In Reception, Jo was acting. Now alone, she could step through the fourth wall, cut to the chase and say, "Listen Ponzi, what the hell are you doing?"

But she didn't. She kept acting. This threw him at first.

'What can I do for you, Mr Baggio?'

He changed completely becoming the true Ponzi. 'You can cut this Mr Baggio crap for starters.'

'I'm sorry?'

'It's me, Ponzi, your scam expert.'

'I think you've got the wrong detective. I interviewed you in the course of a murder investigation. So what new evidence do you have?'

'Okay, play it your way. But I'm not playing your game no more. I've helped you run your last scam, Detective. I'm out. But before I go I want my money. Five per cent of the total scam and cash will be fine.'

As she spoke, Jo took out a notepad and scribbled on a page.

'I have no idea what you're talking about, sir. But I will say one thing. Threatening a police officer is a serious offence.' Ponzi baulked. 'Likewise trying to bribe a police officer can see you taking a holiday in a government hotel with all expenses paid by the taxpayer.'

'You bitch.'

'I suggest you hop on your bike, Mr Baggio, before I arrest you.'

She opened the door. He glared at her. Suddenly she showed him the page in her notebook. He read it.

Friday 6 pm
Park bench
Pigdon Street
Princes Hill

Their eyes met. She indicated the exit. He looked confused then nodded, and walked through Reception and back into the city.

Jo discovered she was shaking.

18

THE SUBURBAN TERRORIST WAS OFF HIS TROLLEY. Martin Fielding was suffering. He threatened his brother who then got himself murdered. Now, with brother dead, Martin should receive what he believed was rightfully his—the old man's entire estate. But the cops came after him. He reckoned they were likely to arrest him for murder. Martin would lose his fortune and go to jail. No wonder he flipped.

Specialist police were on the scene trying to talk the bomb-wearing, knife-wielding lunatic into surrendering. In-house, Henry Dunn tried to do likewise.

'Mr Fielding, I'm sure the police won't try and frame you for something you didn't do.'

'Oh yeah? How many miscarriages of justice have there been?'

'I have no idea.'

'Lots. Look, I've got no alibi, I've threatened my brother, and if the cops can't find the real culprit, they'll pin his murder on me.'

'Well whatever happens, Mr Fielding, taking people hostage won't help your cause.'

Martin knew that, but desperate times breed desperate measures.

Jean was feeling the pinch. She knew the man with the knife was not a terrorist with a political cause. He was a man who felt hard done by in his father's will. And his brother's murder hardly helped.

The atmosphere switched to despair, and everyone jumped when the phone rang again. It was the negotiator.

'I told you,' shouted Martin. 'Give me a written guarantee that I will not be charged with my brother's murder or else.'

'We have that guarantee, Mr Fielding.'

'In writing?'

'Yes, in writing.'

'Who signed it?'

'The Chief Commissioner, the highest law officer in the state.'

Martin went quiet. 'I need to see it.'

'Certainly. If you'll come outside I can hand you the paper in person.'

'Bring it here and slide it under the door.'

The negotiator swore—softly.

At that very moment, DI Richelieu was telling Homicide Squad detectives about the drama in Henry Dunn's office.

'Martin Fielding wants a guarantee the police won't frame 'im for 'is brother's murder.'

'Has he really got a homemade bomb?' asked Billy.

'And a knife.'

'He wouldn't be that stupid,' said Baldwin. 'He wouldn't be holding the knife he used to stab his brother.'

'Well assuming they can talk 'im down, we won't get a crack at 'im for a while.' Richelieu wrote on the display board beside Martin Fielding's photo. *Took solicitor hostage.*

'DI Richelieu.' He turned around. 'Your bottle of champagne may never be claimed, n'cest par,' said Hughes.

Nobody found Billy's attempt at humour funny. Of their three prime suspects, one was on remand for assault, one was dead, and the other was a potential suicide bomber. Solving the two murders just got even harder.

Back at the solicitor's siege, Martin had persuaded the police to push the document, guaranteeing he wouldn't be charged with murder, under the front door. He produced the key to unlock the inner office door. He watched his two hostages as he placed the key in the lock.

'I'm going to lock you in,' he said as he went to close the door.

'You might have trouble receiving the document,' said Jean. Martin stopped. 'The carpet is new and the door's a tight fit.'

He looked at the front door then back at the others.

'If I can't get that document, I'll blow us all to Kingdom Come.'

Martin was in a bind. His mind told him to get that guarantee. He was convinced the document would save him from jail and give him what he deserved, the entire estate left by his father. The police knew they couldn't honour a guarantee but wanted a peaceful resolution.

Henry tried to keep Martin talking. 'I have no idea where that is,' he said, trying to engage the madman.

'Where what is?' Martin needed calming.

'Kingdom Come. People talk about it but I don't know where it is, and I've never seen it on a map.'

'I think it's the Kingdom of God,' said Jean.

Martin lost it. 'Will you shut up about Kingdom Come and God? How can I get that document?'

'You could unlock the front door,' said Henry.

'And have those bastards shoot me? That's what they wanna do. They can't prove I killed my brother so this is how they solve their case. No way.'

'They won't shoot you, Mr Fielding. That might set off your bomb and they don't want to do that.'

Martin considered his predicament. He pointed at Jean. 'You, come with me.' Henry didn't like the idea and moved to stop Jean. 'Stay where you,' screamed Martin thrusting the knife in Henry's direction. 'You, what's your name?'

'Jean.'

'Come here, Jean. You're my insurance.'

Jean and Henry didn't like this. It had danger written all over it. The knife was large and lethal. Jean took a few steps. She kept thinking about her family and especially her daughter and unborn grandchild number 6.

Martin grabbed her arm. 'Stay close or I'll stab you.'

'Mr Fielding,' called Henry, 'please, take me. I'm easy to control.'

'Stay back,' threatened the man with the knife.

A voice sounded outside the front door. 'Mr Fielding, this is the police. We have your document.'

Martin yelled as he and Jean edged closer to the door. 'Slide it underneath.'

Sounds were heard then the police called again. 'It won't fit. Can you open the door, just a little?'

'No way,' shouted Martin. 'Without that guarantee, I'm detonating this bomb.'

Jean said a silent prayer. She wanted to live, and had an idea.

'Let me open the door and get the document. You stay back with Mr
Dunn.' Henry nodded. 'I'll explain to the police who I am. They won't
do anything to me.'

'Okay,' said Martin, moving to Henry and brandishing the knife.
'But any tricks and the old bloke dies.'

Henry was not happy about the "old" bit. Jean moved to the front
door. Her palms were moist. She stood close and whispered.

'Hello, I'm Jean. Can you hear me?'

'Yes, Jean, we can hear you. Where is Mr Fielding?'

'He's in the back office with Mr Dunn.'

'I understand. Are you injured?'

'No, but he's got a knife and a bomb.'

Martin yelled. 'Speak louder—louder!'

The police were poised to burst in. Two marksmen were in a
building across the road. They had a restricted view into both offices.

Jean spoke in a theatrical way. 'I'm going to open the door and you
can hand me the document.'

The cop copied her. 'I understand. Just open the door a little bit and
we'll pass the document through to you.'

'Okay.'

Jean took a deep breath. Her hands shook. She grasped the door
handle, turned it and pulled. Nothing. The door was locked. She
turned back to the inner office.

'It's locked. You've still got the key.'

Martin felt in his pocket and produced the key. He started walking
towards her and tripped. Jean screamed. Martin sprawled on the floor.
The police outside prepared for an explosion.

'What's happened, Jean?'

In a longish trice, Mr Dunn stepped forward and stood on Martin's
hand. He released the key and screamed in pain.

'Quickly, Jean,' cried the solicitor. She picked up the key. 'Go,' cried
Henry. Martin heaved and bellowed. Henry was too frail, not that
Martin was Mr Universe. Jean reached the front door.

'What's happening?' called a police officer.

'We've got Mr Fielding on the floor and I've got the key.'

'Open the door,' yelled the cop, worried that the bomb would go off
at any time. Armed officers stood ready to burst in and shoot.

Martin broke free. He scrambled to his feet and pushed Henry who stumbled and fell. Jean looked back in despair.

Both police marksmen across the road spoke into their microphones. 'Clear shot. I have a clear shot.'

'Hold your fire,' responded the officer in charge.

'No!' screamed Martin as he realised the door was about to be opened. He decided to end it all, and reached for the control button on his bomb. Henry scrambled under his desk and Jean did the same in her office. Martin pressed the button.

'Clear shot,' called both marksmen.

Then it happened. A crackling sound, sparks, and then smoke poured from the device on Martin's belly. He copped a serious fright and a painful sting.

The police didn't wait for an invitation. The door splintered and officers crashed in, screaming. 'Armed police, don't move.'

Martin's act of desperation failed. He suffered burns to his abdomen and a hammer blow to his hopes of being declared an innocent man. If they didn't pin murder on him, he was a goner for armed insurrection or terrorism 101 or whatever.

The detectives at Homicide were right. They would not be interviewing Martin Fielding for some time.

Both Jean and Henry were taken to the Box Hill Hospital. Henry was grateful for the "incident" as he needed a reason to walk away from being a solicitor. He retired that day.

Jean was doubly lucky because her daughter was already in the hospital and the now unemployed grandmother found the right ward in time for the birth of her sixth grandchild—a girl—which made three of each.

Meanwhile on the concourse at Southern Cross Station, Ponzi phoned DS Craven.

'The bitch took the bait,' said Ponzi. 'She pretended not to know anything about the scams. But just as I left, she showed me a note with a meeting place and time.'

'Which is what?' asked Craven.

'Friday night, 6 pm at some park bench in Princes Hill.'

'Where in Princes Hill?'

'Ah, Pigdon Street.

'Right, we'll meet on Friday at 5 in the usual place. You'll get specific instructions and you'll wear a wire again. Don't be late.'

'This had better work out for me.'

'Or what?'

Ponzi swore and hung up.

Craven called DI Steele and relayed the news.

'The cheeky bitch,' he said. 'That's where the journalist was murdered. She's giving herself an out if she's filmed.'

'She'll be filmed all right, and recorded. We're meeting Ponzi at 5.'

'Listen Craven, that woman is a criminal, and we need her caught and thrown off the Force.' Steele ended the call. He wanted her done or dead—either, it didn't matter which.

Jo was genuinely confused. What was Ponzi up to? Surely it was a risk for him to break cover like he did. Surely he was working for Steele. She wanted to talk it over with Michael but knew he was so against any contact with Ponzi. Talking to any of her colleagues was super risky although Dr Gabrielle Strange was the only person she trusted. Then Jo had an idea. She was good on ideas. She walked to the end office and knocked on the door.

'Enter.'

Jo opened the door to her boss's office. 'May I have a word, sir?'

The head of Homicide hid his surprise. He was not expecting Senior Constable Best. He'd just been discussing how she might be arrested for her part in a criminal conspiracy. He assumed she had a question about the two unsolved murders currently on the books.

'Yes, Detective, what's the problem?'

Jo knew she was playing with fire but reckoned that fighting fire with fire was her best option, her only option.

'I'm being targeted by a crim, sir.'

'Targeted?'

'His name's David Baggio known as Ponzi. He's a fraudster I met when investigating a homicide. He was not charged with anything and that was the end of it. But now he's turned up here at the station claiming he has more information.'

'What sort of information?'

'That's the tricky part. He thinks I'm involved in some sort of conspiracy involving fraud.'

Steele was on the back foot and didn't ask the right question. 'And are you?'

'Am I what, sir?'

'Involved in a criminal conspiracy?'

'Of course not, sir.'

'Well why would he think that?'

'I've no idea, sir. Fraud arrested him on serious charges. Maybe because we met over a homicide case, he thinks I can help somehow.'

'So what's this man ...'

'Baggio, sir.'

'What's he want, and what do you want me to do?'

'Warn him off, arrest him, just stop him pestering me, sir.'

'Has he threatened you?'

'Not as such, sir. I know he's up on serious charges but somehow he got bail. It's as if he's protected or been given a second chance provided he helps the authorities.'

'To do what?'

'I've no idea, sir.'

Steele tossed a pen on his desk and stood looking out the window. He spoke with his back to Jo.

'Is this interfering with your work?'

'If it continues, yes sir.'

'Okay, I'll look into it.'

'Would you object if I contacted Fraud to see if they know anything about him?'

Steele tried to keep a lid on his emotions. He wanted to shout but controlled himself—just. 'Don't contact Fraud.'

'It's just that I have a contact there, sir.'

'Who?' Boy, did that come out too loud and too quickly.

'Ah, it's a DS Harry Dale, sir.' He once gave me some help in finding a computer expert.'

'What's his name?'

'I just told you, sir, Harry Dale.'

'Not the cop, the expert.'

Jo had the sinking feeling again. It was like her stomach needed help. She felt trapped. Could she lie? Of course.

'Ah, Mitchell Collins, sir.'

'Mitchell Collins?'

'Yes sir.'

Steele scribbled the name. 'Okay, I'll look into it.'

'Thank you, sir. Anything you can do to get rid of David Baggio will be much appreciated.'

'I said I'll look into it.'

'Sir.' Jo got out fast. Both she and Steele experienced a multitude of thoughts. Jo sweated, Steele fumed. He rang Craven.

'She's on to us.' Craven didn't understand. Steele explained. 'Senior Constable Best has just walked into my office to report your man Ponzi, for harassment. She wants him watched and, if necessary, arrested.'

'Right,' said Craven. 'She's smart.'

'Ah, so you also do the bleeding obvious.

Craven tried to recover. 'Maybe she's guessing and bluffing.'

'For your sake, Detective Sergeant, I hope she is. Because if she's engaging in criminal activity while serving as a detective in my Homicide Squad, then a very large amount of human waste will soon be distributed by the largest electric fan in fucking history. I suggest you slip on your goggles, and catch that bitch holding a smoking gun!'

Steele replaced the phone and Craven's ear hurt.

19

ERNIE AND JOE SIM SAT IN A DEEP, DARK ABYSS. They needed help to regain their money but couldn't ask for help. Well they could but to ask meant telling the world they'd been duped, screwed and sucked in. What a disaster. If news of this scam got out, the brothers would be a laughing stock. If people knew someone ripped them off *and* got away with it, their empire would crash and burn and their egos would be trashed.

Everyone hated the Sims, even other criminals. The brothers treated their victims like dirt so whoever conned Ernie and Joe would become a legend.

Ernie paced the room. Asking his brother was useless. Ernie's BP soared into the stratosphere. His only option was to ask fellow thugs if they knew of any fraudster who was good at internet scams.

The guilty party, Michael Chan, wasn't on the Victoria Police Ten Most Wanted list. Cops and crims didn't know him. Michael flew under the radar.

'What's up, Ernie?' asked the people he called.

Ernie couldn't bring himself to say, "We wuz robbed, and we wanna nail the scum what done it".

Instead he asked a question. 'Have you heard about the Dee-Fat scam?' Nobody knew what he was talking about. How could they? The scam was targeted at one family—the brothers Sim.

Ernie needed to get the word out that he was after a crook who had cheated him. But he couldn't say that. It would be a crook who had gone back on his word. Some bastard had promised to pay Ernie but had welshed on the deal. Ernie could tell that tale and retain a semblance of dignity. He made calls.

'Buddy, how are you, mate?' Ernie never mastered insincerity. 'Listen mate, I need to find the low life who owes me big bucks.'

'You're owed money,' asked the "friend" desperate not to laugh.

'He's a scumbag, mate, but I'll get him. I'm prepared to pay big bucks for anyone who helps me find the bastard.'

'What's his name?'

Now that was a tricky question. Ernie didn't have a clue. If he invented a name, the search would be in vain. If he admitted he didn't know the name, his shame would be up in lights.

Ernie Sim, scammed by an unknown genius.

Wow, that would hurt.

'He's using different names, trying to keep one step ahead. But I'll get him. Just keep it quiet, mate, I don't want to frighten the bastard. If you hear of anyone bragging about not paying a debt to me, let me know, and I'll make it worth your while. Okay?'

'Sure, Ernie. I'll put out some feelers.'

And so it went on. Ernie would spin the same bullshit yarn and his "friends" would make the same bullshit promises. None lifted a finger to help but all lifted a glass to toast the hero who stiffed Ernie Sim.

A couple of brave individuals couldn't resist trying to rub Ernie's nose in the mud. One left a text saying they'd look out for anyone boasting about ripping off Ernie Sim. Mind you, the sender had a bloody good laugh at Ernie's misfortune. What a prick.

Then Ernie got excited when a promising text arrived.

Re your scumbag, check out this address. Guy there is laughing about your news.

Ernie didn't know the address but grabbed brother Joe and they set off to sort out the moron who dared laugh at the Sims.

Joe went armed with his fists, which he found more effective and satisfying than baseball bats and knuckledusters. Joe loved the feel of flesh on flesh. He was quite sensual in that way. Ernie was carrying.

The brothers arrived at this foreign address and bounced up the steps. A burly bloke answered the door, and Ernie opened with a somewhat challenging line.

'Are you the prick who's been laughing at my financial situation?'

The burly bloke had never heard of Ernie or Joe, and didn't take kindly to being accosted on his own doorstep. He told Ernie to kindly self-copulate, which only poured more petroleum products on the fire.

Ernie and Joe assumed the gent was involved in their troubles or knew someone who was, and so pushed their way into the property. Wrong. Ernie and Joe copped another scam, the wild goose chase one.

The house, you could never call it a home, was the abode of a little-known but fierce group of chaps who wore leather, tatts and whiskers, and rode around on large, two-wheeled machines bearing the name Harley Davidson.

The door of the house slammed, and additional burly blokes came into the living-room, surrounding the brothers Sim.

'Oh shit,' murmured Ernie. Joe spoke the same line.

To their credit, the brothers escaped with only severe bruising and cuts when broken bones could well have been on the cards.

Driving home in pain, Ernie asked Joe for the name of the person who tipped them off about the bikies.

'Dunno,' said Joe sucking his swollen lips. 'It was your phone.'

Ernie had erased it and cursed his luck. Getting belted, not finding his cash, and not knowing who set him up—twice—meant Ernie had a lousy day. He used up his full repertoire of expletives.

All this built the rage within Ernie's mind and body. His ulcers were fit and well. His nerves became nervous. He wanted his money and more, much more, he wanted the scammer.

<h1 style="text-align:center">20</h1>

REDMOND LATIMER WAS AMBITIOUS. He liked wealth, fine wine, sex, vintage cars and power. Power ranked high on his list of priorities. At present, he was the deputy leader of Her Majesty's Opposition in the Victorian Parliament. He wasn't the nominal deputy, the Clayton's deputy, the one you have who will never challenge. Redmond wasn't there to make up the numbers. He wanted the top job.

But alas, Red had insufficient followers. With an election less than two years away, the time to move against the leader was now but without sufficient followers, Redmond remained No. 2.

His mate from school days was one Paul Brittain, fellow Carlton supporter, white collar criminal and property developer. The two had a mutual interest. The developer could bankroll the politician, and when in office, the politician could approve the developer's plans. The two men ate a late supper at Southbank.

'I've got no chance, mate,' said Redmond enjoying his Peking Duck. 'No numbers, no challenge.'

'You've got it arse about,' replied Paul, also with succulent food in and around his tongue.

'Here we go.'

'Stop trying to persuade colleagues to join you, and start persuading them to leave him. Undermining and backstabbing are more far effective than bribery and bullshit. Don't give them a reason to join you. Give them a reason to dump him.'

Redmond thought about that. 'You should be in politics.'

'People want a leader who can win and who rewards their backers. As soon as they reckon a leader can't win, they switch, and if they reckon there's a promotion in it for them, they join your bandwagon and bring their mates. They want you to win to get their reward.'

'So I don't promote m'self, I *de*mote him?'

'Shaft him, and the rest will follow. Always back self-interest.'

'Is that how you operate in business?'

Brittain ignored the question. 'The only people politicians hate more than their political opponents are their political allies.'

Redmond remembered the Godfather's advice; *Keep your friends close but your enemies closer.* He did hate his political enemies but he hated his rival colleagues more. Problem for the ambitious Redmond was that he failed head kicking 101.

'So how do I damage my glorious leader?'

Brittain kept eating. This was quality grub. He spoke without looking at his friend.

'Do you want him wounded or killed?'

Panic flickered in Redmond's eyes. He'd stoop low, but murder?

Brittain saw his friend was struggling. 'I mean, do you want him quietly retiring for personal reasons, or scrambling for the exit smothered in scandal?'

Relief for Redmond. 'Ah, what's the difference? I mean which is the quicker and easier option?'

'Six of one,' replied Brittain quaffing the last of his red, and pointing to his empty glass while looking at the hovering waiter.

'I like the quieter method. A family crisis or personal health issue removes the media feeding frenzy.'

'I thought you liked publicity.' Redmond looked at his backer. 'Okay, Understood.'

Redmond changed the subject. 'How goes the developer's empire?'

'Yeah, good. Asian parents want their offspring studying in fine Australian institutions, so we build high rise boxes with shared sunlight and continue raking in their cash.'

'What is shared sunlight?'

'Window-free rooms. You open the door to let in the sun.' Redmond looked confused. 'Saves on building costs, mate.'

'You know if I become leader and we win, all those planning problems you've had will disappear.'

'If they don't, you'll disappear.'

Redmond endured another panic flutter. His friend wasn't joking.

'Help me win, Paul, and we'll all benefit.'

'Good,' said the developer, enjoying his third glass. 'So when do we play the dirty tricks?'

'As soon as.' Redmond raised his glass. 'I won't forget this, mate.'

Brittain tapped his friend's glass then resumed eating. He spoke without looking at the politician.

'There may be a delay due to a small problem.'

The politician baulked. 'What problem?'

'Some journalist was murdered and the cops contacted Charlie.'

Redmond's pulse accelerated. He whispered with a tinge of fear. 'The police?'

'Don't panic. He had nothing to do with it.'

'So why did the police contact him?'

'Some bloke gave the journalist his name.'

Redmond stopped eating. He spoke faster. 'Why, for God's sake?'

'No idea.' Brittain lied. 'But it's all over. The journalist and his source are both no longer with us.' Brittain exuded calmness. 'We might just wait till things settle down.'

Redmond relaxed a smidgeon. 'There are times, mate, when you scare the shit out of me.'

Brittain laughed. 'It's your leader who should be scared. He's about to cop the dirty tricks campaign from Hell.' Brittain pointed a chopstick at the politician. 'And when you're the premier, Redmond, don't forget who put you there.'

Redmond forced a grin. 'Go Blues.'

Later that night, Paul Brittain called Danny Fortune to his office. 'Change of tactics and target, mate. No more cloak and dagger stuff.'

Fortune was intrigued. 'And?'

Our old mate Redmond wants to stick one over his boss, Simon Edwards, our premier in waiting.'

'Oh not political stuff,' moaned Fortune. 'I'm only good at buggery and thuggery. With blackmail and violence, you know your enemy. With politics, your best mate's your worst enemy. Do we have to?'

'If Redmond replaces his boss, and his mob wins the next election, we'll be first best friends with the next Premier of Victoria.'

'Who gives a stuff? Will he make us more money?'

'Yes, and we'll get VIP seats for the Cup and Grand Final.'

Fortune was unimpressed. The only thing he hated more than politics was politicians.

'Okay, what's the job?'

'We need to nobble Redmond's leader.'

'Set him up in a sex sting?'

'Too obvious.'

'Photos of him dining with a mobster?'

'Ha ha. No, I said subtle.'

'I don't do subtle.'

'Look, Edwards needs to be exposed in a sneaky way. We set up something which occurs naturally, allowing him the chance of a dignified exit where he uses the excuse that his health or that of a family member reluctantly forces him to retire.'

'What about a car accident or a mugging gone wrong?'

'No. Something embarrassing, so he takes early retirement.'

Fortune thought about it. 'If it's subtle, I won't need Mr Black.'

Brittain flared. 'And don't tell me names—ever.'

'The job he did on that Rupert guy was brilliant.'

Even more angry from Paul. 'And don't tell me details.'

Danny gave a summary. 'So I think of a scheme, set it in motion and watch Redmond's boss quit on the 6 o'clock news. Yes?'

'Yes. Just make it subtle.'

Fortune left to engage in subtle skullduggery.

Danny had his orders. Nobble the Leader of the Opposition, Redmond Latimer's political boss. This was not Danny's usual brief. If Brittain wanted someone rubbed out, Danny had the contacts. Pizzas delivered, legs broken—Danny's your man. Rupert Lenton was a potential problem for Paul Brittain, so who you gunna call? Danny Fortune.

But this job didn't involve bullets, blades or blood. Danny needed advice, and called on an old geezer, once a mate of Danny's dead dad.

Albert "Bluey" Jackson was long retired and spent his days rolling his own smokes, going to Port Melbourne football training, and getting told off by his middle-aged daughters. In Australia, blokes with red hair are called Bluey. When people ask why, the answer is the same as why blokes with a surname of Clarke are called Nobby. Nobody knows why. They just are.

Bluey's little cottage in Port Melbourne was old enough for a heritage listing and as decrepit as its owner. He was a stevedore in his working days, which is where he met Danny Fortune's late father.

'G'day Bluey,' beamed Danny when the old codger opened his door.

'Piss off, I'm not buyin' nothin,' snarled Bluey.

'It's Danny Fortune, Terry's boy,' said Danny holding up a gift.

Bluey twigged and grinned. His small collection of nicotine-stained teeth bobbed up to say g'day.

'G'day mate,' said Bluey with a rich Antipodean twang.

With Danny carrying a six-pack of full-strength beer, Bluey was doubly delighted to welcome his visitor.

'Come in,' he grinned, and they navigated the piles of newspapers in the hallway to sit on the pre-Ikea chairs on the back verandah. The garden would never feature on *Gardening Australia*, although Bluey grew heritage-listed weeds.

'So how have you been, Bluey?'

'Bloody awful but I'm still above ground.'

Danny laughed. 'Good on ya, mate.'

'I've become a believer in miracles,' said Bluey with a deadpan expression.

Danny couldn't believe this left-wing, atheistic curmudgeon would ever believe in any religion. Bluey explained.

'I wake up in the morning, check to see I'm still alive, and if I haven't carked it, I believe in bloody miracles.'

His eyes had a twinkle and Danny enjoyed being conned. As they enjoyed the beer, Danny made his pitch.

'Listen Bluey, I've come to pick your brain.'

'Gone, mate, long gone.'

'I need to embarrass a politician.'

Bluey's mind snapped into gear, and he looked ready to fight. 'Too easy,' he said. Bluey wrote the book *101 Ways to Vote Early and Often*. He joined the Communist Party as a teenager and considered most Labor politicians worse than the Liberals whom he loathed.

(In Australia, a Liberal politician is a conservative.)

'You'll enjoy this job because the target is one of those toady, useless pricks in the Liberal Party.'

Bluey relaxed. 'Bastards, blood-sucking vermin.'

'Here's the pitch. I need to come up with a scheme to force a prominent pollie to resign.'

'Break his fucking legs.'

'Ah, but it has to be a bloodless coup.'

'There's no such thing, mate. If you wanna seize power, show 'em the size of y'musket balls.'

Danny explained the subtlety of his assignment. He looked at Bluey's face and thought he was wasting his time. Like Danny, Bluey didn't do subtle. Or did he? Bluey scoffed but secretly enjoyed the chance to bring down a hated enemy.

'I could tell you any number of dirty tricks, mate. But if I've understood ya, it's gotta be somethin' that forces him out on the quiet.'

'Spot on, mate. That's exactly what I need.'

Bluey pondered the problem. 'I think some Hungarian geezer invented it.'

'Invented what?'

'Don't rush me. Ah, the six degrees of separation.'

Danny was clueless. 'Right.'

'It means that any two people in the world are connected with no more than five people in between.'

Danny's ignorance settled in for the duration. 'Right,' he said again.

'So you work back from your target. It's a conservative politician?'

'Yep.'

'You'll need a journo who writes hard stories, and who gets to pressers with the pollie you wanna dump.'

'Okay.'

'The pollie is number 6 and the journo number 5. Then you find a close mate of the journo who becomes number 4.' Danny reckoned Bluey had lost his marbles. 'Then you need a mate or associate or even a family member of number 4 who becomes ...'

They spoke together. ' ... number 3.'

'You've got it. Keep working backwards till you get to number 1. Remember, everyone is connected to the next person up the line.'

'Got it,' said Danny. 'But how does that stitch up the politician?'

'That's when you play *Chinese Whispers*.'

Danny didn't want to admit he was lost. '*Chinese Whispers?*'

'I think the Yanks call it *Telephone*.'

'Right,' said Danny wondering how he could escape.

'Now the important bit. You need some dirt the politician doesn't want revealed, such as when he cheated in an exam, when he lied on a job application, dressed up as a Nazi, got busted in a drug raid, that sort of thing; murdered someone'd be good.'

Danny gave a weak smile. *Is he nuts?* 'So where do I get the dirt?'

Bluey looked peeved. 'Come on, mate, what'd your last slave die of?'

Danny forced another grin. 'Thanks, Bluey, you've saved my bacon.'

Fortune didn't believe that. They finished their beers, Danny thanked the old codger, and left, wishing Paul Brittain had ordered an old-fashioned hit.

So Danny had to find five or six people he didn't know from Adam, and some secret dirt on Redmond's leader, and then start a game he'd never heard of. *Too easy. Too easy my arse.*

Bloody hell.

He walked back to his car in the next street and was about to climb aboard when he looked across the road and realised where he was. That's Charlie Brittain's place. Danny went visiting.

When he knocked, Charlie's mutt went crackers. Charles opened his door and wanted to die.

Here was big brother's henchman coming to warn him, check on him, threaten him or, with any luck, put him out of his misery.

Charles didn't say a word. He just walked back into his townhouse holding his yapping dog. Danny entered and closed the door.

'Nice to see you, Charlie. How ya keeping?'

'Can we make this as short as possible?'

'I was in the area and just thought I'd drop in.'

'Oh please, my darling baby brother has sent you to do whatever, so let's just get it over with.'

'Wrong, Charlie.'

'And it's Charles, if you don't mind.'

'Your brother has given me one hell of a task and I don't mind admitting, I'm lost.'

'I don't give advice on how to kill people.'

'No, be serious, Charlie. Hear me out.'

Danny explained the project; everything old Bluey Jackson told him about the six degrees of separation and the game of *Chinese Whispers.* Danny must have been a good storyteller because Charles just sat there and didn't interrupt. When Danny finally finished, Charles spoke.

'Cup of tea?'

'I thought you'd never ask.'

This visit, Danny to Charles Brittain's place, was serendipity writ large, a stroke of fortune for both men. Charles went to school with Simon Edwards, leader of the State Opposition, and knew several "flaws" in the politician's past. Danny got excited. The job he loathed suddenly copped a makeover.

Charles felt good knowing he could do something which might curry favour with his over-critical brother.

But there was more. In his publishing career, Charles knew the journalists who most hated Edwards and who would love to expose the politician, no matter how trivial the incident. Suddenly Danny had a flying start to carry out the wishes of his boss, which, if successful, could propel Redmond Latimer to win the Liberal leadership.

Danny buzzed. If Redmond gets in and wins, my boss will have his first best friend as Premier. This was a win-win-win situation.

Charles was almost chirpy. Danny was dead set delighted. Charles' pooch, Chester, caught the party mood.

21

CHINESE WHISPERS IS A GAME where someone whispers a fact to someone else, who whispers it to a third person and so on. After many whispers, the last listener writes what they heard, which is compared with the original. It demonstrates how stories change in the retelling.

Danny spent time working backwards until he found his five people. He already had #6, the politician to be removed. It went like this.

#6 Simon Edwards (politician to be removed)
#5 Political journo who hated Simon Edwards
#4 Friend of political journalist
#3 Spouse of friend of political journalist
#2 Brother of spouse
#1 Actor who loved to gossip and boyfriend of brother of spouse

Here they were, the six degrees of separation. Danny was chuffed.

Person #1 was a retired actor who turned bitching into an art form. He was a lover of whisperer #2. Danny Fortune found the actor online and posted a cryptic message about the politician's "secret" on the actor's Facebook page. Bingo. Danny struck gold.

The gossip made the former thespian email his boyfriend, who was whisperer #2 on the list. Because the "secret" initiated by Danny—thanks to Charles—was salacious, the *Chinese Whispers* treatment meant the risqué version became more risqué.

And on it went, the "secret" being whispered far and wide, and it wasn't long before the six degrees of separation theory proved itself to work. The journalist Charles recommended, #5, got the "secret" and rolled his eyes. 'That can't be true,' he said aloud to himself having put down the phone from his brother-in-law.

Actually the brother-in-law wasn't #4 in the line but such was the nature of these *Chinese Whispers* that he found himself in the game. The "secret" was verified by the journalist's friend, the real #4.

The journalist wrote an article he called *The Secrets of Simon*. The original tale, upon which the first Chinese Whisper was based, originated about 40 years ago when the now Leader of the Opposition was a Year 12 student. It involved a school camp, a ukulele and a half-naked gym teacher who was the subject of lustful desire by most of the boys on the camp and several of the girls. Charles Brittain was on that camp.

The journo used that sneaky trick where you ring the politician late in the afternoon asking for a comment before the story appeared the next morning. Actually it was due to go online almost immediately.

A staffer took the call and asked the nature of the article. The journalist went all cryptic.

'Tell Mr Edwards it's about his school camp days, a ukulele and the lovely Miss Davenport's undergarments.'

The staffer thought it was a practical joke but stopped the Opposition Leader just before he left for his shack in the Grampians.

'What?' Simon Edwards turned pale. He thought the incidents—there were several—from his past were dead and buried. 'What line?'

'Two. Are you sure you want to speak to him?'

'I do, and you can go.'

The staffer left and with heart racing, Simon picked up the phone.

'Simon Edwards.'

'Just wondered if you'd care to comment on the story we're about to publish, Mr Edwards?'

'What story would that be?'

'You mean you've forgotten? It was only 38 years ago.'

The gist of the article was read to the politician.

'Why would you publish that?'

''So you don't deny it's true?'

Edwards hung up and fell back in his chair. He was well aware of dirty tricks with smears, half-truths, and outright lies but this was way below the belt. He was a teenager at the time. It was a prank that went wrong. He apologised and, after a year or two, everything was forgotten. Until now.

Edwards called his wife to say he'd be late, probably very late.

'What's wrong?' she asked.

'Something's come up and I need to deal with it. I'll call you.'

His Chief of Staff was already on his way home and answered in his car. 'Come back? Why? What's happened?'

'I'll explain when I see you. Just get here.'

By the time his senior adviser arrived, Edwards had already drafted his letter of resignation.

'You're overreacting, Simon. It'll all blow over,' the staffer argued.

Edwards knew better. He knew there were other incidents related to the one in the story. This issue would not go away. There were people who wanted to hurt him. His political opponents of course but far worse were his colleagues with Redmond Latimer leading the pack.

If Edwards tried to ride it out, his suffering would endure. The issue would bubble along undermining him. By 9 pm, the Leader of the Opposition had resigned, cleared his desk and set off for the bush.

Paul Brittain saw it on Twitter. So did Redmond who got in first.

'Paul, you are a genius,' gushed the Deputy Leader. 'Bloody fantastic, mate. I cannot thank you enough.'

'Redmond, I don't know what you're talking about but thanks.'

The politician realised he was speaking on an open line and immediately laughed off his remarks.

'Breakfast in the morning?'

''See you at 7,' said Brittain and life was just fine.

Redmond Latimer received many calls and texts all urging him to run for the now vacant position of Opposition Leader. He had the numbers and it appeared he would be elected unopposed. What a triumph for the ambitious politician. He had already decided who would be in his shadow cabinet to reward those who backed him.

It would be next week before the Party would vote on their new leader but unless the sky fell in, Redmond was heading to the next election as the alternative Victorian Premier.

Jo dropped in on Billy Hughes. 'Got a moment, Sarge?'

The detective sergeant leaned back in her chair. 'If you've solved the murders of John Fleming and Rupert Lenton, I've got all day.'

'Remember the photos in Charles Brittain's townhouse?'

'The one's I failed to notice,' said Hughes, interested because she knew her colleague's observation skills were terrific.

'One featured the politician, Redmond Latimer, and two other men. One was Charles Brittain and now I know the third.'

Jo handed Hughes an open magazine. 'That's Paul Brittain, developer and younger brother of Charles, our man in Fielding's diary.'

'Well spotted, Senior, but what's the relevance?'

'Charles admits he knew Lenton. But has he told us everything?'

'Probably not but without new evidence, any evidence, we've got no reason to question him again.'

'But we've got two powerful people who know or are related to him.'

Hughes stared at her younger colleague. 'If you had balls, Jo Best, I could label you a Son of a Bitch.'

Jo shrugged. 'All's fair in love and law, Sarge.'

'So?'

'Would the successful brother and the prominent politician be happy knowing brother Charles knows a murdered criminal?'

'This is dangerous territory, Detective.'

Jo looked at Hughes then went for it. 'How about we take another crack at Charles?' Hughes went to object but Jo raised a hand. 'But via his rich and powerful brother.'

'Oh please, Senior Constable, that's an unadulterated fishing trip.'

'Sarge, we've got two dead bodies with two of our suspects locked up and the other one dead. We've got zero leads and one diary as evidence. We need a break. Charles Brittain admits to knowing Lenton and the VIP paedophiles. What else does he know? We interview his brother on the grounds that he, Paul Brittain, may know something about his brother's activities. What's wrong with that?'

'A lot. Paul Brittain is mates with a prominent politician.'

'And possibly our next Premier.'

'What?'

'Just been announced. The Leader of the Opposition has resigned for personal reasons. The Brittain brothers' mate, Redmond Latimer, is odds on to take over and could become the next Victorian Premier.'

'We can't do this. The Pope will go spare.'

'Not if we don't tell him.'

Hughes stared at Jo. 'Now I *know* you have a death wish.'

'We could run it past DI Richelieu instead.'

Hughes paused. They had nothing. This was dangerous. 'We're playing with fire here, Senior. Come on, let's talk to the Cardinal.'

Half an hour later Detectives Hughes and Best stood in Reception of the palatial office of Paul Brittain's building empire. The woman on the desk had never greeted a homicide detective before, let alone two.

'Take a seat,' she said indicating the imported furniture.

She disappeared and was gone a while. She returned followed by the head honcho himself. He extended his hand as he approached the women.

'Paul Brittain,' he said with a straight face and even straighter voice.

'DS Hughes,' said Billy shaking hands. 'And this is Detective Senior Constable Best.'

'How can I help?'

'We're investigating two murders, Mr Brittain, and would like to ask you some questions about a statement we've received.'

'What statement? I've got no idea what you're talking about.'

His straight bat defence now turned a little nasty. A smidgeon of aggression crept into his voice.

'It concerns your brother, Charles, sir.'

Brittain hesitated then made an executive decision. 'We can discuss this in my office.'

He gestured and the detectives walked out of Reception with the woman on the desk sad she could no longer eavesdrop.

Brittain leaned on his massive desk. He didn't suggest the officers sit. 'I'm not impressed, Sergeant. You barge in here without an appointment on what is clearly some fucking fishing trip.'

Okay, thought Jo. *Now we know where we stand.*

Hughes paused. Jo noted how she let the anger of a "customer" fade before she replied. And her reply would often be soft and less abrasive than her attacker.

'Perhaps if we could explain our situation, sir, you might have a better understanding of our visit.'

It worked again. Brittain succumbed to logic and politeness. Mind you, Billy's clenched fist crouched inside her velvet glove.

'This had better be good,' said Brittain.

'We interviewed your brother Charles. He told us he knew one of the men who was recently murdered. We are asking people who know your brother if they too knew the dead man.'

'I haven't the faintest idea what you're talking about.'

'Do you know a Robert Lensbury?'

Brittain looked vague. 'No.'

'Do you know a Rupert Lenton?'

Brittain suffered a small change in his body language. 'No.'

'Do you know any of your brother's friends or acquaintances?'

'Oh for God's sake, what is this, *Family Feud*?'

'Your brother told us he knew some men in Sydney in the 1980s. Were you acquainted with any of your brother's Sydney based friends?'

This was not so much a fishing expedition as a flotilla of trawlers all casting their nets simultaneously. Jo was worried Billy had lost her knack of painting a suspect into a corner. Just as Brittain was about to explode and ask to see the officers' fishing licences, his phone rang providing a circuit breaker for both parties. He snatched the phone.

'No calls, Gloria.' She spoke and Brittain faltered. 'Tell him I'll be right out.' He went to replace the phone then spoke again. 'No, ask him to wait in the meeting room. Is that clear?'

He replaced the phone.

'You were saying, Mr Brittain?'

He was about to tell them to get out of his office while he sent a blistering complaint to the Chief Commissioner. Instead, he chose a less aggressive line. He seemed a tad uncertain.

'I can't help you, officers. I know nothing of my brother's life in Sydney. I'm a Melbourne boy. So if you've no further questions ...'

Jo Best had not spoken a word since entering the office. She didn't wait for a look from DS Hughes. Jo felt her boss would support her. They had become a solid team. Jo went for it.

'Can you help us find someone who may know your brother's friends, Mr Brittain?'

Paul copped another polite whack in the face, this time from the previously mute detective. Brittain struggled to control his tongue.

'No,' he almost shouted.

Jo went for the kill. 'It's just that you and your brother appear to be friendly with a number of prominent people, and we would not like to disturb them unnecessarily if at all.'

Wow. Bloody hell, Jesus Joyce and more besides. Talk about unsubtle threats. Tell us what you know or we'll drop in on your high-flying pals just as we've done with you.

Paul's face changed colour. 'Are you threatening me?'

Hughes thought about dying. *Oh shit. Shut up, Jo.*

The young detective switched on her acting skills feigning shock. 'No sir. We're trying to keep your name *out* of the headlines.'

She could have said *gossip columns* or *social media* but she chose *headlines.* Big bold Brittain was thrown. Jo continued.

'This double homicide involves a number of prominent people and we are trying our best to keep important and influential people like your good self away from any media scrutiny.'

How could Brittain be angry? The police were trying to help him. Jo kept up her gentle baloney.

'If you could persuade your brother to tell us about his friends, we'll be extremely grateful, sir, and do our best to never trouble you or your colleagues again.'

Brittain was having a bad day. The euphoria he experienced when his mate, Redmond Latimer, was handed the leadership gift wrapped, was now lost in the mire of awkward questions. He had conspired to murder Rupert Lenton. Did these cops know that? Were they using his brother to set a trap for him? Their presence now put the wind, more like a cyclone, right up his boxer shorts. Paul was thinking.

What do these bitches know? Has Danny blown it? Am I in strife?

Jo, having studied how Billy Hughes handled upset interviewees, said nothing, and allowed silence to add pressure to the suspect.

DS Hughes reckoned enough was enough. 'Well thank you for your time, Mr Brittain.' She handed him her card. 'If you think of anyone who could assist in our murder enquiries, we'd be grateful to hear from you or them. As mentioned, we're investigating a double homicide.'

The detectives left with a smile to Gloria who was busting to know why they were here and what had happened in her boss's office.

Paul looked at the business card. Had he looked at his desk calendar he would have seen the thought for the day.

I've had the kind of bad day no quote can fix.

As the detectives left, Jo spied the meeting room. She whispered. 'Nine o'clock.'

Hughes looked without making it obvious. Both women waited for the lift. They looked at one another. They recognized the visitor. Neither spoke. There were others sharing the lift. But out in the busy city street, Hughes complimented Jo as they walked back to work.

'Nice call, Senior, bloody nice call. Just make sure you put on your body armour when we get back to the office.'

The moment the detectives left, Brittain called Danny Fortune and ordered him to attend forthwith. Danny lived in an apartment in a Southbank tower, one of the many built by his boss. These flats had windows—no shared sunlight for Danny. The normally unflappable Fortune suffered feelings of unease. The boss's voice spelt trouble.

Brittain buzzed Gloria to send in the hidden politician. Paul was fuming when a smiling Redmond Latimer opened the door. His smile vanished quick smart.

'What's happened?' gasped the politician.

'Two fucking cops have just been in this office.'

Redmond experienced a fear he'd never felt before. 'Police!'

'They asked me about ...' Brittain stopped. He realised Latimer knew none of the details of the murder of Rupert Lenton, and to tell a politician anything was akin to posting it on Twitter and Facebook.

'What did they want?'

'It's my brother. He's mixed up in some sordid affair from years ago, and the cops were on a fishing expedition to see what I knew.'

'God, if this gets out, I could be ruined.'

'Redmond, if what happened gets out, we're both dead.'

The politician sat and suffered heart palpitations. 'If what gets out?'

'Don't ask.'

The politician's dream looked over before it began. He'd be leader in the morning and dead man walking by afternoon.

Redmond departed under strict instructions to say nothing. He knew nothing but that wouldn't stop a politician. Danny Fortune arrived and went straight into Brittain's office. The boss and his bagman sat, leaning forward in their chairs. Gloria was forbidden from interrupting unless the building was ablaze or Carlton was about to lift the premiership cup.

'The cops were here asking about Lenton.'

Danny was stunned. 'Why? How?'

'They're fishing but the fact they were here spells trouble.'

'What do we do?'

'How solid is your man?'

'Rock solid, no problems there.'

'Where is he?'

'No idea. I have a number but he could be in this building or in far north Queensland.'

'We might need him again.'

There was a pause. Danny thought he understood. 'Charles?'

Big brother sucked in air. 'He's already blabbed to the cops.'

'What?' Danny was incensed. 'Is he mad?'

'This is tricky. If we do nothing, the cops may get something.'

'Get what?'

'I don't know. Those two women were smart.'

'Women? The cops were women?'

'Bloody clever too. They played me well. And I wasn't helped by fucking Redmond turning up.'

Danny copped more shocks. 'Redmond was here with the cops?'

'I made him hide in the meeting room.'

'Did they see him?'

Brittain wasn't sure. He wasn't sure of anything right now. He was angry, worried and leaning towards desperate.

'This could go pear-shaped, Danny.' Danny looked at his boss. Neither laughed. 'I've got to get my brother out of the country.'

'He won't talk if he's dead.'

That was too much for the hard-nosed, take-no-prisoners brother.

'I can't kill my own brother. But if he thinks I will, he'll piss off.' Brittain looked at Danny. 'Frighten him. Persuade him to move.'

Back at Homicide, Hughes and Jo went to see Richelieu.

'Bonsoir, ladies. 'ave you come to claim your magnum of champagne?'

'We wish, sir,' replied Billy. She explained the latest visit. 'Paul Brittain is well-connected and hated us being there asking questions.'

'So, in summary, s'il vous plaît.'

'As we left, a Mr Redmond Latimer was trying to keep out of sight.'

'The politician, the favourite to become Leader of the Opposition?'

'That's him. Those two are mates.'

'Powerful men,' added the DI.

'We know Paul Brittain's brother knew Lenton and several of the men being investigated by Fielding. But getting Charles Brittain to talk is difficult. And as such we've got half of bugger all.'

'And going back to Charles Brittain is not a good idea?'

'Possibly. But we were definitely fishing today. Returning to his brother would get us nominated for angler of the year.'

The meeting lagged. The investigation lagged. Jo spoke.

'I'd be happy to try Charles Brittain again, sir. Now that we know his brother is in with the big end of town, maybe using the names of heavy hitters might spook him. I think we should strike tonight, just when he thinks the world is winding down.'

'Good idea,' said Richelieu.

'I can't tonight,' said Billy. 'Family birthday, which I dare not miss.'

'Okay, Senior, it's you and me against the world, babe.'

'Right, sir.'

Jo looked at Billy whose face went blank.

The Frenchman stood. 'Meet me here at 2000 hours, and wear your running shoes, s'il vous plaît.'

Jo felt a tingle of excitement.

22

CHARLES BRITTAIN WORRIED. He didn't want to talk to the cops or his brother. He dreaded hearing from those men he knew in Sydney years ago. If Rupert Lenton blabbed then he paid for it with his life. *His fault, not mine.* Charles decided. It was time to sell up and get out of the country. Would he tell his brother?

Later.

Charles rang a friend and cut to the chase. 'I need to sell and quickly. Can you help me make a quick sale?'

'Not a problem, Charlie. How are you by the way?'

'I'll tell you when I see you.'

'Right.'

That sounded ominous. It *was* ominous.

They made a time for a catch up later that night, and when, two hours later Charles' dog, Chester, started yapping and his doorbell rang, Charles didn't hesitate to open the door and greet his friend.

Bad move.

Gary Black pushed his way inside making sure his gun was visible.

'Make a sound, Charlie boy and you're dead.'

Charles' worst nightmare began. His dog snapped and yapped.

'Stop the dog or I'll shoot it now.' Terror gripped Charles.

Now there are certain things a criminal can do and, within reason, get away with. Killing, maiming, or in any way harming the family pet is an exception. Murdering Charles is fine but do not harm even a hair of the dog. But right now Charles had slumped to the depression end of sadness. He needed a hair of the dog. Two.

Charles scooped up his beloved Jack Russell and carried him to the laundry. Gary followed in case the owner entertained thoughts of an escape. There was a basket for the dog, and Charles tossed a chewy treat into the bed. With dog distracted, Charles was dragged out and the door closed.

'Move,' ordered Black, and Charles complied.

'I'm leaving the country,' he said, pleading with his eyes.

'You've been naughty, Charlie; been telling tales out of school.'

'Please, I've said nothing. I know nothing. Please, contact my brother. He'll back me up.'

Gary looked at his target. Charles died inside. Now he knew. Black didn't have to speak. This wasn't the VIP paedo ring's representative. This gunman was here on orders from Paul Brittain. Baby brother had run out of patience. Charles had become too much of a threat. It was time to remove it.

'Let me call my brother. Please, just one phone call.'

Black did his usual trick of screwing a silencer to the barrel of his gun. Charles started to cry. On cue, his dog started to bark. Chester shouted, "Let me out of the laundry," although Charles believed it was a cry for clemency. The dog was saying, "Please don't kill my master. I love him. No-one else does but I do."

Black had been told to collect any diaries, phones, letters, etc., which might link Charles with the VIP paedophiles back in Sydney all those years ago. The killer played an underhand trick. He was more than an assassin; he was a sneak.

'Give me everything that ties you to those perverts in Sydney.'

Charles saw this as the condition of him being spared death.

'Of course,' he said moving to his desk, opening drawers and collecting anything which might save his life. Black smiled thinking of the time he would save, and the possibility of him not finding what was required.

'Everything,' said Black checking the chamber of his Glock.

Charles took photos, memorabilia, letters, theatre programmes, all of which had some connection to his former life in Sin City. Being naturally tidy, and of course wanting to do anything to curry favour with a killer, Charles placed the objects in an expensive attaché case, closed it then placed it on the coffee table for his "guest".

'Tell Paul I'm leaving the country for good. He'll never see or hear from me again. I swear.'

'That's true,' said Black who suddenly raised his gun.

A pathetic moan escaped from Charlie as he slumped to his knees and begged for mercy. 'No, please, no.'

Black pointed his gun at Charles's head. In the second before he would pretend to fire, someone banged on the door and a loud voice rang out.

'Come on Charlie, let's be having you.'

Black froze. Charles froze. Only Chester remained active. His barking moved to frantic. "Let me out, Dad. I'll protect you."

'Don't move,' snapped Black. 'Ignore him. Let him leave.'

'I can't. It's a mate. He's expected.'

'Shut up.' Black hated jobs with problems. He was Mr Clean Kill. He wanted the in-and-out-and-home-in-time-for-cocoa jobs. And anyway, this was only a put-the-frighteners-on job—no killing required.

Charles pleaded. 'He's an estate agent. He's helping me sell this place because I'm leaving the country. He'll tell you.' Charles begged. 'Please, you've got to believe me.'

More door banging and more Chester chat.

Black decided. 'I'll be in the laundry. Say or do anything stupid and the dog gets it first then you. If your visitor is still here in fifteen, I'll kill you both.'

Black went to the laundry. Chester's barking became louder for a few seconds before he yelped in pain then suddenly went quiet.

Charles was a mess. His eyes were wet, his breathing short, his boxers moist, and his best mate was alone with a madman.

'Come on, Charlie,' cried the visitor.

'Coming,' called Brittain, wiping his face and checking his crotch. He opened the door where stood his longtime friend, the real estate agent Malcolm Best, aka Malcolm X, Joanna Best's old man.

'Malcolm,' greeted Charles in a forced and over enthusiastic way.

Malcolm stepped inside and shook hands with his friend of 30 years. 'How are you, my son? You're looking ...' He stopped mid-sentence because Charles couldn't contain his distress. 'Jesus, Charlie, what's wrong?' Malcolm's shock took over.

'Come in,' said Charles. 'I'm in a bit of strife.'

'What's happened?'

'Sit.' They did. 'I'm in debt, Malcolm. I have to sell and fast and get out of the country.'

'Leave the country? What, have you murdered someone?'

Oh dear, that was unfortunate. In the laundry, hitman Gary Black listened intently, holding his gun ready to burst out and shoot. One or two, plus a dog, it made no difference to Gazza.

Now you could never describe Gary Black as nice. He began his criminal life age 14. He stole cars, and ran drugs making good money. When offered serious dough to hurt someone, he did. When his pay grade increased for a killing, Gary took the promotion. He soon discovered good hitmen were hard to find. Most screw up and get caught or get shot.

Gary found plenty of work. Husband wants rid of missus. Missus wants rid of old man. Drug dealer needs to lose a competitor. Tit for tat revenge killing. There is never a recession for assassins.

Gary didn't run ads on Facebook but had plenty of offers. He didn't take every job, and could afford to pick and kill. The money had to be right and the job had to be safe. Gary checked the T&C of every contract and gave preference to reliable employers.

Danny Fortune was reliable.

The assassin cased the joint then, if happy, took the deal. In this case, Charles Brittain was just to be frightened. No killing. Too easy.

But suddenly things changed. Some bloke rocked up. Now it became tricky. Gary thought about the emergency instructions. Danny Fortune had added a rider.

'If you have trouble, kill the prick. I'll square it with my boss.'

In the laundry, Gary listened to Charles and Malcolm. Chester cowered having felt the brutality of Gary's boot. Gary was thinking.

If I'd grabbed that attaché case, I could open this back door and be gone. I can't leave without the stuff. So if Charlie doesn't kick out his visitor, Danny will get my buy one, get one free offer.

Charles explained to Malcolm. 'I owe a lot of tax, I've been a silly boy with some gambling debts, and I borrowed from the wrong people. The ATO want payment and the loan sharks want a limb.'

'Charlie, why didn't you ask for help?'

'I'm scared, Malcolm, terrified. I have to sell this place and move overseas. Can you help me, please?'

'Of course.' Malcolm was in shock. 'Okay, have you got a mortgage?'

Charles answered Malcolm's questions. The longer they spoke, the more nervous Charles became. He formed a plan to get Malcolm out. He'd walk him to the door then tell him to run, and both would take off like the clappers, although at their age it would be more like the slappers. The only worry was Chester. Charles had to save his mate.

Malcolm watched his friend become more erratic. He even thought about calling an ambulance, and having Charles taken to hospital.

The minutes ticked by and the tension kept building. Malcolm took notes, then put down his pen.

'Listen mate, let's take a break. Let's have a coffee and forget about the house sale and all your problems.'

Charles became more disturbed. Now he started to speak in a louder voice as if he wanted others to hear the conversation.

'I'm not well, Malcolm. Sorry, but I think you should go.'

Malcolm thought it weird but got the message. 'Okay, if you're sure.'

'I'm sure.' He spoke louder. 'I really want you to leave.'

'No worries.' He stood. 'What's happened to your dog?'

'Chester.'

'I thought I heard him before.'

'I can't take him overseas so I've given him to a friend.'

Right on cue, Chester let out a yelp. He was not happy with his current surrounds and especially not with his current companion.'

'What was that?' Malcolm heard the dog bark. Everyone heard it.

Charles made a lousy liar. He shrugged and moved to the door. 'What was what? Come on.'

Malcolm stood still. 'Charlie, what the hell is going on?'

Charles panicked. *There's an assassin in my laundry with a real gun. He'll kill us both. Come on, Malcolm, piss off.*

Charles hissed. 'Malcolm, come on,' and gestured frantically. Malcolm shook his head and moved toward his friend. Charles reached for the door ready to open it. With his other hand, he reached for Malcolm and pulled him close. Charles whispered. 'When I open the door, we have to run. Okay?'

Malcolm thought of the word *insane*. Charles started to turn the lock. A voice, dripping with menace, sounded behind them.

'Freeze.'

You can pack a lot into one word.

Malcolm turned and Charles looked back to see Gary holding his gun in both hands and moving to get a clear line of fire.

'Shit,' said Malcolm.

'Oh God,' said Charles.

'Back, come back,' ordered the gunman. The would-be escapees moved away from the door and into the room. They dawdled. 'Move!'

'Sorry, Malcolm,' murmured Charles.

'No problem, old chap,' replied Malcolm.

'On the floor,' snapped Gary, waving his gun. 'On your knees, now.'

Malcolm started to kneel but Charles grabbed his arm.

'No, Malcolm, stand.' Charles threw in some defiance. 'If I'm going to be killed, it won't be on my knees.'

'Killed?' gasped Malcolm. 'Did you say killed?'

'Yes. Sorry about that. Please, make your own choice.'

'I get a choice?'

'Shut up,' snapped Gary. He was seriously pissed. 'I said, kneel.'

He raised his gun when Chester suddenly found his voice and asked to be let out. He let rip and Charles was overcome.

'Chester,' he called, 'you're alive. Hang on, buddy, Daddy's coming.'

Gary lost it. Here was a bloke he was supposed to terrify, defying him, walking away from him to attend to a bloody dog.

Then Malcolm decided now was a good time to leave. He edged towards the front door. This was too much for the hired assassin. He swiveled, raised his gun and for the second time tonight aimed at a victim, this time Malcolm Best. Then, again for the second time tonight, Gary suffered gun-pointus interruptus as aggressive door knocking began. Charles froze at the laundry door. Mal froze at the front door. Gary just froze.

The trio couldn't miss hearing the loud visitor. He sounded foreign.

'Monsieur Brittain, this is the police.' DI Richelieu spoke with his usual Gallic charm. 'Open the door, s'il vous plaît.'

Charles and Malcolm found breathing easier but Gary found himself closer to the high end of the anger spectrum.

'Fuck,' he exclaimed while pointing his gun from Charles to Malcolm, to Charles and back to Malcolm. Eeny, Meeny, Miny, Moe.

The police waited, as the victims waited while the gunman considered his options. Before he chose his next course of action, the police knocked and called again. This time the other officer spoke.

'Mr Brittain, this is Detective Senior Constable Best.'

'Jo!' exclaimed Malcolm. There was a pause. Malcolm yelled. 'Jo, it's me.'

'Dad?'

Gary Black was seriously confused. His one victim had become two, and now the filth were here in numbers ready to play *Happy Families*.

Malcolm called loudly. 'Run Jo. He's got a gun.'

Now Gary reckoned that was seriously unfair. His rules didn't allow victims to help the police. In a panic, unusual for him, he opened fire sending two shots through the frosted glass by the front door. DI Richelieu went down. Jo didn't need encouragement to cease being upright. Charles and Malcolm assumed the prostrate position and Gary fled to the laundry exiting via its outside door.

Chester's barking increased in tempo and volume. Suddenly it stopped. Charles crawled towards the front door, stretched up and unlocked it. Jo burst into the room bending low and holding her gun with both hands.

'He's gone,' said Charles.

'That way,' pointed Malcolm.

'Are you both okay?' asked Jo.

'Fine,' said Malcolm. 'But we can't go on meeting like this.'

Chester was silent. Charles spoke. 'Will you try and help my dog, please? He's in the laundry with the gunman.'

'Call an ambulance and help my colleague outside the door,' said Jo.

Malcolm grabbed his phone and Charles went to his front door. Jo moved to the laundry.

'Jo,' called her father. 'Be careful.'

She grimaced. 'Stay down, Dad, both of you.'

She crouched to one side of the laundry. If the gunman fired again, she'd be out of the line of fire. She called.

'Armed police. Throw out your weapon. Do you hear me?' Nothing. Jo spoke to Charles. 'Is there another way out?'

'That's it. The laundry leads to my courtyard.'

Jo tried again. 'Armed police. Throw out your weapon, now.'

Same lack of response. Jo weighed up her options.

Do I wait for back up or attempt to disarm the intruder?

She could hear DS Hughes speaking in a clear voice.

'Secure the situation and wait for backup.'

Jo stood alongside the door out of the line of fire. She reached with her left hand and grasped the doorknob. It was awkward. Being right handed, her gun was in her right hand. She paused rehearsing the moves in her mind.

Then she struck. She turned the doorknob and pushed. The door opened and Jo pulled back her hand to avoid deadly fire. Nothing.

She heard a strange sound. Again she gave the order. 'Armed police. Throw out your weapon.'

She paused. The strange sound continued. Then came a voice, quiet and strained.

'I can't.'

Jo paused. She looked at her father. Malcolm gave a thumbs up. Charles was outside attending to DI Richelieu. She called to her boss.

'Are you okay, sir?'

'Magnifique, Mademoiselle. Carry on.'

She called again to the man in the laundry.

'Throw out your weapon.'

'Are you fucking deaf? I can't.'

More confusion for Jo. More of the strange sound.

'Why?'

'Will you please just shoot this fucking dog?'

It wasn't a question, more a demand. Jo prepared to look inside. She held her gun in both hands, paused then took a fleeting peak around the laundry door frame. She pulled back, allowed her brain to compute the situation, then, feeling a lot more comfortable, took another look. Then she relaxed, well stopped producing as much adrenalin, and stood in the doorway, pointing her gun at Gary Black.

He was on his back, his feet towards the sitting-room with his gun almost within reach on the floor. He could have moved and picked it up quite easily were it not for Chester.

The strange sound was Chester's deep throated growl. He couldn't bark because he had a mouth full of the assassin's trousers, and what was underneath said strides. Chester's preferred area of biting was adjacent to Gary's groin. The smallest of moves by the gunman saw Chester growl and tighten his grip on the trousers and its immediate contents. Gary was in discomfort with the imminent prospect of massive pain. Chester was not a whole dog and reckoned Gary should join the club.

Jo wanted to laugh. Instead she leant in slowly and collected the gun from the floor. She called.

'DI Richelieu. Are you still okay, sir?'

He called. 'Merci, Mademoiselle, I am, 'ow you say, bonzer, mate.'

Jo called again. 'Mr Brittain, could you collect your dog please?'

Charles was delighted to do so. When he looked inside his laundry, he wanted to laugh but was so overcome with finding his best friend safe and well, all he could concentrate on was Chester.

An ambulance arrived and Malcolm called. 'Ambulance is here, Jo,'

'Thanks, Dad. Go and bring them in please.'

Malcolm did just that wanting to tell the ambos that the superhero cop inside was his daughter. Gary was cuffed and plonked on the settee. Jo radioed for support, and told Charles and her father to wait in the kitchen.

What a night with possibly the best still to come.

23

POLICE ARRIVED IN NUMBERS. When someone discharges a firearm, certainly in an urban area, the local constabulary attend—pronto. When one of their own is shot at, that brings the gendarmes out en masse. And it was a gendarme of sorts who was in the line of fire. DI Richelieu, muttered a few Sacrebleus when a bullet grazed his upper arm. However, the DI's distress was all about his haute couture.

Ambulance officers had no garment repair expertise but were prepared to ferry the Inspector to hospital. His graze needed checking.

DS Hughes left her family function in a heartbeat when she heard that homicide detectives were fired upon. When she arrived, most of Homicide Squad, including the Pope, was there.

Gary Black had adopted a hangdog look, rather appropriate since a dog hanging on his crotch brought him to this situation. Getting caught was the pits. Getting caught by a bloody animal was worse.

Hey Rex, eat your heart out.

Gary took a vow of silence. He made a couple of bad blues, and right now, silence was his only friend.

Detective Senior Constable Best removed his wallet and phone. She looked at his driver's licence and at him. 'Not all that smart carrying ID when you're on the job, Gary.' He wanted to spit.

Steele asked for an immediate report. Jo explained how she and Richelieu arrived, were fired at, how the shooter tried to escape, but was cornered by Chester, the Hound of the Baskervilles—Payne had no idea what she meant—been arrested and placed on the settee.

There he sat and if looks could kill.

'What have you done since the arrest, Constable?' asked the Pope.

'I removed his phone, sir, and checked his messages. He'd been sending and receiving texts to a particular number. I replied to his last incoming text.'

The officers sensed a major error. Best had blundered again.

Steele exploded. 'You sent a text from the suspect's phone?'

'I thought it wise, sir.'

'Explain.'

'Well the suspect and this other person had been discussing the "game" which I believe was his task here tonight. The suspect's last message read ...' Wearing gloves, she looked at the phone. '*Game on.*'

'And?' asked Steele.

'The contact then sent a text 12 minutes later which reads, *Is game on?* So I replied *Game over.*'

'Brilliant,' murmured Billy Hughes.

'Sir, if we can trace this number, we should find the person who ordered the attempt murder.'

'Who said it's an attempt murder?'

'The arrested man fired twice at police, sir.'

'Thank you, Detective,' said Steele, in a manner which suggested her role was finished, and senior officers would assume responsibility.

'There is something else, sir.'

Steele glared. *This bloody woman keeps getting in my way.* 'Yes?'

'Having disarmed and arrested the suspect, I searched him and found the following items.' She moved to a cloth on the bookshelf. She raised the cloth exposing a hunting knife and gun.

'I've placed them there for Forensics, sir.'

'Thank you, Senior Constable. Is that all?'

His question took the form of a sarcastic statement.

Step back, woman, I'm in charge.

But Jo had more. 'It's just that we've never found the weapons used in the Fielding and Lenton murders, sir.' She paused. 'The owner of this house is connected to Rupert Lenton and the weapons seized might give Forensics something linked to one or both of the murders.'

Talk about showing the boss who's boss.

'Excellent work, Detective,' said Hughes. She wanted to say it loud knowing Steele wouldn't. Other officers murmured their assent.

DS Fleming offered advice. 'I think we should act immediately, sir.' Sunny Jim here won't give us anything. The sender of those texts will be hanging out for news. We need to find that person and quickly.'

Steele took action. 'Right DS Fleming and DS Hughes take officers, find that phone and its owner.'

'Sir,' said Hughes, and looked straight at Jo. 'You're with me.'

Officers left. Neither DS grabbed Payne. He was the kid who doesn't get picked for that game of cricket or football at lunchtime at school.

Steele was annoyed when he should have been excited. Out of nowhere the police had evidence and what looked like a significant lead. Payne remained with Steele. They looked at one another. Not only had they nothing with which to nail Best for her criminal behaviour, she was again proving to be a detective who got results.

Forensic officers arrived and got cracking. Under protest, Richelieu went by ambulance to hospital. Payne went with two uniformed officers who delivered Gary to police HQ. He was not happy. Steele was about to leave when a civilian approached him.

'Excuse me, sir, are you the officer in charge?'

'Who are you?'

'I was here in the house when the gunman opened fire.'

'You were in the house?'

'Yes sir.'

'Have you given a statement?

'I have.'

'So why are you still here?'

'I wanted to say how brave I thought the young police officer was.'

'Good.'

'And how proud I am of her.'

Steele looked at Malcolm Best. 'Proud of her?'

'Yes sir. Senior Constable Best is my daughter.'

It was difficult to describe the look on Steele's face.

Jo gave Richelieu's car keys to Fleming then hopped into Billy's car. The women set off for a meeting and plan of action. Jo had an idea.

'Sarge?'

'I don't like that tone of voice.'

'Let's head to Northcote and see my computer friend.'

Hughes looked at her. 'Because?'

'I'm sure our tech staff will be able to trace the number on the suspect's phone but when will they do that?'

'Hopefully tonight.'

'Michael can do all sorts of interesting things online. He might be able to help us sooner.'

'Define interesting.'

'He's good, Sarge.'

Hughes trusted her young colleague's instincts. She knew Jo had a habit of following her hunches which sometimes backfired. But when she got it right, she really got it right.

'What's the address?'

As they drove to Northcote, Jo sent Michael a text.

Need help. On way with fellow officer.

Billy was curious. 'So who is this guy; boyfriend, lover, best mate?'

'Do I have to answer that question?'

Billy laughed. 'Well how come you know him?'

'We've helped one another and he's fantastic at all things digital.'

'You have some interesting friends, Jo Best, Dr Gabrielle Strange being a perfect example.'

Jo felt a tremor of terror. She told the pathetic pathologist about her scamming activities. Surely Dr Strange didn't tell Billy Hughes?

They arrived and Michael met Billy. Jo explained the situation and gave him the mobile number to which Gary had been sending texts.

Michael went to work. Billy was fascinated with the setup. She would have asked for a guided tour but felt her leg being touched as Alan arrived, keen on a chat.

Billy knelt and patted the scientific feline.

'That's Alan,' said Jo. 'He's an expert on Eastern religions and salmon fishing in the Tay.'

'And I guess he's called Alan because of Mr Turing,' replied Billy having seen the wall of computers.

Jo was impressed. She had no idea about that until told.

'I didn't know you were a cat person, Sarge.'

'There's a lot you don't know about me, and let's leave it at that.'

Jo realised she knew next to nothing about the private life of her detective sergeant.

Michael called. 'I may have something.'

The women moved to him.

'Something to Michael usually means everything,' said Jo and she was right. Michael had the name of the phone's owner, and its current location. Billy was sure illegal data retrieval was in play here if not straightforward hacking. She said nothing.

Michael looked at them 'Well good hunting, officers. Just don't tell anyone where you got the information.'

Jo grinned and Billy mused. 'Thanks for this, Michael. It's been a brief but fascinating meeting. I hope not our last.'

'Perhaps, but in future, please leave your handcuffs at home.'

Billy smiled and he walked them to the door. Michael and Jo's eyes met and she gave him the briefest of eyebrow raises.

The address of a D. Fortune was in a Southbank tower. At this time of night, that was a good 20 minute drive.

'Should we let the others know we've got a lead, Sarge?'

'Okay, and you can explain how we got it.'

'Right.'

'I think the less said about your friend and his computer expertise, the better. How did you meet?'

'Fraud Squad recommended him.

'You're kidding.'

'I needed a computer expert, asked Baldwin I who recommended a DS Harry Dale in Fraud. He had only one name—Michael Chan.'

'I assume your search for a computer expert had nothing to do with your job as a homicide detective?'

Jo fell silent. 'You could say that, Sarge.'

'And is this why DI Steele is so keen to sack you?'

'You should be a detective, Sarge.'

Neither spoke. Billy wanted to know the truth behind her colleague's situation, and Jo wanted to tell her. Neither was willing to take the next step—enquiry or confession.

Billy drove and Jo looked at Michael's notes.

'He's given us two addresses. The phone's registered owner, a D. Fortune, lives in Southbank. But the phone, when Michael last checked, was at an address in Glyndon Avenue, Brighton.'

'Where the poor people live. Let's try there.'

They travelled in silence. Billy knew Jo had been in a traumatic situation which so easily could have been tragic. Jo and Richelieu were shot at and fortunately only the DI was hit suffering a fabric more than a flesh wound. Jo had disarmed, with great support from a Jack Russell aka Chester, an armed and dangerous criminal. Normal procedure would require she have a medical check and be debriefed, yet here she was, still on the case. Hughes kept an eye on her colleague.

They pulled up outside a substantial property in Brighton. All the properties in the street were substantial but this was at the high end of classy. Lights shone subtly in the house, and a number of expensive cars preened themselves in the driveway.

The cops walked up the gravel drive past box hedges, each sporting an immaculate coiffure. The lawn was of MCG quality. The watering system effects were out on show and, in a word, the garden was lush.

They approached the solid front door. A police raid via this opening would struggle. Billy pushed a button. They heard a sound from inside. Celebration noises drifted from the rear of the house.

A woman approached the door laughing and calling. 'I bet that's Gordon and Clive. They're always late.' She opened the door and underwent a major facial expression change.

'Oh. You're not Gordon and Clive.'

'Good evening, madam,' said Billy, showing her ID. 'We're police officers. I'm Detective Sergeant Hughes and this is Detective Senior Constable Best.'

'What's happened? Is someone dead?'

'Is that someone in particular, madam?'

'What? No, isn't that what you do after an accident?'

'We do but in this case we're trying to trace a person by the name of D. Fortune. Would such a person be here?'

'Who is it darling?' A voice called from inside the house. The officers looked at one another.

Oh shit.

'It's the police. They wish to speak with Danny.'

Paul Brittain came to the door. He didn't rush. He looked at the two women who had been in his office only hours before. He experienced a sharp internal pain.

'Good evening, Mr Brittain.'

His wife experienced a sharper pain. 'You know these people?'

'This is harassment,' was his opening salvo.

'We wish to speak to a Mr Danny Fortune, sir. Is he here?'

'Why?' Brittain was stalling. That, and he was angry and nervous.

'It's a police matter. Is Mr Fortune here?'

'He might be.'

'We need to speak to him. Would you mind if we came in, sir?'

This was Billy's way of politely issuing a command.

We're coming in, Sunshine, so kindly step out of the way.

Brittain changed tack. 'Look, officers, I'm having a drink with a few friends. Whatever you want can wait till the morning, surely. Please, give me a call and I'll see that Danny makes himself available.'

Billy was having none of these stalling tactics. Mrs Brittain was having none of the hoi polloi invading her property. A woman's home is her castle with walk-in robe and imported bidet. She edged closer to a hissy fit.

How dare the police embarrass me in front of my friends.

Billy looked straight at Brittain. 'I hope I won't need to arrest you, sir.' He sucked in air. 'Or you, madam.' She just sucked.

Controlling their outrage and with a dash of fear, the couple stepped aside, and the detectives entered the spacious hallway. Jo considered wiping her feet. Brittain headed into the house.

'This way,' he spat and refused to look at the police. His wife was floundering, furious that two ridiculous women—*I wouldn't be caught dead in those clothes*—should invade her home.

My God, imagine if this gets out. The Brighton coffee shops will be ablaze with gossip.

Brittain entered the spacious under cover outdoor room where a dozen guests were drinking, nibbling, laughing and celebrating. Chief partygoer was the Honourable Redmond Latimer, soon to be elected unopposed as Leader of the Opposition in the Victorian Parliament.

As Brittain appeared, guests looked to him for yet another of his witty barbs but his words killed the atmosphere stone dead.

'Danny, these people would like a word.'

"These people" stood side by side. Everyone knew they weren't Seventh-Day Adventists or selling Timeshare holidays. You could smell they were police officers.

Billy slipped into her charm mode. 'Good evening, ladies and gentlemen. We apologise for interrupting your soiree.' Brittain was so

incensed he thought about calling the police. Then he remembered.
'We'd like a word with Mr Fortune.'

That's all she said. Jo once again admired her style and technique.
People looked at Danny. He was not in a position to run. All he could
do was pretend this was all a mistake, and the cops had made a
mistake. Inside, he wasn't thinking that. He whipped up a fake smile
and approached the police.

'Mr Fortune?'

'That's me.'

'We're police officers.'

Brittain, and particularly his wife, were hoping the word *police*
would not be spoken, not even hinted at within a country mile of their
home. It was spoken and the Brittains cringed. Redmond Latimer
considered crying. He was hours away from political victory when
suddenly the rug upon which he stood was being tugged—hard.

Brittain took control. 'You can discuss your enquiry in my study,' he
said walking into the house.

Billy followed and led Jo to the study. She thought it was bigger
than her entire flat. Danny tagged along. What else could he do?
Brittain and he made eye contact. No smiles there then. Brittain went
back to his guests, the study door closed, and the hubbub at the party
instantly changed key from Major to Minor.

Hughes and Jo showed their ID and Billy went for the jugular.

'We're homicide detectives, Mr Fortune, investigating an attempted
murder. We have reason to believe you may be involved.'

'Ridiculous. I've been here all night, with a dozen witnesses.'

'May we see your phone, Mr Fortune?'

'Why? I told you, I've been here all night.'

Billy showed Fortune her notepad. 'Is this your number, sir?'

He looked at it. 'I'm saying nothing without my lawyer.'

Hughes didn't muck around. 'Danny Fortune, I'm arresting you for
conspiracy to murder.' She looked at Jo. 'Senior Constable.'

Jo handcuffed the furious suspect as Billy finished advising him of
his rights.

'I assume you don't wish to say goodbye to your friends,' said Billy
in as flat a voice as possible.

Fortune wanted to swear but decided that silence is golden. Right now he was snookered, and wanted to know what happened at a certain townhouse in Port Melbourne. Surely Gary would never grass.

Fleming and Baldwin interviewed Gary Black. 'What were you doing in the Port Melbourne townhouse where you were arrested?'

Gary's solicitor, paid for by Paul Brittain, did the talking. 'My client has made a statement and has nothing further to add.' The statement was based on the less-is-more principle. It read as follows.

I went to burgle the Port Melbourne townhouse, and was attacked by the residents and later the police. I acted alone.

Fleming had been around the block. He knew formal questions would get nowhere with an experienced crim, and a likely killer to boot. He adopted the chummy, informal approach.

'Gary, how are you buddy?' Black sneered. 'Jeez, mate, being arrested by a dog must have been terrible. Mate, I understand. I sympathise. Oh, and how's the wedding tackle?'

'Fuck off.' The solicitor coughed and looked at his client.

Fleming kept goading. 'It must have been bloody scary having your nuts in a vice that growls. And a male pooch at that. You haven't got anything against gay dogs have you, mate?'

Gary slapped the table. Baldwin felt uncomfortable and the solicitor exploded.

'Detective Sergeant, I strongly protest at this infantile and egregious behaviour.'

'Infantile and egregious?' Fleming turned to the solicitor. 'You'll have to use one or two-syllable words with me, Mr Hyde-Williams. And you might try some of that language on your client. Attempted murder of two police officers is more than a wrist slap. Then there's the attempted murder of the two men in the townhouse. And cruelty to animals is always a big no-no for juries.' Fleming paused. 'Oh, and not forgetting the murder of one Rupert Lenton.'

That last incident was new to the solicitor. He had no instructions on that matter. Under his breath, Gary said, 'Shit.'

'So I suggest, Gary, me old mate, you need to think about talking because with your record, and this list of charges, you're odds on to cark it inside.'

'My client has made a statement and has nothing further to add,' repeated his solicitor.

Fleming leaned closer to the suspect and spoke intimately.

'I'd grab as much prison time as I could, Gary, because the stories about you being the dog's bollocks are gunna haunt you, mate.' Fleming paused and spoke softly. 'Woof woof.'

Gary wanted to smash the detective who grinned, and reached across to the recording device. 'Interview terminated at 2257.'

Danny Fortune had the same solicitor, again funded by Paul Brittain. Fortune's main fears were what had happened with the "game" that night, and what Gary had told the cops. His solicitor showed Danny the statement Gary had signed. Danny was relieved.

But not for long. His phone contained a variety of cryptic texts to Gary and although that put pressure on Danny, the police needed more. Richelieu, wearing a new suit, was back in harness with Payne his sidekick.

Neither Gary or Danny would roll over so Richelieu played a joker. It was a gamble and possibly deceitful. Well, no, not possibly deceitful, it was clearly and absolutely deceitful.

'Monsieur Fortune,' began Richelieu using the odd French phrase, which annoyed the suspect and infuriated his solicitor.

'I 'ave 'ere a statement from Monsieur Brittain in which 'e states you are the conspirator who ordered Monsieur Black to go to Port Melbourne with an order to commit murder.'

Danny was terrified. That had to be a lie. He could not believe Paul would cut him loose. Richelieu continued.

'Furthermore, Monsieur Brittain's statement claims it was you who ordered Gary Black to go to the flat of Rupert Lenton to discover if 'e 'ad told the police or the journalist John Fielding anything about the VIP paedophile ring in Sydney in the 1980s.'

'You're lying,' snarled Danny.

Holding out a hand, the solicitor spoke. 'May we see that statement?'

Richelieu passed it across. Danny leant in and started to read.

'The lying bastard. He's rolled over. He's fucking rolled over.'

'Shut up,' snapped the solicitor.

Danny dribbled. 'He's rolled over to save his own neck.'

The solicitor grew angry and held the statement away from Danny. 'It's a trick. The police have conned you.' Danny looked confused. Matched with his anger he looked, well, unattractive.

He glared at his solicitor then the police. 'What?' he screamed.

The solicitor explained. 'This is Charlie's statement, not Paul's.'

Danny had been conned. He raged. Charles had decided enough was enough. He would flee the country to avoid his brother ordering the death of his own flesh and blood. But my God, once Chester became fair game, Charles grassed.

The solicitor tossed the statement back across the table. 'Pretty low trick, Inspector,' said the solicitor, 'and no hope of my client's comments ever being allowed in court.'

Richelieu feigned shock and horror. 'Oh, forgive me, gentlemen. Did I not say Monsieur *Charles* Brittain. Forgive me, s'il vous plaît.'

Danny would happily have smashed the police officer who rubbed even more salt into Danny's gaping wound.

'I wonder what Monsieur Paul Brittain will say when 'e's told your response.'

'You can't do that,' threatened Danny.

'Be very careful, Detective Inspector,' threatened the solicitor.

Richelieu ended the proceedings. He stood and walked to the door. He mimicked Danny.

'The lying bastard. 'e's rolled over. 'e's fucking rolled over.'

Richelieu left with Payne almost running to catch up with him.

24

THE NEXT AFTERNOON, AFTER WORK, Jo drove to Princes Hill, to the murder scene where John Fielding died. She had a date with Ponzi. She looked around. No sign of him. She stood by the bench where the late journo breathed his last. The police tape was gone. Nothing to indicate murder most foul happened on this spot.

Nobody had sat on this bench since the murder. Would you?

She knelt and examined the ground. It was all a show. Forensics had been over this place with a bespoke toothcomb and recovered everything of interest, so far to no avail.

'So you turned up.'

She knew the voice. It came from behind. She remained kneeling not looking around.

'Mr Baggio, are you stalking me?'

Ponzi laughed. 'You're good, I'll give you that.'

'I've reported you to my boss asking that you be arrested if seen anywhere near me.'

'Clever. Play the innocent victim when all along you're the crook posing as an honest cop.'

She stood, turned and faced him.

'I've warned you twice now. Keep this up and you'll be arrested.'

She walked to her Peugeot 313 and got inside. She was about to drive off when he tapped on the passenger side door. He looked around trying to spot a car with undercover cops. He saw nothing. She unlocked the door and he got in. Before he settled, her radio blared some FM station's rock music.

'Bit loud,' he said and she turned the volume up louder.

She leant towards him and spoke quietly.

'I have a new job for you.'

His eyes lit up. 'But what's with the music? Turn it down.'

Jo smiled. 'The walls have ears, Ponzi.'

He reluctantly accepted what she was saying. The wire he wore would give a crappy result at best. The cops listening nearby were frustrated and then some.

'Get him to turn off the music,' shouted one of them.

Jo ran the show. 'Now let's get one thing straight. Never contact me again unless I contact you first. Got that?' He nodded. 'And never come to my place of work. If you do, I'll have you framed for everything from littering to mass murder.'

He looked at her and could see she was angry and serious.

'Okay. So what's this new scam?'

'It's big. We're ready to roll but need your help.'

'What about my money from the last job?'

'It's coming.'

'So's Christmas.'

'You'll get your cash next week. Just do your job, which at the moment is to stay away from me, keep your head down, and wait till we contact you. Got that?'

'He nodded.

'Now piss off before I arrest you.' He looked at her then opened his door. 'Oh and this next job will pay very well.'

Ponzi got out and Jo turned on her engine. She drove home to recover and plan. She didn't notice a car which started to follow her.

As Jo drove home, Ernie Sim got a phone call from one of his victims. With no lead on his thief, Ernie's rage festered. He'd failed to find even a trace of the bandit. He'd been set up and robbed, and beaten up by bikies. Most of the people he'd extorted money from for years were too afraid to tell him anything. He needed a break. Finally, *finally* it came.

'What can you tell me, Mr Yeung?'

'Mr Sim, one of my customers, who I haven't seen for quite a while, came to my restaurant last night and seemed very happy. I heard he'd lost quite a lot of money in a bad business deal but tonight, he and his wife seemed to be celebrating.'

'Celebrating what?'

'I have no idea.'

'And what's their name?'

'The husband is Mr David Chan.'

Ernie felt a tremor of pleasure. He knew David Chan, the man he ripped off with a phony Chinese company fraud.

'Thank you, Mr Yeung. I will not forget this.'

'Thank you, Mr Sim. You are most kind.'

Now Mr Yeung didn't mean that. He hated the Sim brothers and wrestled with snitching on David Chan. But by using twisted logic, Mr Yeung believed, hoped that by sacrificing his customer, he might get less grief from the Sim gangsters. Some hope.

Ernie felt good. If David Chan ripped him off, Ernie would easily crush the thief and regain his money. Chan was a soft target.

David Chan and his wife Jai went over the day's business at the back of their main furniture store. They were fastidious in balancing the books and preparing for the next day's trading. The staff had long gone and the couple went about their work with quiet efficiency.

Ernie and Joe Sim dressed for the occasion—in black. They parked their van close to the rear of the Chan store. They watched and waited. They knew this store, having called there before, always after hours.

David told Jia they should leave. He went to switch off the lights and switch on the alarm as his wife unlocked the back door.

Crash!

It was smashed open thanks to Joe Sim's massive frame. Jia fell back in terror and David ran to investigate. Their nightmare began as the Sim brothers invaded their premises and lives—again.

Michael's parents knew not to struggle. The ferocity of the criminals was impossible to oppose. To save your life, do not resist.

The couple was bundled into their office where they cowered in fear. David wrapped his arms around his wife.

'Right, you miserable shit,' spat Ernie. 'Where's my money?'

David knew it was futile to do anything other than comply yet something encouraged him to make an effort.

'Do you mean the money you stole from me?'

Ernie saw red and swung a sledge hammer against a computer monitor. Carnage.

'You are going to regret ever opposing me, you little man. Nobody messes with Ernie Sim and lives. You and your pathetic family are dead.' He screamed. 'Give me my money.'

David knew it was madness to oppose the gangster but tried.

'You let my wife go and I will do whatever you say.'

Ernie went ballistic. 'Don't fucking tell me what to do. I give the orders. Now do exactly what I say.' He spoke to his evil sibling.

'Get her.'

Jia screamed as Joe grabbed her hair and dragged her across the floor. David went to help his wife and was kicked by an enraged Ernie. The married couple were in their 60s, wiry and healthy but no match for the younger, fitter criminals. Helpless, they cowered on the floor and wept in silence.

'Now I want to know who set up that phony Dee-Fat web site.' The Chans had no idea. They knew their son was responsible for their money being returned but had no idea how he did it.

'If you won't tell me, I'll have my assistant here snap a few bones.'

David tried to prevent the torture they knew could be inflicted.

'We don't know.'

'Ahhh!' screamed Ernie and smashed the phone system.

'All we know is our bank balance received a mysterious deposit.'

'So who paid that deposit? Who set up the sting?'

'It wasn't us. Surely you can see we could never do such a thing.'

Ernie believed the older man. He and his wife would have no idea about creating that fake DFAT web site.

Sim moved close to David. 'But somebody helped you. And I want to know who.' He screamed into David's face with spittle and hatred a part of his fury. 'Who helped you?'

David was prepared to suffer many things for his family and would do almost anything to protect his wife and children. The pressure increased.

Ernie moved to Jia, being held by the hair by Joe. Ernie grabbed Jia's hand, placed it on the floor and raised the hammer.

'No,' begged David. The hammer began to fall. 'It was our son,' cried David as the hammer smashed into the floor missing Jia's fingers by a whisker. David sobbed. He was a broken man.

'Where is he?' Pause. Ernie turned up the volume. 'Where is he?'

'In Northcote,' blubbed Michael's father.

'Take her,' ordered Ernie, and the Chans were dragged outside and pushed into the Sim van. The Chan store was left open for the world to help itself. Sadly, David and Jia's misery was only just beginning.

Michael Chan sat at the island bar in his kitchen eating his homemade risotto, and telling his cat, Alan, to get his own food.

His warning system kicked in showing a visitor on the property. Michael looked at his monitor and saw two uniformed police officers making their way along the side of his converted warehouse. His meal was put somewhere Alan couldn't get it, and Michael opened his door.

'Mr Michael Chan?'

He felt his stomach do strange things. 'What's happened?'

'May we come in?'

This sounded like one of those car accident moments when the police arrive with devastating news. Michael stepped back and the cops entered. They stood waiting for him to turn. He didn't want to turn. Every part of his mind and body told him this was bad news.

He turned. 'What's happened?' he asked a second time.

'There's been a break-in at your parents' furniture store.'

'Are my parents hurt? Are they okay?'

'We don't know. They're missing.'

'Missing?' Michael was in shock. His mind struggled to focus.

'Another shop owner noticed the back of your parents' store was open, went in, and found the office had been badly damaged. There was no sign of your parents.'

'Blood, was there any blood?'

'We don't think so. The shop owner told us your details. Could you please ring your parents? We sent a car to their home but it was dark and unoccupied.'

Michael had already dialed his father's mobile, which went to Voicemail. 'Dad, this is Michael. Please ring as soon as you get this.'

'Voicemail?' asked an officer.

Michael nodded and was already waiting for his sister to answer. 'Taz, it's Michael. Something's happened to Mum and Dad. Please ring as soon as you get this. Please.'

Michael's face wanted to collapse. He stayed strong because he wanted to be able to do whatever he could to help his parents. He looked at the police. It was their turn to ask questions.

'Is there any reason why your parents would go missing?'

Michael knew. The Sim brothers had discovered who had stolen their money, the Chan money, and done what they always did—

resorted to violence. Michael's chest was on fire. He wanted to vomit. His mind screamed at him. *I've killed my parents.*

He thought about things then shook his head. 'What can I do?'

'Stay here, sir. If your parents don't show up in the next hour or so, a detective will contact you and a proper search will begin.'

'A proper search?'

'It's what happens with a misper, a missing person. And look, there may be an innocent explanation, sir.'

Michael couldn't speak. Well he could but to tell the police about the Sim brothers might make matters worse—for everyone.

He thanked the police, and they left. Immediately he dialed the number he was always reluctant to ring. If anything went wrong with the scams he created, and the police got wind of them, he wanted the authorities to discover as little about Joanna Best as possible. He didn't want her to suffer. But this was different.

She was at home, recovering from her latest skirmish with Ponzi. She answered her phone, surprised and worried.

'Michael?'

'It's my parents, Jo. They're missing.'

'Oh God, Michael. Sorry, but are you sure?'

'Yes.' She knew he would have checked.

'Michael, you have no choice. You must contact the police.'

'They told me. They've just been here.'

Jo's mind filled with questions and fear, the fear she thought about ever since she and Michael joined forces. Their "games" were dangerous and, if caught, she would be in serious trouble. But right now, going to jail seemed of little importance. Two people were missing and could be in danger. Worse, they could be dead.

'Are you at home?'

'Yes.'

'I'm on my way.'

25

DAVID AND JAI CLUNG TO ONE ANOTHER. They huddled in a factory in an industrial park in outer Melbourne. It was deadly quiet and no-one outside could see or hear them.

They knew they were in serious trouble and why. Their clever son had retrieved the money David lost in a scam set up by the Sim brothers. The gangsters had discovered who reclaimed the cash, and now wanted not just the money but blood. Nobody stands up to the Sim brothers and survives.

Ernie screamed. 'Tell me about your son.' The Chans were desolate.

'He is clever,' said David. 'He runs his own computer business.'

'So what did you tell him to do?'

'Nothing, I told him nothing.'

'You lie, Mr Chan, and you and especially your wife will suffer.' He moved to Mrs Chan. 'Tell me now or ...'

David panicked. 'Wait! I told him I lost some money and that you had received it. But that's all. He did what he did without my knowledge or permission.'

'What's his address?' David hesitated then gave the address. 'Does he live alone?' David nodded. 'Does he have weapons?'

'No,' cried David through tears. 'My son is a good boy, an honest and law-abiding young man.'

Ernie roared. 'Who stole my fucking money.'

David wanted to roar back. "Who took back what you stole from me," but couldn't bear to see his wife suffer any more.

Ernie took Joe to one side. 'I'll check out this computer guy. You stay here and be ready to make the woman scream when I call. And don't stuff up.'

Joe nodded. *Torture, I do.*

Michael and Jo sat in his darkened warehouse. Outside in the street, the person who followed Jo from her meeting with Ponzi, to her flat and now here to Michael's warehouse, waited in a darkened car.

Michael was broken. Jo felt his pain. She started this whole adventure. She approached him. She suggested this scam-the-bad-guys routine. If Michael's parents die, Jo knew she would live with that agony for the rest of her life.

She wanted Michael to tell the police everything. 'It's the only way, Michael. Your parents are our only concern.'

'But that will mean you'll be arrested and lose your career.'

'Michael,' said Jo with a low but determined voice, 'excuse my French but fuck my career. It's worth nothing if your parents are hurt. The Sim brothers are clearly evil. We pulled off the perfect sting. How they found out it was you, we don't know. But we do know the Sims have done what we expected. They'll torture, maim and even kill to retrieve their cash. For them, Michael, it's pride. Their egos are smashed, and people like them want revenge. You do not bargain or negotiate with these guys. You have to contact the police now.'

'You're the police.'

'Stop it! Michael, I've told you. If I'm arrested, it's no big deal.'

'Bullshit.'

Jo was shocked by the normally well-mannered geek but hit back. 'We both knew the risks before we started these scams. We both knew they could fail or, as happened with my mother and now, with your folks, the bad guys fight back. We have to call the cops.'

She spoke with passion. Her sincerity and common sense came pouring out. Michael knew she was right.

He paused. 'Okay,' he said. 'What do I do?'

He looked at her. Tears glistened in his eyes. Before she could speak, his warning system did its subtle thing. They looked at his screen and saw a man creeping along the side of the warehouse.

'That's Ernie Sim,' gasped Michael.

'What?'

'My father showed me a picture. That's Ernie and he's armed. Have you got a gun?'

Jo shook her head. Michael was genuinely scared; scared for his and Jo's safety but more scared that this man had already hurt or killed his parents. Jo took over.

'Stay calm. Don't make him angry and do whatever he says.'

Jo snatched her phone and dropped it. 'Shit,' she whispered bending to pick it up. It wouldn't swipe. 'Shit,' she gasped again. 'Where's your phone, Michael?'

He pointed to a desk. Before they could move, heavy banging on the door added to their fear. Jo swiped again and her phone worked.

'Open the door now or I start shooting. Now!' More door banging.

Michael hurried to the door. Jo dialed emergency. The person answered. 'Fire, police or ambulance - which service do you require?'

'Police,' said Jo and that's all she said as Michael had to open the door and Ernie Sim barged in waving his gun.

'Drop the phone. Drop it!'

Jo didn't fancy being shot at twice in two nights so placed the phone on the floor without turning it off. Ernie slammed the door.

'Kick it over here. Do it!'

She did and Ernie picked it up. He turned off the phone and pocketed it. He waved his gun and moved towards Michael.

'So you're Michael Whiz Kid Chan, the prick who stole my money.'

Ernie shoved Michael towards Jo, and checked out the place.

'Who are you?'

'I'm Jo.'

'Who else is here?'

Michael spoke. 'No-one, it's just the two of us.'

'Right, get over there and sit, both of you.'

Michael and Jo sat. Ernie watched them while looking around.

'What is this place?'

'My home.'

'Weird.' Ernie got down to business. 'So this is how it goes, Mikey. We've got your parents ...'

'Are they all right?' blurted Michael, desperate for news.

'For now and their lives depend entirely on you.'

'I'll do whatever you want but please don't hurt my parents.'

'You don't know what I want yet.' Ernie was playing with them. 'First I want my money back.'

'I'll do that if you release my parents unarmed.'

Ernie flared. 'Listen you little prick, I'm in charge so shut up.'

Jo squeezed Michael's arm. Her message was "don't annoy him".

'Then, Michael, digital genius, you are going to spring that scam you dumped on me on my biggest enemy. You are going to make me a lot of money, my friend. So settle in for a long night.'

What could Michael say? His parents were being held against their will, and could be dead or tortured.

'Whatever you say,' said Michael in a humble, pleading way.

Ernie waved his gun. 'Right, get on with it.'

Michael moved towards his equipment. Ernie followed him but kept an eye on Jo. He spoke to her.

'So who are you? What are you doing here?'

'I'm his girlfriend.'

'And was this scam your idea or his?'

Jo scoffed. 'You're joking. I know nothing about computers.'

Ernie yelled at Michael. 'Get on with it.' Then back to Jo. 'So what do you do, apart from shagging your boyfriend?'

'I'm an accountant.'

'God, how boring.' She must have been because Ernie lost interest and moved closer to Michael. 'Come on, show me the fake web site.'

Michael's problem was that the fake DFAT web site no longer existed. That was the whole point of his scams. Once they work, you grab the money then destroy the evidence—everything. When people come looking, there's nothing to find. Michael pulled up the real DFAT site, working slowly without making it obvious. He co-operated.

Jo calculated how long it would take to reach Ernie's gun hand. Would Ernie have enough time to see her running to attack him, turn the gun and fire? What were her chances? She started breathing faster.

Ernie wanted action. 'Listen Mikey, hurry up or I'll have my team break another of your mother's bones.'

Michael almost died. His throat felt restricted. Jo inwardly groaned. Michael believed his beloved mother was being tortured and he was going to fail the one test that might possibly save her.

He fiddled with the real DFAT site and tried to pretend it was his. Ernie saw the site and moved closer. He was side on to Jo but had moved further away. She would take longer to get to his gun arm. But now wasn't the time for a debate on whether she should try to disarm and arrest the criminal. It was try and risk being shot, or not try and risk being shot. She decided to try.

She waited for Ernie to turn a touch further away from her line of sight. She eased herself a tad more behind him. She took a deep breath, made sure her back foot had a solid cabinet to help her launch and prepared to go. Michael's alarm sounded.

Ernie pulled back and Jo's rescue mission was over before it began. Michael and Jo looked at the monitor. Ernie looked at them, moving his gun from one to the other.

'What's happening?' snapped Ernie.

'It's the cops,' said Jo trying to scare the mad man.

Ernie lost it. He moved towards Jo holding his gun in both hands.

'Did you call them? You bitch.'

'How could I? You've got my phone.'

Ernie pointed his gun straight at the woman he thought was an accountant. God only knows what he might have done if he knew she was a cop. She tried to save herself.

'It's the local cops.' She pointed at the monitor. 'Look.'

Ernie looked and saw two uniformed officers walking calmly.

'How do you know?'

'They came before to tell us about Michael's parents. They said they'd come back to tell us what happened to them.'

'Stall 'em,' snapped Ernie to Michael while grabbing Jo and holding the gun to her head.

'What if I can't,' blurted Michael.

'Michael, remember they said they would search the warehouse.'

Jo was winging it with Michael two steps behind. He caught up.

'Yes, they said they had to search my home.'

Ernie needed a quick decision. 'Where's another way out?' Michael hesitated. 'Come on,' barked Ernie waving his gun.

The doorbell rang.

'Through the kitchen,' said Michael, pointing.

Ernie pushed Jo towards the kitchen as the doorbell rang again.

The back door closed just as Michael opened his front door where the uniformed constables stood under the lamp from *The 39 Steps*.

26

JO WAS SHOVED ALONG THE STREET and bundled into the back of Ernie's van. He followed her in and grabbed her hair. Now was the time to strike, and as she went to stamp on his foot and elbow his throat, she felt a dull pain and everything went black. She lay unconscious and Ernie drove off unaware they were being followed.

Jo woke bouncing around in the van. Her hands were trussed like a Christmas turkey, her mouth gagged, and her head throbbed.

They drove in to the factory parking area. A groggy Jo was dragged out and marched towards the small wicket gate in the large door. Ernie knocked with a particular rhythm. The small door opened, and Jo went through at a dangerous speed. She fell at the feet of a grinning Joe Sim. He liked women with his preference being those in bondage.

For Jo, things went from bad to bloody awful.

The wicket gate snapped shut. Outside in the dark and empty street, the person following the van, pulled up in a car sans headlights.

Michael had no idea what to do. His parents had been kidnapped. Maybe they were being tortured. He didn't dwell on the other possibility. His friend Jo Best had been kidnapped while he, the scammer was free and in the company of uniformed police officers.

It was decision time. Will he tell the police everything and hope that will save the captives? If he speaks, will that send Jo to jail?

'Good evening, sir,' said the male constable. 'Any news?'

'Come in, please,' said Michael and the officers stepped inside. 'I've heard nothing. Have you?'

'Sadly no, but we're gearing up for a search.'

Michael was scared and sad. He remembered Jo's words.

'It's the only way, Michael. Your parents are our only concern.'

'I've got something to say.' The police stared at him. 'I haven't heard from my parents but the man who kidnapped them has just left.'

The police came alive.

'Here?'

'Yes.'

The drew their guns. 'Is he still here?'

'No, he's gone, and I don't know where.'

'How long ago?'

Michael shrugged. 'Two minutes.'

'Describe him, quickly.'

'Medium height and build, 40, Chinese, wearing a black tracksuit. And he's armed with a Glock 45.'

The cops exchanged glances. The female cop took off, racing back to the street.

The male cop kept asking questions. 'And the man who was just here is the man who kidnapped your parents?'

'Yes.'

'Are you sure?'

'Yes, I know him, and he said he had my parents.'

'Did you try and stop him?'

Michael felt exasperation. 'What, and get shot?'

'What's his name?'

'Ernie Sim. His brother Joe is part of the gang.'

'It's a gang?'

'They run an extortion racket targeting Chinese Australian business people. Everyone's terrified of them. They're violent and dangerous.'

'Do you know where they live?'

'I guess their home address would be easy to find but they probably have a secret business address and my parents will be there.'

The female constable returned puffing. 'No sign.' The male officer contacted their station and reported the events. Ernie Sim was now a wanted man. The female constable questioned Michael.

'And you've got no description of the vehicle?'

'No, I saw nothing.'

'Did you hear the vehicle leaving?'

Michael was confused. 'No, and there's something else.'

The constable waved to her partner who rejoined the conversation.

'My girlfriend was here and she was kidnapped by Ernie Sim to stop me chasing him, and to force me to carry out another scam.'

Whoa, hold everything. This was getting too hard for the uniformed duo. Speeding tickets, drink driving, and a domestic had been their lot this week. Now they had a violent business invasion, a couple kidnapped, another kidnap by an armed man and, for good measure, a suggestion of serious fraud. If they were shocked, they hadn't heard the half of it.

'And your girlfriend's just been kidnapped by this Ernie Sim?'

Michael was following his new, honesty-is-the-best-policy policy but for the first time lost his even composure.

'Didn't I just say that?'

Inside, his organs were generating adrenalin at a world record pace. He knew his and Jo's secret life was about to be exposed. She had urged him to come clean, and as she was definitely in harm's way right now, the sooner Michael told all and got the police involved in saving one of their own, not to mention his parents, the better. He felt sick.

'And you've no idea where your girlfriend has been taken?'

'I assume to the same place where they're holding my parents.'

'What was that bit about being forced to carry out another scam?'

What a question. It was confession time for Michael. He began.

'I set up a scam to rob the Sim brothers.' The police continued to be amazed. 'The kidnappers robbed my father, well defrauded him. But he was too scared to tell the police. The criminals said they would kill my parents if my father went to the police.'

'When was this?'

'Oh weeks, months ago. My father made me promise never to speak about his loss. But I couldn't let him suffer.'

'How much money was involved?'

'A lot, over 300 grand.'

'So what happened?'

'Without telling my father, I set up a sting and got back the money these men had defrauded from my Dad.'

'And the Sim brothers found out?'

'Well they found out they'd been defrauded immediately but it took time to discover who conned them. I guess they've only just found out and now you see how they've reacted.'

'Who told them?'

'I've no idea. Look, I assume you've reported all these facts.'

'We've reported the identity of the kidnappers. What else?'

'That's it. They took my parents to make me return the money.'

'Have you done that?'

'No. I was about to when you arrived and the kidnapper fled.'

'With your girlfriend?'

'Yes.'

'And you've got no idea where these men are?'

'No. I've told you that—twice. Do you think if I knew I wouldn't tell you?' The admonished police pulled back. 'And there's something else. The kidnapped woman is not really my girlfriend.'

'Oh?'

'She's a friend who's been helping me recover stolen money.'

'What's her name, sir?'

'Joanna Best.' He paused at looked at them 'Detective Senior Constable Joanna Best from the Homicide Squad.'

The cops suffered jaw drop, a condition brought on by 'you've-got-to-be-kidding' shock. They recovered, told Michael to remain at home, contact the police if he heard from the kidnapper, and went out to do … they weren't sure what to do.

Joe was glad to see his brother. He worked well as an underling taking orders and wasn't called Dim Sim for nothing. But being in charge of an operation made him nervous. Even guarding two middle-aged and terrified kidnap victims who were bound, caused him worry. Joe did what big brother said, and earning Ernie's praise made Joe happy.

Ernie indicated the fallen cop. 'I bought you a little present, bro.'

'Who is she?'

'The thief's bimbo and accountant. She'll know where the money is.'

'What do we do?'

'Contact lover boy and get back our cash.' He took Jo's phone from his pocket and turned it on. He pointed at Jo. 'What's his number?'

Jo struggled. A thumping head made any thinking difficult. Ernie moved towards her and kicked her leg. That hurt.

'What's his number?'

She fought the pain and spoke. Ernie punched the numbers and hit the speaker phone. Everyone heard the ringing sound.

Michael spoke. 'Hello.'

His parents experienced great emotion. Even Jo felt stronger.

'Speak,' snapped Ernie at the detective.

'Michael, it's me.'

'Oh hi, are you okay?'

'I'm okay. I'm with your parents.'

Michael's body was bursting with anxiety. 'Are they okay?'

Jo looked at Mr and Mrs Chan. They wept and nodded.

'They're fine, Michael. They're nodding and I think they're fine.'

Ernie took over the conversation.

'Okay, everyone's fine. Now, first things first, Michael.' Ernie said the name with a sneer. 'If you want your parents and accountant to keep all their fingers and toes, transfer my money right now. Understand?'

Ernie was shouting. Even Joe was edgy.

'I understand,' said Michael but I'll need your banking details.'

'It's a trick, don't tell him, bro,' cried Joe.

'Shut up,' spat big brother and Joe retreated.

'I'll give you my account number and BSB. I'll give you five minutes. Then I'll check my account and unless the money's been repaid in full, we start on the digit removal. Understand, Michael?' Again the word *Michael* was given a salacious treatment.

'I understand. I'll start work immediately. Please do not harm my parents or girlfriend.'

Jo heard her description and wondered if that was wise.

Ernie told Michael his banking details. 'Five minutes, arsehole.'

'I understand,' called Michael. 'I'm working on it now.'

Ernie went for a pee with an ominous comment to his brother.

'Play your cards right, baby brother, and you might get some play time with the tart. Have you ever had an accountant before?'

Ernie laughed and left. Joe chuckled. He'd enjoyed a variety of females in recent times but only because he paid for the experience.

Outside in the darkened and desolate street, the person who had followed the van got out of their car and closed the door—softly.

27

BILLY HUGHES WAS ASLEEP when her phone rang. She was on call. When a homicide happens, call the duty officer. She answered.

'DS Hughes.'

'Sergeant Hughes, this is DS Cartwright from Northcote. Two of our uniforms have been called to a shout where the resident claims to have witnessed a kidnapping.'

'I'm Homicide, Sergeant.'

'I know that but the bloke reckons the person kidnapped is one of yours, a Detective Senior Constable Joanna Best.'

'What?'

'You know her?'

Billy was wide awake. 'Yes. Have you got police looking for her?'

'We have.'

'Have they found her?'

'Not yet, they're obviously still looking.'

'What's the address in Northcote, where the bloke reported the kidnap?'

Billy knew it and was dressed and out of her flat in record time.

The person who followed Ernie's van became an intruder, and crept onto the property. The small wicket gate in the main door was locked. The intruder crept around the side of the factory. The solid and locked back door had no window. The door could be smashed but any such action would make a hell of a racket and besides, battering rams were thin on the ground right now. The element of surprise was the key to success in raiding this building with access being a major problem.

The intruder looked up and saw light in a narrow window. The window seemed the only viewing opportunity. A shipping container

173

stood against the factory wall. Once on top of the container, the intruder showed athletic prowess and climbed a downpipe. There was a clear view of the interior through the narrow window. Three people, tied, slumped on the floor. Two armed men stood guard. But the narrow window was fixed. Clinging to the downpipe, the intruder threw a leg up and onto the roof. This was the crucial moment.

Would anyone inside the factory look up? Would they hear anything? Would the intruder make it?

Hoping the guttering was strong, the intruder strained leg and arm muscles, and heaved their body skywards scrambling onto the roof. Did the noise carry to the people below? The intruder lay still. Heavy breathing seemed loud but the voices below remained normal.

The roof had a gentle slope up to its apex on which stood a large skylight. Many factories had as much natural light as possible.

The intruder crept up the slope towards the skylight. This vantage point provided a bird's eye view of the situation below.

Joe stood above Jo. He dragged his gun barrel across her face. With hands tied, resisting the creep was futile. Her health, her life was on the line. The intruder crept around the skylight to get a better view.

Ernie Sim was impatient at the best of times. He looked at his watch. He wanted his money now. He spoke to Michael's parents.

'Let's hope your darling boy has shifted that money because if not, both of you are going to lose a pinky.'

He waggled his little finger at the kidnapped couple. They felt helpless and terrified before this latest ordeal but now felt worse not doubting their captor would carry out his threat.

Jo decided to try some reasoning. 'You know, Mr Sim, you can get your money, all of it ...'

'Oh I will, darling, and if it means your future in-laws spill some blood and you get to play with my baby brother, then that's what's going to happen. So let's call the scammer, on your phone of course. Tell me your name again, Miss Accountant?'

'It's Jo.'

Joe reacted with his unattractive smile. 'Hi Jo, I'm Joe.'

Ernie hit redial, Michael saw Jo's ID and answered immediately.

'Hello.'

'Have you done it?'

'I'm about to make the transfer.'

Ernie exploded. 'About to? Listen.' Ernie nodded to his brother.

Joe grabbed Jo's hair and yanked. She yelped at the sudden pain.

'Can you hear that, wise guy,' shouted Ernie? 'That's your babe getting a touch up before the main event.'

'Please don't hurt her or my parents. I've done what you asked.'

'Not yet you haven't.

'It's at your end. The bank is saying it won't accept the transfer.'

'You're lying, arsehole. Time for a finger chop.'

'No,' screamed Michael. 'Look, I'll send you a screenshot.'

Ernie heard a ping as a message arrived on Jo's phone. He opened the message and there was a screenshot of his bank with a message indicating the bank's computer was offline being serviced. The gangster hesitated. Michael sounded desperate.

'I've rung your bank and they'll be back online at 2300 hours.'

Ernie checked his watch. It was 2251—less than 10 minutes.

'I'm counting, Mr Scammer. Now, in the meantime, get your fake Dee-Fat web site up and running and send that same crappy email you sent "accidentally" to me to an address I'll give you in five minutes. Have you got that?'

'Yes,' said a terrified Michael. 'Please, are my parents and Jo okay?'

'Tell them, people,' cried Ernie holding the phone in their direction.

Michael's parents gave pathetic replies.

'We are okay, Michael,' said his father.

'We love you, Michael,' cried his teary mother

Ernie pointed at Jo. 'And here's your accountant?'

'I'm okay, Michael. Stay strong.'

'Stay strong,' mocked Ernie. To Michael he gave a blunt warning. 'I'll ring in five, Michael. No transfer means no mercy. Got that?'

'I understand,' called Michael and the call ended.

Michael was in panic mode when his warning software got busy. He looked at the screen and saw a woman on his property. He knew Detective Sergeant Deborah "Billy" Hughes. She slapped the front door.

Michael ran to open it. She showed her ID.

'Remember me? I'm DS Hughes, Jo's boss.'

'Yes, yes. Come in. Have you heard?'

She came in and Michael gave her the latest news.

On the roof of the factory, the intruder watched proceedings below. The skylight gave the spy the best seat in the house, none of which helped the three victims below. Was the intruder in the best place to launch a rescue mission? It was time to get off the roof, and through the front or back door. The intruder decided to call for help but in standing, made a sound. The intruder froze as one mobile phone bounced on the roof then slid towards the edge and disappeared.

'Shit, shit, shit,' whispered the intruder.

Below, Ernie could fidget no more. He hit redial on Jo's phone and Michael jumped. With Billy Hughes beside him, they had a plan of how to handle the situation.

Billy located the officer in charge of finding the kidnapped couple, informed them of the third hostage, one of their own, and gave them Jo's mobile number. Police technicians were soon working on its current location. Thanks to Ernie—many crims are thick —keeping the phone operating made tracing easier.

Michael reckoned he could trace it too but Billy urged him to concentrate on the money exchange.

Michael told Billy about Jo pretending to be his accountant. Billy thought about this. Would it help or harm Jo and the Chans to reveal Jo's true occupation. Would the brothers hesitate to harm a serving police officer? Would they take greater delight in torturing, even killing a cop? Tough decision but they chose to stick with the accountant ruse.

Ernie made the call. Michael couldn't control his shaking hands. Even with an experienced cop by his side, Michael worried he'd lose it.

'Hello,' his voice cracked.

'Time's up, Michael. It's the money or Mummy. Your call, arsehole.'

'I'm about to send it. Please don't hurt anyone; my parents or Senior Constable Best.'

Michael died inside. He said what he said while his mind was in a chaotic mess. Billy Hughes felt ill and held her breath. Silence from the factory. Would Ernie be so concentrated on the money that he'd miss Michael's words?

No, he wouldn't.

Ernie's voice went all soft and inquisitive. 'What did you just say?'

'The money's ready to be transferred.'

He got louder. 'Not the money. You said Senior Constable something.'

Michael struggled. Billy wanted to speak but feared she'd make things worse. Three people could lose their life right now.

'I'm sending the money now,' called Michael.

Ernie moved to Jo. The other Joe wasn't following the finer details of the current conversation. Ernie stood over Jo and placed his gun against her head. She shook, sweated and wanted to vomit.

I'm going to be shot lying on a factory floor.

'What is your job?'

That's all Ernie said. Simple question but in the current situation, any question was tough right now. Jo looked at him. She was afraid but determined not to cower. He shouted.

'What is your fucking job, Ms Accountant?'

Jo paused then tried but failed to speak in a calm voice.

'I'm a servicing police officer, a detective in the Homicide Squad, and you and your brother are under arrest for kidnap and assault. You do not have to say anything ...'

The veins on Ernie's neck bulged. He roared. He raged. Even Joe was shocked by his brother's fury. Ernie moved the gun and now held the weapon by its barrel. He raised his hand preparing to pistol whip the helpless senior constable.

Back in Northcote, Michael and Billy were neck and neck in the race to see who would crack first.

Up on the roof, the intruder stood to get a better view of the action below. This meant moving around the edge of the skylight. Ernie let out a roar and started the downward movement of the gun to smash Jo's face. He only stopped because of another sound.

Up above Ernie, the intruder slipped, and pitched forward into the skylight. It smashed and, adding a scream of fear or pain or both, the uninvited visitor imitated Isaac Newton's apple and gatecrashed the party. Perhaps that was skylight-crashed.

It was a short journey but a concrete floor doesn't take prisoners, and the intruder could expect a broken neck if lucky.

Ernie was put off his stroke in woman bashing, thanks to both the scream from above plus the smashing shower of glass raining down from on high. The factory occupants cowered in fear. The intruder arrived. Talk about a dramatic entrance. Everyone screamed. The brothers tried to flee sideways, any ways. Big Joe Sim tried to step back but fell and, unintentionally became the firefighters' blanket. The intruder used Joe's abdomen as the landing spot. The adventure meant cuts for the intruder and one enormous bellyache for Joe.

But now the anonymous intruder was revealed. It was a he and well-known to Jo Best, being a fellow senior constable attached to the Homicide Squad, by name, Stephen Payne.

Detective Payne smashed a pane and suffered pain. It was his first practice parachute jump, (sans chute), and Joe's first time at wearing a large X on his chest.

Dim Sim was unable to cry, "Medic". Ernie was the only person still standing. He recovered sufficiently to point his gun at the now sprawled and defenceless flying constable. It *is* true—pigs can fly.

To say Ernie lost it would not do justice to his behaviour. His scheme to retrieve his money had not worked. His scheme to scam wealthy crims using the DFAT fake web offer had not worked. And now, his uninsured factory had significant damage and would require Emergency Services to prevent the rain and any other airborne coppers from dropping in.

In short, he was mightily pissed, and his immediate reaction was to enact revenge. This was simple to achieve by pointing his gun and squeezing the trigger.

The first target in his line of fire was Detective Senior Constable Payne. The cop was about to go from hero to zero; a pity because he'd just saved the life of the woman he hated and wanted sacked. Such a noble deed did not deserve so unjust a reward.

Payne was there because he wanted to impress DI Steele. Payne reckoned his boss didn't rate him, which was true. The Pope had as good as told Payne he was useless on more than one occasion.

Payne decided. The joint mission with the Fraud Squad to catch Jo Best in the midst of her scam operations had failed. Payne's plan was simple. He would track her, find her, and arrest her as she held the smoking gun. But whatever he thought he would do to catch her, falling through a skylight on a factory roof, and landing on the overweight Dim Sim, a Chinese Australian gangster, was not part of the plan.

Now he was sick and sorry on said factory floor, aching like buggery despite landing on half of the Brothers Crimm, and looking at the wrong end of a firearm held by a lunatic, the emotionally unbalanced big brother.

'How dare you land on my little bro. You are for the long jump, buddy.' Ernie didn't say those words but they described his thinking. 'And look what you've done to my beautiful skylight.' Again, not his exact words.

Ernie pointed the gun at Payne and chose to squeeze the trigger. Just as he did and the gun discharged, at the critical moment before the bullet began its journey, Jo, sprawled on the concrete floor, let fly in kung fu style with one of her untied feet. It landed amidships in Ernie's scrotum forcing him to react in an over-acting kind of way. He felt sharp pain, threw up his arms and the bullet sailed skywards through the now defunct skylight. Ernie uttered the appropriate sounds. He was upset in what could only be described as a major way.

But Senior Constable Payne, having collected parts of the skylight, and bypassed certain death twice, launched himself at the older brother and floored him as Special Forces officers smashed their way in from the front and rear of the factory. Jo's phone being used meant Ernie brought the cops to his hideaway.

It was all over bar the shouting, and there was plenty of that. The words, "Armed police" seemed to be on a loop.

Michael and Billy heard the audio version of the Gunfight at Taylors Lakes not knowing what had happened. The sound effects would have impressed a top Hollywood specialist.

Police trained in hostage and counter terrorism took control. For the good guys, the danger was over. For those wearing black hats, cells loomed large. And if this scenario was to be depicted in cartoon form, the screen would light up with *That's all folks!*

28

DETECTIVE SENIOR CONSTABLE PAYNE WAS IN HOSPITAL. He wasn't dying but the act of removing splinters and shards of glass from various parts of his face and body was a time-consuming and ouch-type procedure. He was a first-time skylight jumper.

Just when he thought he could watch a football replay on the telly above his bed, visitors arrived and entered without knocking—DI Steele was followed by DS Craven.

The senior constable wanted to swear in displeasure but of course wouldn't do so in front of his boss. Payne couldn't stand.

'Don't get up,' said Steele who invaded Payne's personal space standing as close to the patient as possible. Intimidation was Steele's second given name and Bully his third.

'Senior Constable Payne,' greeted the Fraud Squad officer who stood on the opposite side of the bed, in a not-so-threatening position.

Steele seemed almost flippant. 'I've spoken to the doctors and you'll be fit for duty in a couple of days.'

'Thank you, sir.'

'Don't thank me, Payne, just tell me what the fuck you were doing on that factory roof. We'll get to your aerial acrobatics later.'

Payne was miserable. He thought his plan to please his boss would earn him brownie points—alas, not so.

'I was following Best, sir.'

'On whose orders?'

'No orders, sir.'

'You thought you'd play the hero?'

'I only wanted to help you nail her, sir,' he said meekly.

'And instead you've compromised the whole operation. You're a bloody fool, Payne. What are you?'

Payne didn't answer. Craven tried to help.

'Did you see or hear anything which may help prosecute our case?'

Payne shook his head.

'What, nothing?' Steel was angry. 'Nothing at all?'

Payne explained his stop-start journey from the Princes Hill murder site to Clifton Hill then to Northcote, following the female detective in question.

'I waited outside the Northcote address where that tech guy lives. The criminal Ernie Sim turned up then came out with Best as his prisoner. I followed them to the factory.'

'Did you see or hear them doing a deal?'

'Best and Sim, sir?'

'No, Best and Father Christmas. The computer nerd is her partner in crime. Did you see or hear anything between them?'

Payne shook his head.

'And with Sim?'

'No, sir. He kidnapped her at gun point.'

Steele swore. 'Well what happened at the factory?'

'I couldn't get in so climbed on the roof. I saw Best and the others and I thought she was going to be assaulted or killed, so I ...'

'... jumped through the roof,' finished Steele. 'You're a bloody idiot.'

'It was brave, Senior,' said Craven, not pleasing the angry DI. 'You saved your colleague's life.'

'Thank you, sir.'

'What did Best say to you after the cavalry arrived?'

'Nothing, sir.'

'Nothing?' Steele grew more impatient with his junior.

'We finished up in different ambulances.' Steele fumed. 'How is Best, sir?'

'Fit for duty.'

Steele was about to give Payne another rocket when interrupted by a door knock.

Steele dropped his voice. 'Get rid of them. We need to discuss new tactics for Detective Joanna Best.'

Payne felt shithouse. He called. 'Come in.'

Steele turned towards the window and the door-knocking person entered.

'Hi.'

Steele turned and the three males were stunned as Senior Constable Joanna Best entered holding a brown paper bag filled with grapes. She nodded to her boss.

'Sir,' she said then nodded to Craven. She knew who he was but had not been introduced. Steele wasn't going to do that.

'Senior Constable,' began Steele. 'Shouldn't you be resting?'

'Thank you, sir, I'm fine. I think the brave patient is the one who needs the rest.' She held up the bag. 'I've brought you some grapes, Detective.' She looked at the others. 'Well, I can see you're busy, I'll leave you to it.'

She placed the grapes on the table with wheels, the one that slips over the bed, then stopped when Steele spoke.

'No you stay, Senior Constable. We're leaving.' He headed for the door and Craven followed. Steele spoke to Payne. 'End of the week, Detective. And remember, you're always on duty.'

'Sir,' replied Payne and the senior officers left.

An awkward pause dominated. Then both spoke at once. Each gave a weak laugh as often happens in that situation.

'After you,' said Jo.

'No,' replied Payne, 'you first.'

'I was going to say I never know whether bringing grapes to someone in hospital is really the done thing. I mean you see it in movies and TV shows so I guess it must be right.'

He was struggling. 'Look, thanks for helping me back at the factory.'

'God, I'm the one who should be saying thanks. You saved my life, Stephen.'

'But you probably now know your criminal behaviour is common knowledge around the Squad. You can't be a cop and a crook and the boss and the big brass are out to get you.'

'Really?'

Payne didn't do sarcasm. More pausing. Payne started.

'I was following you trying to collect evidence to have you arrested.'

'And?'

'And I just told the boss and the DS from Fraud what I know.'

'Right.' She moved to the foot of the bed. 'Fancy a bet, Detective?' He hesitated. 'I'll bet you fifty bucks you can't tell me one thing about the so-called crimes I'm supposed to have committed.' He went to speak but stopped as she held up a hand. 'Tell me who's involved, what happened and why?' She opened her wallet, removed a note and placed it next to the grapes. 'Fifty bucks.'

He glared at her. She was right. He knew general things but nothing specific about her misdemeanors. She held up the $50 note.

'It's all yours, Detective, for one specific detail.'

He was about to offer a feeble reply when someone knocked. Payne was relieved as he had no chance of collecting the money. Jo pocketed her cash.

'Come in,' called Payne, and David Baggio entered.

It was hard to tell who was more surprised—Ponzi or Jo. They stared at one another. Jo played dumb. She spoke to Payne.

'Well you've got a visitor, Stephen. I'll get out of your way.'

Payne stopped her. 'Don't you two know each other?'

Jo shook her head. 'I don't think so.'

'I saw you both talking at the murder scene in Princes Hill.'

'Not me,' said Jo and opened the door. 'Stephen, you need to go to *Specsavers*.'

She left and Payne received another bag of grapes.

'That's one cool lady,' said Ponzi. 'What did you get on her?'

'I think that's for police ears only, Mr Baggio.'

'So you got nothing.'

'Piss off.'

Ponzi was annoyed. He needed Jo Best arrested, charged, found guilty and sent packing. His life outside jail depended on the cops bringing down one of their own. And what really got up Ponzi's nose was the fact he knew she was guilty. She hired him to work on her criminal activities. They talked about her scams, face to face.

Ponzi swore. 'How hard is it for you lot to make an arrest? She's running a scam, *two* scams, and getting away with murder.'

'How did you know I was in here?'

'Listen, mate, my life depends on you lot doing your job. I make it my business to know what you're doing. I've got first-hand evidence she's breaking the law—I even helped her do it for Chrissake—so why is she not in a cell or at the very least suspended?'

'We're working on a sting. It's just a matter of time.' He reached for the TV remote. 'Now I've got a game to watch so bugger off.'

Ponzi shook his head and left. He stopped at the door and pointed to a second bag. 'I brought you some grapes.'

Payne grabbed a handful and threw them. Ponzi ducked. He looked at the TV and rubbed salt into Payne's pain.

'Collingwood lost.'

Billy Hughes discovered most of the truth about the Michael and Jo scams on the night of the kidnaps but chose to leave well alone. She was impressed by Michael Chan, and already had serious admiration for her protégé, Jo Best. She would talk to the detective later.

The big loser in the kidnap scenario, apart from Ernie and Joe Sim, was the fraudster David Baggio. Ponzi failed to entrap Jo Best as she outwitted him. He was back to square one. He clung to his one last chance, the third scam. Jo Best had told him about it. Well, no specific details, but there was definitely another scam. Ponzi was needed. But to the cops involved, he said nothing.

Once Best explained her new sting to Ponzi, he would set the trap to nail her once and for all. He would make it happen.

I'll catch the bitch m'self. That'll impress the cops and get me that get-out-of-jail-free card.

29

DAYS PASSED WITH THE TWO MURDERS still unsolved. The Sim brothers were in custody facing multiple charges. Gary Black looked a goner for attempted murder in Port Melbourne, and Danny Fortune with his phone full of texts to and from Black about that very plot, needed more than luck to get out of jail.

But his boss, Paul Brittain, was home free and worse, those who murdered John Fielding and Rupert Lenton were unknown. Or was that "not charged"?

Jo Best and Stephen Payne returned to duty with plenty of gossip flowing around the squad about their spectacular adventure. Steele's frustration continued.

DI Richelieu, having recovered from his tailoring wound, ran the Homicide meeting. 'Bonjour Mesdames et Messieurs. We 'ave, as they say, a murderer or two to catch.' He referred to the board. 'Did Rupert kill the journalist? Or was it the Irish cuckold Desmond, or the terrorist brother Martin, 'e with 'is 'omemade bomb? Or maybe someone else? And then, who killed the now deceased source, Rupert? My free champagne offer remains, naturellement.'

'What news on the gun and knife taken at the Port Melbourne shooting, sir?' asked Jo.

'Still in the 'ands of Forensic Services. If they find something, we may make progress. Until then, we 'ave solid police enquiries to make, n'est-ce pas?'

Jo persisted with one of her hunches. 'I think the two students who did some work for John Fielding may be involved.'

There was no support from the room.

Baldwin knew about Jo's hunches. 'But what was their motive? They had huge respect for their lecturer so why kill his source?'

Fleming had a theory. 'Are we missing an obvious candidate?' Everyone looked at him. 'Charles Brittain was in Sydney with the VIPs. He didn't know Lenton named him. He may not have been involved in the paedo rings but he knew those who were. What's his alibi for the Lenton and Fielding murders?'

More murmurs from the masses. Frustrations grew when a murder had multiple suspects but insufficient evidence to make an arrest let alone charge someone.

Whodunit?

The Pope observed from the sidelines then slipped in a comment. He knew how to ask awkward questions.

'Have we cleared the man in Brittain's townhouse on the night of the shooting?'

Steele knew this was Malcolm Best, father of his least favourite squad member. Most of the squad knew that. Yet still the boss tossed in a live grenade.

Richelieu killed the ordnance. 'That gentleman 'as been cleared, sir. A friend of Mr Brittain who 'ad nothing to do with the crime.'

Jo fluctuated between rage and shock.

Why would he ask that question?

'Okey dokey, Mesdames et Messieurs, I appoint DS Hughes teller for the Ayes and DS Fleming teller for the Noes. Kindly choose your suspects and again check every interview, statement, alibi and timeline. If you can positively eliminate a suspect, please do so. Tempus fugit, n'est-ce pas?'

One cheeky officer chimed in using a broad French accent. 'Pardon Mon-sewer, but what 'as 'appened to s'il vous plaît?'

Groans with the odd laugh as officers broke to attack their tasks. Richelieu approached Jo.

'I am off to Forensics, Senior Constable, and should be delighted if you would accompany me, s'il vous plaît.'

He smiled. A senior officer requesting a fellow officer to provide assistance. It was almost like being asked on a date. Jo looked at him.

I wish.

He drove. Jo pondered. 'And your injury, sir, is everything okay?

'Merci, it is but a graze. The real catastrophe is my suit. I 'ad it made in Saville Row.'

'I'm sorry.'

You 'ave been to London, Senior Constable?'

'I have, sir, with my parents when much younger.'

'And Paree?'

'Unfortunately, no sir. But one day, perhaps.'

'It is the City of Light, and the City of Love. My mother 'as an apartment on the Rue Crémieux, a beautiful part of Paris.'

'Sounds wonderful.'

'It would give me great pleasure to show you around, 'ow you say, my old 'ome town.'

Jo struggled with her reply. Her mother's chat to her about certain men many years ago, did not include a chapter on suave Parisians wearing bespoke tailoring from Saville Row. Jo wondered if this basic Gallic charm was a standard Parisian pickup line, and if so, whether she should join the French Resistance.

Bugger that. I'm in.

They arrived at Forensics and entered a lab. A scenes of crime officer looked up from his desk, and over the top of his in-need-of-repair glasses. He sounded like a scientist who was totally absorbed in his profession and work. He was.

'Oh, good morning Detective Inspector.'

'Bonjour, Professeur. And 'ave you have met my colleague, Detective Senior Constable Joanna Best? Professeur Alastair Dean.'

The scientist was impressed with the attractive female but gave her limited attention as he looked for a file.

'I may have some news.' He found the file. 'Ah, here. The knife you delivered has been cleaned thoroughly but not thoroughly enough.' He showed the police a photo. 'Here there is a small opening between the blade and the handle. From within this tiny aperture, we have been able to extract some blood and have sent it for analysis.'

'Magnifique. And this will give a DNA reading n'est-ce pas?'

Wrong question. Alastair was a walking encyclopedia when it came to all matters DNA. Off he went about how STR or Short Tandem Repeats was a process where even a small amount of material could, in time, produce excellent and potentially incriminating results.

Jo's mind clouded over. She kept thinking about being wined and dined in Paris by the Detective Inspector standing beside her.

Alastair prattled on until Richelieu caught him taking a breath.

'And when do you expect the results, Professeur? Later today, per'aps?'

'Oh you'll be lucky. It could be days, even weeks. I really can't say.'

The possible hope for a breakthrough was put on hold. Richelieu thanked the scientist, and was preparing to leave when Jo stepped forward standing quite close to the scientist. Despite being obsessed with his work, and still being dressed by his mother, Alastair was a closet heterosexual. He almost froze when Jo made her pitch.

'We would count it a great favour, Alastair, if you could have your colleagues expedite the tests.' She smiled.

Alastair developed a stammer. 'Well, I, I …

Jo used her eyes as weapons. 'I would be especially grateful.' She paused allowing a generous serve of feminine charm to stroke his imagination.

He gave in—willingly. 'I'll do my best, officer.'

'Call me Jo,' she said and gave him a smile to remember.

Richelieu broke up the seduction. 'May we 'ave the knife, Professeur, s'il vous plaît?'

'The knife, of course,' said Alastair fetching the exhibit in its container and handing it to the DI who signed for it.

'Merci and au revoir,' said Richelieu heading for the door.

Jo followed her boss but stopped at the door. 'Goodbye Alastair. I hope we meet again.'

She left her smile and Chanel No. 22 fragrance behind, and Alastair wasn't sure if he should tell his mother about the policewoman he met today. Mother hadn't approved of the other "girls" he'd brought home to tea. Mind you, they hadn't approved of her.

The detectives drove to consult Dr Strange. Jo worried that Richelieu would think her behaviour towards the scientist a bit, tarty. She discovered he wasn't judgmental. Instead, he thanked her.

'Merci for your efforts to expedite the DNA results, Detective. Let us 'ope the pathologist can give us some instant 'elp.'

'We can only hope, sir.'

'And if I'm not mistaken, I would 'azard a guess you are wearing Chanel No. 22.'

God, he was a charmer.

The pathetic pathologist could help and did. After the usual banter, she was given the knife found in the possession of one Gary Black after his arrest in Port Melbourne.

'We 'ave two stabbing deaths, Doctor,' said Richelieu. 'Are you able to confirm this knife may 'ave been used in either case?'

She examined the knife then referred to her notes and photos.

'I can confirm, Detective Inspector, that this knife almost certainly was used in the murder of Rupert Lenton.'

'And John Fielding?'

She moved her hands and shrugged. 'Possibly. But the wound on Fielding is not the same as on Lenton. I would make a good witness for Lenton and a poor one for Fielding.'

'Merci, Docteur.' He took her hand and kissed it. 'As always, it is a pleasure doing business with you.'

He smiled and Gabrielle smiled. She looked at Jo who poked out her tongue at her friend. Richelieu turned and Jo was caught in flagrante delicto. Her tongue vanished while Strange grinned.

Driving back to HQ, Richelieu raised a new topic. 'Are you still fascinated with the two uni students, Mademoiselle?'

'I wouldn't say fascinated, sir. They lied about their involvement with the journalist. That made me curious.'

'Well it would appear they are not involved. Gary Black is looking like the murderer of Rupert Lenton.'

'I agree, sir.'

'But, as you 'ave, 'ow we say, a track record in picking the guilty party, I would like you to continue to investigate the young people.'

'Oh, really sir?'

'Oui. Unless of course you 'ave another theory.'

'No, sir, and thanks for the encouragement.'

She looked at him and smiled. He took his eyes off the road for a moment and smiled back.

Rue Crémieux, did you say?

30

JO HAD TWO TASKS. Finish investigating the RMIT students, Tommy and Hannah, and set up a phony scam to get Ponzi off her back once and for all. The first task involved research. She went over her interview notes finding nothing new. She worried her antennae were broken. In the past when she got a hunch, she investigated to test the hunch. This time it seemed her hunch was wrong.

The students could not be the murderers. It looked almost certain that Gary Black owned the knife which killed Rupert Lenton. If DNA testing found Lenton's blood on Black's knife, he was a goner.

But the murder of John Fielding remained unsolved. Did Lenton kill him or did Black? He shot at Jo and Richelieu, and could easily have murdered Charlie Brittain and Jo's father.

But what about the mad brother and the mad ex-husband? What should she do? Where should she start? What do all the suspects have in common?

Of course, the victim.

She researched, looking for anything to do with Fielding. As an investigative journalist, his legacy included many articles.

Did he write something about someone who was so offended they murdered him? Possibly.

Could his murderer be one of the VIPs from Sydney all those years ago? Possibly but Fielding had not written about them—yet. And what had the attempted murder of Charles Brittain got to do with anything?

She studied Fielding's articles. Her eyes hurt. Her back ached. Then a headline caught her eye. It was nearly 15 years ago. A company director had killed himself following revelations about the failure of his company. That in itself was not special. What did grab Jo's attention was the name of the dead man. Howard Glenister.

I know that name. Where do I know that name?

She searched her notes then twigged. Of course. The student Tommy Glenister. Could the dead man be a relation of the student? She searched some more then found another article about family man Glenister. The photo featured his young son, Thomas.

Jo's mind raced. What was the girl's name? Hannah. Hannah what? Vine. Hannah Vine.

Now a new search. Was there anyone connected with John Fielding with the name of Vine?

Without a search engine, Jo might have been on the job for hours, even days. Then she found it—the missing link. Mr Bartholomew Vine sued the paper in which John Fielding's article appeared. Mr Vine lost and declared himself bankrupt.

Jo went looking. In the social pages she found a family photo of the Vine family. The little girl beside the bankrupt business man was five year old Hannah. Jo tingled.

Co-incidence? Possibly but unlikely, and if not, it certainly gave the students a motive. But hang on. They admired their lecturer. They worked for him pro bono. They couldn't speak highly enough of him as a journalist. They cried at his murder. He was their mentor.

And yet John Fielding's articles had been the basis for Tommy's father's suicide, and Hannah's father's bankruptcy.

Wow. Maybe my hunch about the students was right after all. But I thought they murdered Lenton not Fielding.

Jo pondered taking her discovery to DI Richelieu or, at the very least, to DS Billy Hughes. But Jo wanted to be sure. She needed more research first and thought it better to have a chat with the Media Studies boss, the lovely Hesketh Spade, to get his take on the situation.

If he confirmed the facts, she could confidently approach her superiors requesting another arrest. She would have their blessing.

She told Baldwin she was off to interview people who might help in the investigation. She lied. She had a plan to keep her job.

Jo and Michael had not seen one another since that terrible night with the Sim brothers, who were now securely in custody.

As the illegal scam operations were at an end, Jo had no concerns about contacting her criminal chum.

'Michael Chan speaking,' said the voice. Jo remembered the first time she heard those words. It seemed an eternity ago with her mother's scam, and the brutal Connie Kruger. Then came Michael's father's scam and the near-death experience with the brutal Sim brothers. All were now in the past.

'Hello Michael Chan, this is Jo Best speaking.'

He laughed. 'Hello stranger. What's news?'

'Nothing new. Both my parents are behaving. But how are yours?'

They're not too bad. They're full of praise for the police and especially a certain Detective Constable.'

'Senior Constable.'

'Of course, Senior Constable.'

'Listen, are you free? I have an idea I'd like to run by you.'

'I thought we agreed to give up crime.'

She laughed. 'Never, I'm only just starting. I'll see you soon.'

It was an open secret that Steele was after Jo's blood. She needed to expose David Baggio, and his plan to undermine her. She had an idea, which required expert advice from her genius partner.

Michael greeted her with his trademark mini smile. Despite their close working relationship and occasional moments of intimacy, nothing romantic had happened between them although respect and friendship were always present. Both were hugely grateful for the way the other had helped their respective families.

'Here's my situation, Mr Chan,' said Jo, tickling Alan's ears and whiskers. 'As you know, certain influential people in Homicide want me out. They're now using Ponzi to try and trap me.'

'So it's really happening?'

Jo nodded. 'I've told Ponzi there's a new scam, a third one.'

'Jo,' he protested, 'we agreed to stop.'

'We have, almost.' Michael got up in frustration. She tried to pacify him. 'Michael, it's not what you think. Hear me out, please.'

He settled. 'This had better be good.'

'I have this idea for a sham scam.'

'A what?'

'If Ponzi's working for my boss, the only way he can avoid jail is to trap me, have me arrested, and thrown off the force.'

'So?'

'So if we can set up a sham scam, and have Ponzi buy it, he'll make a fool of himself and be dumped leaving both of us free to get on with earning an honest living.'

Michael sat and looked at her. 'What's a sham scam?'

She told him.

Jo headed for the city. She wanted a chat with RMIT School of Media and Communication lecturer Hesketh Spade. If he confirmed Jo's theory about the journalism students, Tommy and Hannah, Jo would report to her bosses and, hopefully be responsible for helping to solve the murder of John Fielding.

She found a car spot more by good luck than good management, and walked to the university.

At the Media Studies Department, she headed to Hesketh's office. His face lit up when she stood in his open doorway and spoke.

'Knock, knock.'

'Detective Best, what a delightful surprise, come in, come in.'

'Just a little chat, sir, if I may.'

'Of course, but only if you call me Hesketh.' He stood. 'How about we grab some fresh air.'

'Ah, this will only take a few minutes.'

'Perhaps, but I'm dead set gasping,' he said producing a pack of cigarettes. 'I'm a social pariah these days.'

'Sure,' said Jo following the white-haired academic. They took the lift to the top floor than climbed some stairs to the rooftop garden.

'There used to be a view from up here but now our purpose built building gives us a view of other purpose built buildings.'

'I think it's called progress,' said Jo.

They moved to the edge of the rooftop space and Hesketh was correct. They had a perfect view of skyscrapers. He lit a cigarette.

'So how can I help you, Detective? Have you found my friend John Fielding's killer?'

'I think I have, Hesketh.' He looked interested. 'In fact, I think there were two killers.'

Hesketh was intrigued. 'Two?'

'I've discovered that John Fielding's students, Tommy Glenister and Hannah Vine, have fathers who suffered greatly as a result of things written by your colleague.'

Hesketh looked confused. 'I'm afraid you've lost me.'

'Many years ago, John Fielding wrote about two separate businesses both of which collapsed as a result of his articles. Tommy's father was a CEO who killed himself, and Hannah's father was declared bankrupt.'

Hesketh blew smoke. 'I'm impressed with your research. Have you ever considered investigative journalism?'

She smiled. 'Thanks but I wondered if the students ever spoke about their fathers?'

Hesketh shook his head. 'Not to me but maybe to John.'

'Did John Fielding ever talk to you about the fathers Glenister or Vine, and their death and ruin?'

'Sorry, no. But that's the type of man John was.'

'I'm sorry?'

'The story was everything to John. Anyone hurt as a result of his search for the truth was collateral damage. All that mattered to him in journalism was the truth.'

Jo had to think. This wasn't what she expected to hear. She made a subtle switch.

'Did you ever work as a journalist, Hesketh?'

He smiled. 'Oh yes, indeed. I was once reckoned as the next best thing when it came to investigative journalism.'

She paused again. 'What happened?'

'Well, you know what they say—those who can do, those who can't, teach.'

She looked at him. 'Is that what happened to you?'

He ignored her question. 'I've lied to you, officer.' Jo's pulse accelerated. 'I did tell Tommy and Hannah the truth.' Jo was surprised. 'They had no idea the journalist they admired was the same man who investigated and wrote about the companies in which their fathers worked.'

'You told them about their fathers?' He nodded and blew smoke. 'Why?'

He shrugged. 'Because they deserved to know the truth about the man who cared nothing for people but only for his career.' He sucked hard on his cigarette then threw it on the ground. He ground it with force then looked out over the balcony. 'I wanted those kids to treat Fielding like he treated their fathers.'

'But they didn't.'

'No, they didn't. I wanted them to kill that bastard, the plagiarist who stole my best story, and used it to further his career at my expense.' He paused, still not looking at Jo. 'He deserved to die.'

Jo said nothing. Hesketh switched personality. His hatred gave him motive, and his plan to use his students as killers failed. Jo now knew. That left one glaring possibility.

She spoke in a soft voice, wanting to calm, not spook him, or cause him to do something reckless. But Jo needed to ask one question.

'Do you know who killed him, Hesketh?'

He kept staring at the skyline, and said nothing. Jo moved closer and stood behind him. Again she paused. 'Hesketh?'

He paused. 'That it should come to this.'

'I'm sorry?'

He suddenly turned and grabbed Jo by the shoulders. He gave her a Glaswegian kiss, which would have done any Sauchiehall Street thug proud.

Jo grasped her bloodied face, snatching a handkerchief to stem the blood flow. Hesketh lost it. His years of jealousy and frustration bubbled over. He knew they might come for him, and now they had, well she had—and his rage exploded. Jo became his punching bag.

He spun her around, grabbed her hair and her slacks and heaved her towards the metal railing on the edge of the concrete wall. Jo was younger, fitter and trained in hand to hand combat, yet the surprise of Hesketh's attack, and his first decisive blow gave him the advantage. She tried to fight back but he slammed her against the wall.

Hesketh went for the kill. He heaved Jo up on top of the wall. The busy city location was busy below. Cars, cyclists, students, workers and shoppers went about their business unaware of the impending death above them.

Jo's will to survive meant she kicked back—literally. Hesketh screamed in pain and rage as Jo's boot punched his face. He refused to let go. Jo teetered on the wall. He grabbed her belt with both hands and shoved. There was nothing for Jo to grasp. She swayed.

Hesketh ducked below her kicking legs, stood tall with his head between her thighs, wrapped his hands around her and heaved. She had a fabulous view of where he wanted her to go—the long drop. It was hopeless. Harder he heaved. Now half of Jo's body was over the edge. Her flailing arms signaled her imminent death. She screamed but Hesketh screamed louder.

He too was attacked, and from behind. Jo felt two hands grab her right ankle. It was bloody painful with her abdomen on top of the metal on the wall, and strange hands tearing at her ankle. Jo reached back and put her hands on the inside of the wall. She tried to press backwards. Hesketh kept shoving and screaming. She teetered some more than tipped and fell backwards, landing on a fallen Hannah Vine. Jo looked to her side.

Hesketh was lying on his back with Tommy kneeling on his lecturer.

Jo was safe and had cracked the case of the murder of John Fielding. Mind you that didn't necessarily mean all would be roses with Steele and Hughes.

31

BILLY HUGHES ANSWERED HER PHONE. She was used to bad news from Jo Best. 'Yes, Senior, what have you done now?'

'I've just made an arrest, Sarge.'

'And? There's always an *and* for your statements, Detective.'

'I may need an ambulance.'

Billy switched from sarcasm to serious. 'What's happened?'

'The academic at RMIT, Hesketh Spade, confessed to the murder of his colleague, John Fielding then attacked me.'

'Are you hurt?'

Jo was pleased her sergeant first asked if her colleague was okay.

'No bones broken but I'm a scratching for this week's *Love Island*.'

'Where are you?'

'On the roof of the RMIT building in Latrobe Street.'

'Stay there. I'll call an ambo.'

'Thanks, Sarge.'

Jo looked at Tommy and Hannah. Both were sitting on Professor Spade. He'd been flipped on to his belly and cuffed with his hands behind his back, his stuffing well and truly removed. Jo kept holding a handkerchief to her face.

'Thanks. You two saved my life. But how did you know I was here?'

'We saw you getting in the lift,' said Hannah. 'We ran downstairs thinking you'd arrested him. Then realised you were on the roof.'

''We wanted to tell you the truth. We did a really dumb thing,' added Tommy.

'You knew he killed your teacher.'

'We weren't sure,' said Hannah, who became their spokesperson. 'John saw our surnames and looked into our backgrounds. He told us about his articles and the impact they had on our families.'

'He told you?'

They nodded. Hannah continued. 'We studied the articles and couldn't see how John wrote anything but the truth. Then Mr Spade ...'

Jo held up her free hand. 'I don't think you should say any more about the case or Mr Spade, and certainly not in front of him.'

'I don't care,' said Hesketh. 'I'm glad he's dead.'

Jo waved her free hand indicating their conversation must cease for now. They waited until Hughes, Baldwin and two uniformed officers arrived only minutes before the ambos.

Jo briefly explained the situation then, after treatment, went to hospital.

She'd done it again.

The word in Homicide was again all about Jo Best. DI Steele found it irritating in the extreme that the officer he was hell bent on removing kept solving homicides his other officers had failed to do. They looked at three suspects, and came up with nothing. She went for a wander around town, grabbed the guilty party who put up his hand. Does she also walk on water?

Payne changed. He and Best began to form a relationship, well, he stopped his aggression and rudeness. Each had arguably saved the life of the other. Payne's nastiness softened and the pair got to the stage of saying "Good morning". Holding hands was never going to happen.

Back at work, complete with flesh-toned sticking plaster, Jo copped plenty of ribbing about her lucky arrest and her "pretend" war wounds. Her phone rang.

'Homicide, Detective Senior Constable Best speaking.'

'Good morning Senior Constable. This is Assistant Commissioner John Crowley.'

Jo gulped 'Good morning, sir.'

'I'm ringing to congratulate you on your latest arrest.'

'Thank you, sir.'

'You seem to be making a habit of this.'

'I was just lucky, sir. I actually went to arrest someone else.'

'I didn't hear that, Detective. Never admit you're lucky. Now, apart from ringing to congratulate you, I wanted to ask a favour. Could you spare the time to speak to some students at my daughter's school?'

'Of course, sir. I'd be delighted.'

'That's very kind. Can you drop by my office in the next day or so and I'll fill you in on the details.'

'Certainly, sir. Actually, I'm free at the moment.'

'Now there's another thing, Detective. Never admit to being free. Right then, shall we say in half an hour?'

'Thank you, sir. I'm not free but I'll make the time.'

He laughed, said goodbye, and hung up. Jo had a horrible thought it was a con. Someone sounding like the AC Crime was pulling her leg. She looked around the incident room. Nobody looked at her. She felt exhilarated.

The high-ranking officers of Victoria Police have larger offices, thicker carpet and support staff more likely to shop at Chanel than Target.

Jo was greeted with enthusiasm. 'Senior Constable Best, do come in. Please, take a seat.'

Jo settled in AC Crowley's office. Had a bomb gone off in the office next door, they wouldn't have heard it.

'May I ask where you went to school, Detective?'

'Yes sir, I went to Canterbury Girls' Secondary College.'

'Excellent. Well I have a daughter at Cheltenham Grammar and there's a real push to encourage the girls to consider all types of careers. I've been asked to have a chat to the Year 12 gels and I thought a highly successful woman would make a far better choice.'

'I'm happy to help, sir.'

'Thank you, most kind. May I call you, Jo?'

'Please do, sir.'

'Well Jo, I'll get the teacher in charge to give you a call and arrange the date and time. I'll tell her how successful you've been in your short but brilliant career.'

'Thank you, sir, but I'm not comfortable with such a description.'

'And my offer of a job remains opens, Jo. If ever you want a different challenge or some advice, I'll be only too happy to help.'

'Well, now that you mention it, sir ...'

She paused. How could she ask for help? How could she avoid admitting to being a criminal?

'Something troubling you, Detective?'

Oops. He's back calling me Detective. What happened to Jo?

'There is, sir. I'm afraid I've done something wrong.'

She dreaded telling the man who respected her and wanted to help her that she'd failed him—big time. She decided to confess, to admit to her criminal behaviour and possibly see her career disappear. She didn't want to receive plaudits for her police work only to be exposed as a criminal.

'This hasn't got anything to do with those scams you're running?'

Jo copped another Glaswegian Kiss, at least metaphorically.

'Sir?'

'Come now Senior Constable, you didn't think you could keep your life as a criminal private, did you?'

Jo struggled. 'I don't know what to say, sir.'

'Well let's look at the facts. Thanks to you and your so-called scams, at least three professional criminals have been charged and should be off the scene for years. People defrauded have their funds returned. Justice has been served, and taxpayers have been saved a fortune. How am I going so far?'

Jo shook her head. 'I still don't know what to say, sir.'

'And I've heard that some of your colleagues are trying very hard to have you not just sacked, but charged and jailed.' He paused and looked at her. 'Is my intel any good? Am I even close to the mark?'

'More like spot on, sir.'

''Excellent.'

She came clean. 'I hope you haven't heard about the latest scam.'

'Another one?' He was intrigued. 'No, do tell.'

She explained her sham scam, designed to thwart the officers and real criminal who were working to bring her down.

'What a brilliant idea. But can you pull it off?'

32

TODAY WAS THE DAY. Jo buzzed as she drove to Northcote. Ponzi too trembled with excitement. His misery over the last few weeks drained him. He'd been arrested, charged with serious fraud offences, abandoned by fellow criminals, had his wife file for divorce, and found life to be the pits. Then came a stroke of luck.

The cops were prepared to waive or certainly downgrade his charges provided he helped them snare one Detective Senior Constable Joanna Best from the Homicide Squad. A lifeline. Yes!

He knew she was guilty. She'd been to his house to recruit him as part of her scam team. They'd sat in his car while she gave him a payout in cash. She was definitely bent. He *knew* she was bent. But so far the cops had failed to catch her in the act.

Under instructions, Ponzi took matters into his own hands and confronted her, in her own backyard at Homicide. But she was clever.

Then, just as desperation set in for Ponzi, the bimbo had asked him for help on one more scam. Yes! At last! He would play along but make sure this scam was her last, as she became his ticket to freedom.

With Best arrested and out of the Force, Ponzi could get his life back. His phone pinged. He had a text. If was from Best.

Ponzi. We need your advice on the wording of our next venture. See attachment. Can you help?

Of course he could. Even if he couldn't, he could. And this text was gold. This alone would put that bitch in the dock. Ponzi wanted in on this latest scam so badly it hurt. He read the attachment. Pretty simple.

Best and co needed marketing advice, the sort that drove readers or customers to take action—a CTA, a Call to Action.

He put his advice in writing and sent a return text with the suggested corrections. Then he got thinking. He wanted details of who was being scammed, when and where. With that information, he would be the ideal source for the police. This time they would nail the bent copper and he, David "Ponzi" Baggio, would be a free man, or, an incarcerated man with a heavily discounted sentence.

But how could he ask for such intimate details without making it look obvious? *They must know I'm working for the cops.*

What's this? He received another text with another attachment. The message was a thank you with the re-written attachment using Ponzi's advice.

But no, they'd sent the wrong attachment. It was a screed with details of how and where the latest scam would work. The Michael Chan ruse of deliberately sending an email to the wrong person, or in this case the wrong attachment to the right person was again in play.

This scam involved blackmailing a top politician by claiming to have explosive material about his past. But there was no politician or explosive material—it was a sham scam.

Ponzi could not believe his luck.

He replied saying that the re-write of the pitch was perfect, and could they please pay him once the scam was complete. He said *please.*

He almost lost interest in his fee. Their mistake in sending him details of the scam was his guarantee of avoiding jail. 'Beautiful!' This was brilliant. But Ponzi needed to play this with great care. He phoned DS Craven in Fraud and Extortion.

'DS Craven.'

'Detective Sergeant, this is David Baggio.'

'Yes Ponzi, what news?'

Ponzi hated being called Ponzi. His Italian ancestry now seemed a handicap. Had he been born George Smith in Nar Nar Goon, he would never have earned the nickname Ponzi. He soldiered on.

'Big news. The third scam with Detective Best is up and running.'

'How do you know this?'

'I've helped them write the CTA.'

'The what?'

'The Call to Action.'

'And?'

'And I know the target and where she and the scammers will meet.'

'They're going to meet? Why? All their transactions are online.'

'This scam involves blackmail.'

'Blackmail?'

'Yes, it's a prominent politician paying to keep something secret. And the handover's today at 5.30 at Southern Cross Station.'

'How do you know this?'

Ponzi lied. 'I cracked their code. They don't know I know.'

Craven's mind buzzed. The crimes to date had been fraud related. Blackmail was a whole new ball game—different charges and different penalties. If Ponzi's intel is correct, Victoria Police will be well rid of Best and any of her other rogue coppers.

'We need a meet, Ponzi. In one hour, usual place. Be there.'

Ponzi was frightened. This was his final throw of the dice, his last chance saloon, and worse, he'd run out of metaphors.

Southern Cross Station is Melbourne's busiest. Suburban, country and interstate trains arrive and depart from here. 5.30 pm on a working day was peak hour and people hurried in and out of the terminus.

Ponzi told DS Craven all he knew. In turn, Craven reported to DI Steele. This sounded too good to be true. It might be a ruse. But if true, it was a chance they simply couldn't afford to miss.

Jo, through Michael, had accidentally on purpose given Ponzi all the details. He told his handlers. Fraud squad officers were in place well before the pick-up time. Some were in uniform but dressed as railway staff. A couple pretended to work as cleaners.

Everyone knew the rendezvous spot. Photos were circulated of Detective Senior Constable Best.

She was to meet the representative of the politician being blackmailed. He wore a black cashmere overcoat, a black Homburg, and carried a furled black umbrella. His codename was Mr Black. George Smiley was nowhere to be seen.

The cash would be in a black attaché case, to be exchanged for the embarrassing original documents the politician wanted returned. These documents would be dynamite if made public. Jo had the documents, and worked for the blackmailer.

She checked her watch. 5.15. She looked at the meeting point from a distance. If this sting failed to trick her enemies, she would cop the wrath of Ponzi and DI Steele and all who had it in for her.

People brushed past en route to their train. The time was 5.17. Jo's heart rate got busier.

She set off and as she approached the rendezvous point, in the distance, she saw a man wearing the right clothes. The exchange was on. The man was on an escalator heading up to reach her level. He disappeared amongst the crowd. She checked her watch—again. Her hands shook. She looked for the man again and couldn't find him.

Shit! It wasn't him. It's going to fall over at the death.

She weaved in and out of passengers. Her meeting place was straight ahead. She moved close to the pole and froze. There were hordes of people but no mystery man. Where is he? Then a hand grabbed her arm from behind.

'Don't turn around.' Jo froze. 'Have you got the documents?'

'Yes.'

'Don't turn around.'

'I thought you wanted a face to face meeting.'

'Show me the documents.'

'Money first,' said Jo having zero experience in blackmail drops.

Jo felt something pressing against her thigh. She looked down and there was an attaché case being held by a gloved hand.

'Now the documents.'

'I need to see the money. You'll have to open the case.'

'Bitch,' said the man who snapped a couple of locks and opened the case a little. Jo looked inside and saw the contents.

'Is it all there?'

'Are all the documents there?'

'Yes.'

'And all copies have been destroyed?'

'Yes. Look, just give me the case and I'll give you mine.'

'The Minister will be very cross if you've kept anything back.'

'And if you've shortchanged my boss, the deal's off.'

The man thrust the case forward and Jo took it. He grabbed her case. The man growled.

'Now stay there and don't look around for 30 seconds.'

'Is that when I call, "Coming ready or not"?'

'Bitch,' he snapped. He turned to leave and yelled.

Three burly police officers grabbed Mr Black. Jo copped the same treatment only she had two cleaners in her raiding party.

'Joanna Best, you're under arrest for blackmail.'

'What?' yelled Jo as she was frog marched along the concourse towards Spencer Street and Police HQ.

Her fellow criminal, the politician's agent, copped the same treatment. The officers grabbed the case he'd taken from Jo and handcuffed him. Mr Homburg got himself nicked.

One of them said, 'You're under arrest', and another said, 'Oh shit.'

The others looked at their swearing colleague then at their captive.

Wearing a bemused grin, a cashmere overcoat and Homburg hat was the Assistant Commissioner of Crime, John Crowley.

The arresting officers were stuffed. They knew who he was but had serious doubts about his arrest. "Oh shit," was correct. The AC spoke.

'I think this is called a sting, gentlemen, and you've been had. I suggest you check the contents of the case.'

An officer opened it to reveal a copy of the current issue of the *Australian Police Journal*.

The officers gripping the arms of the AC went decidedly limp.

'My train leaves in exactly 4 minutes, gentlemen, so if you don't mind, I'll leave you to get on and make your report.'

'Sir,' said each of three officers who all wanted to swear and now dreaded the bollocking and ribald laughter they would soon receive.

The situation with Detective Best was not so fortunate. The arresting officers knew their mark, and that she was a bent cop. They took delight in escorting her back to Police HQ. Her life as a crooked cop was over as was her life as a cop. During the frog march, Jo tried to explain. She cared more for the arresting officers than herself.

'Gentlemen,' said Jo, 'I can explain this.'

They ignored her and kept walking. Dozens of people stared at this unusual sight; three big males, half-carrying one average-sized female. Fare evasion was getting heavy handed.

'Shut up,' said the Fraud Squad officer. 'You can explain all this to AC Crime, Mr Crowley.'

'But he already knows.'

'Shut up,' said two of the officers together.

Jo persisted, and spoke louder. 'He was the man I was talking to. Your mates just arrested him.'

That caused the convoy to slow. They exchanged glances. That couldn't be true. Or could it? They stopped and looked at one another. Then they looked at Jo.

'Oi!' cried a voice. The police looked back to see their colleagues fast approaching. One of them called.

'Let her go.' The Crowley arrest party reached the Best arrest party.

'What?'

'The guy we arrested is Crowley, Assistant Commissioner Crime. We've been stitched up.'

Jo's captors slowly released their hold. She adjusted her clothing.

Her main captor challenged his colleague. 'Are you joking? The Assistant Commissioner Crime?'

'I did tell you, gentlemen,' she said in a matter of fact way. 'May I have my case, please?'

After a pause, the officer with the case, handed it to Jo. She opened it and took out a handful of blank sheets of paper each with a Victoria Police letterhead. The cops adopted the expressionless expression. Steam seeped from their ears. Egg yolk trickled down their faces.

The leading officer departed and the rest followed with much gesticulating and what looked like threats. Jo called after them.

'Good luck with the debrief.'

The men didn't look back. The travelling public lost interest and Jo copied Julie Andrews in Austria, doing a sort of swing around with her arms extended on the concourse of the busy station. She sported a Luna Park grin.

DI Steele needed a new string to his bow—the ability to kill a story. When told the news by DS Craven, Steele turned a deeper shade of crimson. Not only had his scheme to destroy Detective Best failed, she'd played him for a fool in cahoots with an Assistant Commissioner, an officer with whom Steele had to work, and to whom he needs must metaphorically bow.

Damn and blast. They were not Steele's exact words but boy was he off his Weet-Bix. His task now was to limit the damage. His mind raced. *My God, imagine how this will look.*

A simple sting and he, DI Steele, had been sucked in. He couldn't kill the story. And to make things a thousand times worse, the top brass knew the tale or soon would. An Assistant Commissioner was part of the fiasco.

The final humiliation being that Steele now had to work with the clever bitch Best. She was opposed by the Pope but supported by God.

When Stephen Payne heard the news, he surprised himself by feeling a tinge of pride and satisfaction for his fellow senior constable. Wonders will never cease.

When Ponzi heard the news, he started to cry. He sat in his motel room and imagined it as his cell. He soon sat in a real one.

Of course Jo Best was lucky. Was she ever? She landed on her feet. But even Jo knew such a result might not always happen. She knew happy endings may bob up in fairytales but not always in real life. Her next case might bring tears and sadness.

Gary Black copped it in the neck. DNA testing, thanks to Mummy's boy Alastair, found traces of Rupert Fenton's blood buried in the handle of Black's knife, the one he carried to Charles Brittain's townhouse. Black was charged with murder and attempted murder. Good luck with that.

Danny Fortune lost his fortune thanks to his phone. His text messages with Black meant he was charged with conspiracy to murder. Danny said nothing about anything and even less about his boss.

Paul Brittain escaped police charges but not the press. Investigative journalists went after him. His dodgy buildings were exposed. His donations to political parties and politicians were exposed. His old school chum, Redmond Latimer became unelectable. And far worse, Paul's missus, Davinia Brittain, was sent to Coventry. No coffee in Church Street for you, darrr-ling.

And Malcolm Best's assault charges were dropped while his former work colleague Gordon Hayward and his girlfriend were charged with various offences.

Charles and Chester remained in Port Melbourne walking every day. And Martin Fielding was lucky, receiving a suspended sentence but sole ownership of his father's estate.

33

IT WAS TEN DAYS AND TEN SLEEPLESS NIGHTS since toddler Candice "Candy" White went missing from a busy park in suburban Richmond. Her parents lost weight and gave birth to all sorts of nasties within their bodies. Stress is bad for people. The Whites' stress worked hard to damage arteries, organs and cells.

Inspector Ronald Graham slumped in his chair, exhausted. It was his retirement case, his final task and he could not bear to fail. Telling a parent their child is dead didn't rate on his list of difficult jobs. It was beyond difficult.

For the last few months, Ron and wife Barbara had been fixing their caravan, preparing to become grey nomads exploring Australia. They fancied discovering the land of their birth.

'You'll miss your grandchildren,' said their daughter.

'Have you made your wills?' teased their son-in-law.

It was all good fun and proof that 90% of the enjoyment of an adventure is the anticipation.

But as retirement drew closer, Ron became more miserable. He brought his work home and his moods caused his wife to worry.

He tried to find the little girl; by God he tried. He left no stone unturned, interviewed every paedophile twice, some three times, and investigated every alibi. Every lead was checked and re-checked.

There were moments of hope. A sighting, a report of a child who looked like Candy, and even a confession from a mentally-ill person who had no concept of the pain he caused. But in the end, nothing.

Ron had a meeting with his team at 1000 hours. The DI had a sinking feeling it would be their worst meeting by far.

The police had no answer to the following questions. What happened to Candy? Where is she now?

Graham entered the incident room, and the hubbub ceased. The case killed frivolity and levity. Officers fell silent and listened.

'Good morning,' said the DI.

Everyone responded in soft tones. Did they know what was coming?

'I have bad news. The powers that be have asked for the search and investigation to continue but with fewer officers.' Immediately people groaned, complained or protested.

'It's not even two weeks, sir. They can't shut it down now.'

You're not listening, Constable. We carry on but with fewer resources.'

More hubbub. Another complaint. 'What do we tell the parents?'

'*We* tell them nothing. I'm in charge. I tell them. I'll be at their home tonight and tell them then.' Unhappiness ruled. 'But there is to be no mention of staffing changes to anyone. Is that clear?'

Murmurs of agreement. DI Graham began his final speech.

'For those of you leaving, I want you to know I'm proud of you. I could not have asked for a more dedicated team. I've been putting in more than 60 hours a week and I'm one of the lazy ones. Thank you. Thank you all for your dedication and outstanding professionalism. We cop a lot of criticism and some of it, in my humble opinion, is deserved. But I would like the public to know that you, this group on this case has gone way, way, way beyond the call of duty.'

He paused. They knew he was retiring. They wanted him to stay. They wanted everyone to stay and find Candy—alive.

DI Graham concluded his remarks in a softer voice.

'As you know I'm retiring, and it breaks my heart to quit without finding the kiddie.' He had a granddaughter about Candy's age. He paused to keep control of his emotions.

'I'll announce who'll be leaving later today. In the meantime, let's go as hard as we possibly can.' He tapped the notice board behind him. 'Any new leads, no matter how small, log them and put them here. We stop working on this case the day we find little Candice.' He looked at them. He eye-balled them and spoke slowly. 'Never give up.'

They didn't. DI Graham didn't. Even after he took retirement, he thought about the missing toddler, and kept in touch with a couple of officers still working on the case.

His replacement came from outside. DI Patricia "Trish" Goddard was a career cop and a good friend of a certain homicide officer, DS Billy Hughes. The two women met for their regular Friday drink.

Whoever arrived first got them in. Billy was there well ahead of Trish who sent a text apologising and giving her ETA. When she did arrive, Billy was on her second—her limit.

'Sorry, sorry, sorry, said Trish, dropping her bag and raising her glass to her friend. Trish looked knackered.

'I believe congratulations are in order,' said Billy.

'Thanks but it's a poisoned chalice, and I reckon you lot should take over now.'

'Still no body?' Trish shook her head.

'No body, no homicide,' said Billy.

'No body, no sign of a body, and I've lost two-thirds of my team.'

'Speaking of which, I may be able to help. How would you like a really smart detective?'

Trish almost choked on her drink. 'You, leave Homicide?'

'Not me, you daft bitch.'

Billy told Trish a potted history of one, Joanna Best, a redacted version. Billy reckoned Jo having a break from Homicide would be a good thing for everyone. DI Steele was ropeable after the sting at the railway station. Jo could escape the pressure, and time might soothe a savage breast or two.

'She's big on ideas and follows a hunch, which sometimes spells trouble. But she has a nose for the truth and a strike rate better than anyone I know.'

'What, even you?'

'Even me. If you're keen, I'm sure I can persuade the Pope. He'd prefer to sack her but this is the next best thing.'

'Okay, send her across.'

And so it came to pass, as a temporary measure, Detective Senior Constable Joanna Best moved from Homicide to Major Crime working under DI Trish Goddard in the case of the missing toddler; the little lady who vanished.

The Detective Joanna Best Mysteries

www.cenfoxbooks.com

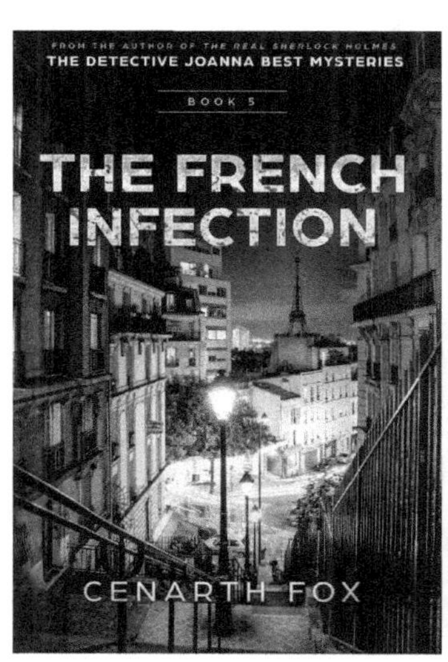